WE DON'T TALK ABOUT EMMA

J.D. BARKER
E.J. FINDORFF

We Don't Talk About Emma

Published by:
Hampton Creek Press
P.O. Box 177
New Castle, NH 03854

Worldwide Print, Sales, and Distribution by Simon & Schuster

Hampton Creek Press is a registered Trademark of Hampton Creek Publishing, LLC

For information about special discounts for bulk purchases, please contact Simon & Schuster Special Sales at 1-866-506-1949 or business@simonand-schuster.com

Cover Design by Domanza
Book design and formatting by Domanza
Author photograph by Bill Peterson of Peterson Gallery
Manufactured in the United States of America

ISBN: 979-8-9907461-5-2 (HARDCOVER)
ISBN: 979-8-9907461-6-9 (PAPERBACK)
ISBN: 979-8-9907461-7-6 (EBOOK)

ALSO BY J.D. BARKER

Forsaken
She Has A Broken Thing Where Her Heart Should Be
A Caller's Game
Behind A Closed Door

4MK THRILLER SERIES
The Fourth Monkey
The Fifth To Die
The Sixth Wicked Child

WITH JAMES PATTERSON
The Coast to Coast Murders
The Noise
Death of the Black Widow
Confessions of the Dead

WITH OTHERS
Dracul
Heavy Are The Stones

WEDNESDAY

1

WAVES FROM LAKE Pontchartrain pounded the seawall, adding spray to the sweeping rain on Lakeshore Drive. Nikki white-knuckled the final three blocks of the drive without headlights until parking behind a public bathroom at a picnic rest area. Combine the storm with the January chill, and it made for a desolate road at two in the morning—perfect conditions to rid the world of a predator.

February in New Orleans could get bone cold. Nikki turned off the engine, letting the heavy downpour invade her ears. The interior's heat lost the battle with the outside chill. Her eyes searched for anything odd, or witnesses who might've seen her stop. An ominous crack of lightning flashed in the distance.

Subsequent thunder rumbled while latex gloves snapped snuggly onto her fingers. A black knit ski mask slid over her head, smashing her ponytail. Her mouth filled with saliva, an obvious symptom of nausea. Fighting to keep it down would be worse.

She lifted her mask just enough to throw up outside her door. It resulted in a mash-up of baby carrots, which she loved to snack on while nervous. They didn't settle her stomach as intended. She wiped her mouth and closed the door again.

Nikki shivered from perspiration under black sweatpants and a plain black hoodie. She pulled a snub-nosed revolver from under a set of folded clothes on the passenger seat. The gun was secured in a Velcro holster on her right ankle. With no safety, she had to be careful not to blow her foot off.

She straightened, looking around again. To the left, the black lake extended to a blacker horizon. To her right, the grassy levee that hid the Lakeview neighborhood just beyond. Fingers tickled her spine as headlights crept by on the road. Its rear red glow soon faded.

Random cars passing are normal, she told herself.

Nikki's heartbeat filled her ears, drowning out the rain. The more she thought about taking a life, the less likely she'd open the door, the less likely she'd climb that levee, exposed to the weather and possible witnesses.

Another sip of water wet her dry lips. She took in air, filling her lungs.

Go home, Nik.

She placed a black umbrella across her thighs, gripping it tight. The object grounded her, like something real in an abstract painting. Like a foot on the floor while lying drunk in bed. Like holding your little sister's hand as she takes her last breath. Three years had passed since Morgan's death, and the sensation was still there on her fingertips.

The car door opened enough for the umbrella to expand while stepping out. Amplified rain on the plastic sounded like sizzling steak, or an electric chair. The carrot vomit had created a tiny island in the watery slush, but her discount tennis shoes avoided it, splashing in the ice-cold water. With one step, her left ankle rolled on a bottle, but she caught herself. Six more inches, the tire would've crushed the glass and caused a flat, and that evil man would get to live.

Outside the claustrophobic car, the surroundings became clear. Her heartbeat eased when she reminded herself of the girls that would be saved by this act. She headed for the levee, unbalanced on her right side due to the gun's weight on her ankle.

She leaned forward while ascending the slick levee. The umbrella hovered close to her head while her feet squished in the spotty, weeded grass. The levee protected the Lakeview neighborhood from storm surge as well as kept anyone enjoying the lakefront from wandering into the neighborhood.

At the top of the incline lay a muddy trail from joggers with remnants of overlapping footprints. Nikki took in the beautiful houses along the secluded curved street while at the summit. Both her, and the homes, were protected and exposed at the same time. Short gusts of wind encouraged her to keep going.

Herman Napleton's majestic home stood dead center on the street, at the forefront of the affluent Lakeview area. Nikki imagined Napleton had never taken advantage of being a stone's throw from the lakefront. It was all about *prestige*.

His porch light wasn't a criminal deterrent, however, with frequent patrol, not much traffic made it to this street. Along the right side of Herman Napleton's house, the driveway led to a two-car garage in the back. When people thought of New Orleans, they didn't picture modern homes in affluent neighborhoods.

Nikki descended on the slippery grass until falling on her backside with all the grace of a newborn deer. The cold wetness soaking her clothes was immediate. *Great.* At least she didn't slide all the way down.

She righted herself, side-stepping to even ground with tiny steps. Headlights surprised her while nearing the street. She froze, exposed in the dark rainstorm with nowhere to hide. She stood still as a tree while Herman Napleton's Mercedes pulled into his driveway. The garage door opened on the right side. This was perfect.

2

THE RELENTLESS RAIN forced Herman to concentrate on the road. Every time he stopped at a light or a stop sign, the windshield turned into a movie screen, playing the girl's straining eyeballs as he choked her out. Her breath had been so bad, and yet—*so good*.

The wipers did their best to clear the deluge, but streetlights were still only a fuzzy glow. Traffic never congested his neighborhood. Making it back home without any issues was a relief, but expected. Inside the dry garage, he placed his Mercedes in park.

An unseen force pulled his head back against the seat. His aging reflexes couldn't stop the knife from sliding across his frail throat. He witnessed the spray of blood, dotting the inside of the windshield. It was the oddest thing; there was no pain.

A revelation materialized as the light dimmed and death was imminent. *Every single thing* Herman Napleton did today was for the last time. Would he have chosen a fried seafood basket instead of salad? He might have taken the time to enjoy his eggs and grits. Five extra minutes under the jets of a hot shower.

He would apologize to the women he killed, if only Heaven awaited.

The knife wasted no time plunging into his stomach. He wouldn't call it pain, as much as *devastation*. The attack stopped long enough for this person to squeeze between the seats and write something on his face. The attacker's eyes met his.

Of course, it's you.

3

NIKKI'S NUMB FEET avoided the freezing puddles while crossing the street toward Herman Napleton's open garage door. Heavy, wet clothes clung to her back. Once on the driveway, she hugged the side of the house, keeping the umbrella close to her head. She stopped, still exposed to the rain. Napleton hadn't exited the car yet.

The Mercedes's headlights lit up the back wall, making harsh shadows from the shelving unit. Thin mist came from the tailpipe. Was he drunk? Did Herman Napleton fall asleep against the wheel?

Nikki tracked mud into the garage. It wasn't too late to turn and run. Once he identified her, she had to commit. She couldn't panic and lose her senses. *Shoot him and get out.*

Herman Napleton looked to have passed out against the steering wheel. With the umbrella still low, Tom Jones sang his pussycat song from inside the car as weak exhaust fumes crinkled her nose. The driver's side door had been cracked open a hair in an attempted to exit.

She squatted to pull the snub nose from the ankle holster. Her thigh muscles burned as if she'd done a full set of squats. The visual was like being immersed in a television show. Her fingers lost strength while wrapped around the gun. Her aim trembled toward Herman Napleton's head.

"You're just cold," she hissed through her teeth.

As her finger touched the trigger, the saturation on Napleton's clothes jumped out at her. She stretched and ducked to get every vantage point, but she couldn't tell shadows from solid objects. A bright lightning strike almost caused her to pull the trigger. She managed to glimpse a partial of Napleton's sliced throat. Without pressing her face against his window, she saw fresh blood on his clothes.

A large handle extended out from his crotch—*a kitchen knife?*

The subsequent thunder vibrated the earth, and the rain crashed down. Mixed with the smears of blood on his face, something had been written. His profile wouldn't allow her to see what. It could be a number, or a symbol.

Leave.

Nikki inched over to look in the back seat. A shadow's movement caught her attention. The rear door opened so fast, it knocked her over, like being tackled. Momentum forced her into the shelving unit, then to the ground. Random items fell around her. The headlights blinded her.

The snub nose never left her grip. Nikki squirmed on the ground next to a crumpled umbrella. A hooded figure exited the back seat and tumbled toward the exit. Nikki couldn't shoot and risk exposing herself.

"Emma?"

The figure halted, still facing away at the edge of the garage. This person's long shadow stretched out into the rain. The frame in the baggy clothes appeared to be Emma's size. Her hands were gloved. She aimed her gun at the killer who wouldn't turn around. This person stood like Emma Courtland.

"I'll shoot."

The person bolted into the soaking rain without a shot fired.

"Emma!" Nikki attempted to stand.

The Tom Jones song mocked her.

Don't panic, Nikki told herself. She couldn't leave the scene without taking inventory.

The snub nose went back into the holster. *Check.*

Nikki patted the key fob in her zippered pocket. *Check.*

She collected the mangled umbrella. *Check.*

Nikki used the umbrella to hide from the video cameras while leaving the property under the relentless rain. *Why was she moving so slow?* Adrenaline alone carried her across the street to the levee. She collapsed the bent umbrella best she could, this time climbing on all fours like a monkey, nearly stumbling again down to the other side.

She stopped just yards from her car to catch her breath, stemming an imminent heart attack. Her hand rubbed over the rapid beating. The rain lightened. Her feet carried her past her parked car to Lakeshore Drive, still absent of travelers. She crossed over the road until reaching the edge of the seawall facing the agitated waves.

The mangled umbrella went in first, hitting the water's edge before being swept back. That wasn't the main concern. She pulled off her ankle holster with the snub nose, performing her best underhanded softball pitch. It flew twenty yards out into the lake. Even though the snub was innocent, it had to go.

Nikki's clothes weighed on her frame while walking back to the car. No activity came from across the levee. She was the only person on the planet. The passenger door unlocked with a touch of the handle. She pulled out her key fob, tossing it across to the driver's seat. Every stitch of clothing came off except underwear, shoving the items in the plastic garbage bag. Last were cheap gym shoes that left mud prints in the garage.

She fell into the passenger seat to dry her cold feet. A giant shiver rendered her useless for a moment. With a huge groan, she forced her body to slide from the passenger side feetfirst into the driver's seat. The heater went on full blast. Dry clothes on the passenger seat were welcomed as they slipped on, but they didn't stop her tremors.

The Tom Jones song had imprinted in her brain.

4

KEITH TEAGUE RECLINED in the bathtub. He slid the gun into his mouth, aiming at his brain stem. There was a chance of survival when pointing at the side of the head. People jerked or twitched. A deflection was likely. He could find himself hooked up to a machine or blow out his optic nerves to be left blind with no pension.

Clamping his mouth down on the barrel didn't cause the same visceral reaction like the first time he attempted suicide several years ago. That initial, desperate act had offered an adrenaline rush he never attained again. At this point, it was more like an exercise.

He embraced the ceremony. A gun in his mouth relaxed him enough to think, which made no sense. Perhaps being that close to death put life in perspective. It made suffering through the hard parts easier, knowing a pull of the trigger would end it all. What was one more day, if this was all it took?

Apologies to Nik swam in his head. She had forgiven him, but those words were hollow. His tongue buckled under the gun barrel as he swallowed. Deep within his subconscious, if he didn't leave a letter explaining things, he wouldn't pull the trigger.

That's enough, now.

He placed the weapon on his chest flat, pressing down with his hand. The metallic residue of gun oil lingered. He sat forward with his mouth over the drain, letting saliva drool from his mouth. The gun oil coated his tongue. He spit water out from the faucet.

A well-worn *The Simpsons* episode filtered from the living room. He stepped out of the tub, which he considered his psychiatrist's couch. *Gun therapy*, he joked in his head. The wave of guilt passed, and his slate was clean once again. The rain ended, but grayer clouds were always on the horizon.

Without warning, his cell phone rang with a unique ringtone that a fellow cop downloaded for him. The voice of Roy Kent from Ted Lasso yelled *no* three times in his rough British voice, then ended with the soft, drawn-out *fuuuuuck* before the voice mail came. Sometimes, he made a game of answering right after the profanity.

He cleared his throat, slapped his face, and answered his boss's call on Roy Kent's second *no*. "Tran, to what do I owe this early morning pleasure?"

"You sound chipper. Are you up already?"

"Lightning woke me. What woke you?"

"Herman Napleton was murdered. I need you on the scene."

5

A LIGHT DRIZZLE continued as Nikki pulled onto the curb outside of her condo building. She parked on the street the day before to avoid the parking garage's cameras. She discarded every shred of evidence. Every detail counted.

The condo residents complained about the broken surveillance camera in the front lobby. She used the blind spot to her advantage. Being New Orleans, some of the younger tenants came home at all hours, but drunk witnesses were horrible witnesses.

Did Emma beat her to killing Herman Napleton?

No one had called or texted. Her vigilant, overly friendly next-door neighbor stayed inside his own place at that hour. She sat cocooned in a blanket at her kitchen table where a nearby vent blew heat on her numb, wrinkled toes. The lights from the Crescent City Connection over the Mississippi could be seen through the sliding glass door to her balcony.

A laptop's bright screen faced her. It added to the outside illumination. She opened an old news article about Emma Courtland's rape accusation against Herman Napleton posted three months ago. Emma couldn't be named in the story, being a sixteen-year-old minor.

The article focused more on the police ineptitude in the investigation. The reporter speculated on how crucial evidence against a rich, white businessman disappeared from the evidence room as if managed by bumbling idiots. No charges were ever brought.

But—*what about the copy of the video*, the reporter speculated.

Somehow, someway, the file became corrupted while on the NOPD's secure network. District Attorney Simone Collins refused to charge Herman Napleton, the owner of the Grande Esplanade Hotel. That didn't ingratiate Collins to Nikki.

She pulled the plaid blanket tighter over unruly, damp hair. Her body heat rose enough to stop the shivering. *What would her day look like when word got out?* So much had gone wrong, but at least nothing was left behind. Even if identified as the suspect pointing the gun, nothing other than being placed at the scene would come from this.

Well, except obstruction of justice.

Nikki switched to a bookmarked tab with Emma's social media. Nothing had been posted beyond the time of becoming a *gutter punk* a year ago. The next bookmarked article described the infiltration of gutter punks in New Orleans. It informed the reader of twenty-somethings scouring the Quarter, begging for food and alcohol, harassing tourists. Hardly any were teens, but there wasn't an age requirement.

Emma would be the same age as Nikki's little sister Morgan if she had survived the car accident. These two girls could've been best friends.

The little rebel had grown on Nikki more than she would admit. Emma wasn't a replacement for Morgan, but maybe just a *placeholder*. Nikki shared in Emma's heartbreak when the DA announced the devastating news of not pursuing her rapist. The justice system's failure had been the last straw.

Stale microwaved coffee sat untouched next to Nikki's cell. She wanted to make a new pot, but the motivation drained. Dawn would arrive soon. A sudden blast of a Neville Brothers ringtone jerked her into the moment. The ID indicated Lan Tran.

Nikki disguised her voice to be groggy. "Lan, what's going on?"

"Sorry to wake you. Something happened. Take a minute to clear your head."

Nikki let a moment pass. "I'm sitting up. What is it?"

"Herman Napleton was found murdered."

"You're kidding." She focused on Napleton's picture in the article.

"One of his staff found him dead in the garage. Considering your involvement and the special circumstances, it's time for Detective Nikki Mayeaux to make her homicide debut as lead."

"Lead?" Her burning eyes closed. "Okay, I'm getting up. I'm guessing no one is in custody?"

"No. Despite the victim, it's still a homicide."

"I've only been in the squad a month. You think I should handle point?"

"Simone Collins might have something to say about that, but yes, I do."

"Why would the District Attorney object?"

He laughed. "Uh, *you*—Emma. She somehow still blames you for Napleton's cell phone disappearing from the evidence room and the video getting corrupted."

"Get in line."

"Don't worry about Collins. You won't be alone. I'm sending Teague to help."

"Do you have to?"

"Keith told me you two settled things when you transferred. Is there a problem?"

"No problem. Yeah, okay. I'm on my way. Um, anything I should know?"

"Don't talk to the media."

Nikki closed the laptop. "Ironic, isn't it?"

"What?"

"I transfer out of Special Victims because of the Napleton case, just to end up in Homicide investigating his murder."

Lan yawned. "Stranger things."

Nikki ended the call with a sliver of relief that cops weren't banging on the door. It was best she controlled the investigation. At worst, she might have to arrest Emma Courtland, a girl she fought hard for a few months ago. Her blanket fell onto the chair as she stood on weak knees.

Warmed toes led her into the bathroom. A brush helped calm her hair into a ponytail, then she applied a light touch of makeup and concealer over the irritation from the ski mask. *Good enough.*

It was going to be a long day.

6

NIKKI ARRIVED ON the Napleton murder scene about thirty minutes after receiving Lieutenant Tran's call. The Third District cops had blocked off the street. Some early morning gawkers collected atop the levee in the nosebleeds, mushing her earlier tracks.

Red and blues flashed in a disco rhythm from atop the squad cars. The caution tape hung from anything useable, encompassing the Napleton property. Nikki bypassed the uniforms with her shield hanging from her neck. One pointed her to the first responder in the driveway.

Nikki read the name tag. "Morning, Officer Perez. What we got?"

Perez appeared to be in his late thirties, with a mature look. "The maid…"

"Housekeeper is fine, go on."

"Housekeeper. She was dropped off at 5:30 this morning. She discovered the victim in his car in the garage, but she found him *after* entering the house. She says the house was locked up, but the right garage door was open. Left garage door was closed. She called 911."

"Nothing was touched?"

"She said no. My partner and I secured the scene."

"Hang tight, I *will* need you later." Nikki moved past him, glancing at the video cameras mounted on the front and back corners of the house. This was her fourth official visit to the house since the rape investigation. She pulled out latex gloves. An officer handed her plastic baggies for her feet.

The Mercedes still idled. This time, an annoying radio host voiced some stupid morning show instead of the song that shall never be named again. Nikki opened the passenger-side door first. She reached in to shut down the engine.

Napleton's Android Galaxy phone sat in a holder on the dash, dotted with blood. She slid it from the cradle, pressing the side button, but it wanted a passcode. Herman's face was out of the question. She walked around to the driver's side, opening the door.

Nikki took the index finger from Napleton's left hand, pressing the print against the sensor in a natural holding position. The cell unlocked.

"Nice," she whispered. "Do you have any new videos, Herman?" She scanned through his gallery. He wouldn't be that stupid to keep them on his personal phone.

It took a few seconds to turn off the lock screen security. She reached over the hunched body and placed it back where she found it.

Next, Nikki needed a better view of Napleton's face. Her fingers attempted to pull his head back, but rigor mortis prevented easy access. She used extra force and managed to make out the number *five* stretching from the top of his forehead down to his chin.

"Are you touching the body?" a voice said from behind.

Detective Keith Teague folded his arms, wearing slacks and a jacket, dark bags under his eyes and blue bags over his shoes. His bedhead looked styled with product. Stubble grew on his face like dark algae.

"I'm sure CSU won't mind that I got a look."

"You must be happy."

"Happy?"

"That he's dead. Not about who did it."

She shifted her weight. "Oh, and who did it?"

Keith tapped his gloved finger on his temple. "Hmm, if we wrote down all the possible suspects on playing cards…"

"It's too early for this." She freed her unruly ponytail to tighten it up again.

"You have your cards with the suspects. I have mine." He pretended to hold them like a poker hand. "Do you have any Emma Courtlands?"

"I can't do this with you."

"Look at me." Keith turned serious. "If you and me are *good*, prove it."

"Playing along with your bullshit will prove it?"

He emphasized holding playing cards. "Do you have any Emma Courtlands?"

Nikki walked near items knocked from the shelves. "Go *fish*."

"*There she is.*" Keith appeared sincere, with those puppy-dog eyes that always used to get his way. "So, are we good to work together?"

"We are. It's not going to be the same, so turn down the charm. I don't need it."

"Fine, as long as there are no eggshells."

Nikki smirked. "Look, I'll admit Emma is a possibility. But a man like Herman Napleton would have many enemies. Just the anonymous video sent to me proves that."

He presented Herman's lower region like a lawyer in a courtroom. "A knife to the groin is personal. That mark on his face looks like black lipstick, and Emma Courtland wears black lipstick."

"Murder solved," she snipped.

"Someone on the wrong side of a bad business deal wouldn't shove a knife in his groin."

"Did Lan send you to spy?"

"Not at all. He just wants me to second chair."

Nikki offered the open rear door in rebuttal. "The back seat rest is down. The killer hid in the trunk, then released the mechanism to climb out as he parked. He or she grabbed Napleton's head from behind, drawing the blade across his throat, then stabbed his torso. Then, he or she ended with one in the man bits."

"And they took the time to write the number five on his face."

"You can tell it's a five?"

"Well, look how it starts." His finger traced the air while speaking. "And then comes down, and if you use your imagination—process of elimination, you can guess it's a number. It looks like the top of a five."

She blinked a few times. "Aren't you wonderful."

"That's my daily affirmation." He continued, "Does the number five have meaning to Emma?"

Nikki leaned in close to him. "Do not say her name in public until it's confirmed."

"You're right. So, what do you make of the items that came off the shelf there?"

"The killer lost their balance?"

Three CSU members stepped into the garage carrying gear. Troy Ozwald led the team, referred throughout Headquarters as Oz. He was middle-aged and came off as chill thanks to a tween daughter. Nikki appreciated that his team was on the job.

He combed his thin blond California hair back with his fingers. "Morning, detectives. Who's lead this fine morning?"

"I am. Can someone make a coffee run?"

"Let me know if you find a sucker." Oz moved away to instruct the other forensics techs and photographer on where to start. He turned back to Nikki. "Anything out of the ordinary?"

"Where do I start? Can you process his phone first? Also, I want to keep the black five on his face out of the media. Tell your people."

Keith added, "Nikki touched his head."

WE DON'T TALK ABOUT EMMA

"Tattletale. You got beat up a lot in school, didn't you?" She fell into their old routine without even realizing it.

"Play nice." Oz offered a fatherly expression. "You see those gloves she's wearing, Keith? I'm sure it's fine."

"I also turned off the engine."

"Not a problem."

As Nikki and Keith started for the house, the responding officer, Miguel Perez, chipperly approached in a pressed uniform. "What can I do, Detectives?"

Nikki swept her arm around. "Find some helpers and question the neighbors about anything they heard or saw."

Perez backed away, diligent with his duties.

"Hold on, Nikki," Oz called out. "You need to see this."

"What is it?"

Oz held up a small bloody gym shoe accented with yellow trim. "It was tucked under the front passenger seat. Maybe it came off as the suspect ran?"

"Is there another shoe?" Keith asked.

"Haven't found one yet." Oz held it at the shoestring.

Imaginary tingles returned to Nikki's feet. "No one would leave barefoot in that cold rainstorm if they didn't have to."

7

THE HOUSEKEEPER WAS questioned while she sat on a stool in a spectacular white and black trimmed kitchen. The refrigerator seamlessly blended into the modules. Nikki set her HGTV wonder aside, giving the young housekeeper, Cristal Dominguez, her warmest smile. A tepid cup from a fancy expresso machine waited on the marble counter.

Nikki faced her from the opposite side of the island. "So, Miss Cristal, did you make this coffee before or after you found Mr. Napleton?"

Cristal spoke with a Hispanic accent Nikki couldn't place. "I make before."

"When did you realize Mr. Napleton wasn't home?"

Her pursed lips indicated she was trying to hold it together. "He is always up when I make coffee. He make no sound, so I go check. He's not in bedroom. I look outside and garage door open." She stopped before crying.

"His death is shocking, Miss Cristal, but I need to know if anything was disturbed in here this morning? Anything odd stick out at you?"

"Everything normal. Who did this to such a nice man?" Cristal asked.

Nikki swallowed down her reaction to *nice man*. "So, I take it Mr. Napleton is good to you."

"Muy bien."

"I hate to be this direct. Has he ever forced you to have sex?"

Her deep, brown eyes widened. "Oh, no. Why would you ask such a thing? He help me send money back to El Salvador."

"A kitchen like this must have a nice set of culinary knives. Where does Mr. Napleton keep them?"

"There. Just give a push." Cristal pointed at a large drawer between the stainless-steel sink and the Viking stove.

Nikki used her knuckle to push it in a tad. It glided open on its own with a soft click. Inside, a wood display case had been custom built, with narrow slots for each knife. None were missing. The handles didn't match the one used in the murder. "These are beautiful."

"He was killed with a knife?" Cristal clutched her chest.

"Has anyone threatened Mr. Napleton?"

Cristal's eyes wandered. "Ever since the…trouble, he try to be private."

"Trouble?"

"The, ah, false truth—the lie." Her cheeks blushed. "Such a shame. It hurt him. Mrs. Napleton move out. That girl just shows up."

"What girl?"

"That *liar girl*. She came several times. She stand out on lawn. She stare at the house. I tell Mister Napleton about this. He says *don't you worry about it*. I tell him I worry."

Nikki presented a photo of Emma on her cell. "This girl?"

"Si, but she was—ah—much makeup." Her hand swirls around her face. "Dark makeup. Scary."

"When was the last time you saw her?"

"Saturday—yes." Her head swiveled, looking up at the ceiling. "What do I do now? Is Mrs. Napleton coming back here to live? She liked me."

"I don't know." Nikki sympathized with her.

Keith entered the kitchen, putting his cell away. "I updated Tran. You mind if ask Miss…"

"Cristal," the housekeeper said.

"Miss Cristal. Mr. Napleton had an extra key fob for the Mercedes?"

She pointed to a corner drawer. "All keys are kept there."

"Push and it opens," Nikki explained. "You think the suspect had it?"

"Oz found a second one." Still gloved, Keith used his thumb to press against the drawer. He knocked a few junk items around. "We'll get prints for the drawers."

"No key?"

Nikki didn't answer. "Has that girl—Emma Courtland—ever come inside the house?"

Her head shook. "Not while I'm here. No."

"Emma must've been in here at some point."

"Keith." She moved behind Cristal, making a face.

"Oh, sorry. Didn't mean to say that."

"Be right back, Miss Cristal." Nikki walked Keith by the arm into the living room. "Are you sure you're a detective? Don't talk about suspects or evidence in front of witnesses."

He pinched the bridge of his nose. "My bad. I'm used to gang killings or domestic murders. No one gives a shit what we say there."

"I'm not so sure that Lan doesn't want me to babysit *you.* A spotlight will be on us from here on out. I'm lead, not your ex-girlfriend. The press is bound to find her and ask questions. Discretion, please."

His dimples appeared. "You're cute when solving murders."

Nikki took a breath. "So, our *un-sub…*"

"*Un-sub.* So FBI.

She ignored him. "Our suspect somehow managed to acquire the key fob unless Mary Napleton took it when she moved out."

"We need to question his wife."

"Thanks for the tip. C'mon. Let's search the house."

Herman Napleton's home decor reflected the Grande Esplanade Hotel, which he owned. Nikki figured his estranged wife Mary could be responsible for the interior design. Mardi Gras items, New Orleans memorabilia as well as Impressionist paintings and modern art were on display.

He had a *Blue Dog* painting by Rodrigue, another status symbol. A gigantic mirror with Grande Esplanade etched in the glass hung on the main wall. Either Herman didn't spend much time home, or Cristal kept it perfect.

"No weird sex stuff," Keith said, leaving the bedroom. "Nothing was disturbed. I'd say not a robbery."

"Come see this." Nikki opened the door to a small room containing several stacked monitors. A computer tower was underneath a table. Despite every urge to destroy the hard drive, Nikki knew she hadn't made a mistake. "It's Herman's security room with video. Go get Oz."

8

A TICKLING ON Dread's face woke him. He swiped at his cheek, swearing when the insect bounced off his fingers. A roach jetted for the nearest shelter. Those flying creatures were the most annoying thing about New Orleans.

He pulled the blanket over his head in an attempt to keep sleeping. Every tickle or itch felt like a bug. Both arms pushed the covers down to his waist in frustration. The other *traveler kids* in the warehouse slept hard, dead to the world. Most didn't wake until noon.

Dread sometimes slept in his clothes. Baggy jeans, a torn tee shirt, and a fake Aztec hoodie kept him warm enough during the southern winter. His armpit reeked so he didn't lift his arms. Deodorant wouldn't be found amongst the traveler kids' toiletries.

First check of the morning showed no one contacted his prepaid phone.

He scratched at three-day-old stubble. His dreadlocks would need to be palm rolled again soon, despite the pain. Maybe his Afro could go natural. His own yawn caught him by surprise.

Before sliding on his boots, he turned them upside down and patted the soles, in case more roaches had tried to find a home. His neck cracked when he stretched left and right. Hunger pulled at his stomach. He craved a Lucky Dog.

His mother, when sober, had cooked him pancakes on the weekends up in Oklahoma. They volunteered at the shelter when she was *straight*. Her sobriety mimicked a rollercoaster. Then one night, a *john* killed her in an alley.

He never knew his father—or *a* father, for that matter. Running away from a bad situation was a common story with these *traveler kids*, who weren't kids at all.

The vacant warehouse on the West Bank offered premium shelter, as if they were all roaches themselves. The designated mattresses were private islands. Original art made by traveler kids, books, and food was shared between them. The leader named Rot ruled the warehouse, so everyone respected each other. In their little kingdom, the *Rottweiler* wore the crown.

Dread dodged discarded items on the floor on the way to Emma's corner. They accepted her despite being so young. Someone had given her the name *Peewee*, but it didn't fit. Emma used her real name. Her mattress was empty. Her backpack was gone.

The industrial metal steps led up to the second-floor catwalk. No one stirred at the pounding of Dread's soles on the grates. His rings tapped every time he gripped the railing. Some of the kids stirred. The view of ten or so people living in commune conditions comforted him to know he wasn't alone.

He knocked before walking in on Rot and the company he brought to his private room. They were both naked under the covers. Drug paraphernalia was scattered on the floor. Clothes dotted the place.

Rot was over six feet tall, with long muscles that sported various tattoos on tan skin. The pale girl looked fragile. *Translucent* came to Dread's mind—and young. Sex filled the room like a scented candle.

"What?" He turned over, tugging the blanket off the girl, exposing her breasts. The pretty girl didn't show a bit of modesty.

"You seen Emma?" Dread leaned against the door.

Rot lifted the covers. "Emma? You here, girl?" He looked to his date. "Where's Emma? Here, girl!" He whistled, waiting for a comment that didn't come. "How the fuck would I know?"

Dread's eyelids dropped. "She's never up this early. I'm worried."

"You're worried your mocha princess fucked someone and didn't come back last night. You just won't pull the trigger because you're scared of the *law*. She moved past your ass."

"Fuck you, man. I'm heading out."

"Hey, is there coffee down there?"

"Do I look like Starbucks?"

"Why don't you make us some coffee, you fuck."

"I'm out."

"Hey, hey, hey!"

Dread returned to the room with mild interest.

Rot waved his hand over the naked girl. "What do you think of *Flower?* She's a year younger than Emma, and cops haven't slapped cuffs on me."

"That's not something to be proud of."

"You have pride? I'm bringing her by The Crush for Percy to check out. Beautiful tits, right?"

"Don't ask me that." Dread conveyed sympathy. "You're fifteen?"

"And four months." She lit up a cigarette.

"Jesus…" Dread rubbed the bridge of his nose.

Rot leaned into her. "Remember. Outside these walls, you're eighteen, babe." He looked back at Dread. "Percy has to let her dance."

"He'd be stupid to let you in the door. No offense, Flower. You're ten to twenty without parole."

The girl frowned. "I've been with older men."

"I found Flower outside Tipitina's. When I saw this face, this body. We are going to make some money."

Dread pushed off the doorjamb. "Careful with this guy. He's a heartbreaker. And not in a romantic way."

"You're right. He's uptight." She giggled.

"Go—get!" Rot threw an empty plastic cup at Dread that fell way short.

Dread exited the West Bank warehouse, conveniently located near the river, opposite the Quarter. He could see the Crescent City Connection if he stood on the warehouse roof. No immediate ride was available. He needed to walk several blocks to take the ferry across the Mississippi. He stuck his hands in his pockets and started the journey.

Exploring the streets gave Dread time to clear his head. He inhaled and sighed, releasing a breath of fog. Emma stayed out last night. A pit grew in his stomach with each passing hour. A sixteen-year-old girl needed protection in their world. Emma needed someone to make sure a guy like Rot didn't sink their teeth in them, like with Flower.

Funny, he'd left Oklahoma so he wouldn't have to give a shit anymore.

9

HERMAN NAPLETON'S SURVEILLANCE video would reveal mistakes Nikki made—Emma's as well. Nikki and Keith waited in Napleton's spy hub for Oz to change gloves and booties. The housekeeper spoke in a one-sided Spanish conversation in the kitchen. When it became evident that Oz wasn't coming right away, Nikki sat to settle her butterflies.

Keith looked out the window. "Dating anyone?"

"You don't have to fill the silence."

"Just curious."

Oz entered the room with an excited face. "Video. Perfect."

"Yeah, nothing bad ever happens to video."

"You won't let that go, will you?" Oz eyed her. "The malware that destroyed the video came from the phone that recorded it."

"And the phone disappeared."

"The tech resigned, and we installed new virus protection. It won't happen again."

Nikki asked, "Do you have to take the system back to your office to crack the encryption?"

Oz spun the tower around, locating a list of crossed-off passwords taped to the side of the tower. "He wasn't worried about hackers. I'll run a gauntlet of tests to make sure nothing harmful is on it."

"Lovely."

With three clicks of the mouse, a video played from earlier that morning. The outside recorder's lenses had awnings, offering a clear view of Herman's Mercedes pulling onto the property in the drenching rain. The back camera continued to pick up footage. Most of the garage's back wall was out of view.

"This is a nice Lorex setup. It's continuous, which most people don't do." Oz glanced at both of them. "He's recording on a forty-eight-hour loop."

Keith asked, "Why record no activity?"

"Motion detectors have a shorter range than the actual camera's vision."

Nikki caught on. "So, continual footage will catch stuff the motion detector won't, like a person walking across the street."

Despite the light source in the garage, the video was dark and distant. The brake lights on the Mercedes shook for a few moments, then settled. Seconds later, Nikki saw herself on the screen, hidden under the umbrella. She held her breath.

"*What the what?*" Keith said. "Isn't the killer in the car?"

"I don't know. I thought so. Go to the front camera, Oz. A minute or two earlier."

As it played, they made out a blur falling on the levee's slope. Then, the figure crossed the street.

Keith said, "They came from across the levee. We should have uniforms canvass the whole area leading to the lake."

"I'll have the levee taped off. When the ground dries, there might be some useable shoe prints." *Not a chance, but it sounded good.*

"Fast forward?"

"Yeah, let it play out." Nikki's peripheral was on Keith. The video was clipped at the top of the garage door, only allowing a blurry visual of Nikki's bottom half.

"I can't tell. Is that a gun?"

"Looks like it," Nikki said. "Napleton could have a bullet wound we didn't see."

The rear door opened with the force, knocking Nikki out of frame. The rest of the video played out with an individual in baggy clothes running off the property after pausing at the entrance.

"You were right. Killer hid in the trunk. Killed him from the back seat. Still doesn't explain the mystery guest or the person missing a shoe. Did you notice they stopped for a moment?" Keith asked.

"It's like they heard something. Did the other person call out?" Nikki wondered aloud.

"Too bad the audio didn't pick it up."

Oz broke in. "Either way, they both got away without showing their faces. We can analyze it better with my software back at my office, but in my experience, I'm not going to ascertain much."

Nikki remade her ponytail. "That's an interesting wrinkle."

"A second person wanted to kill him?" Keith pondered.

"Popular guy," she said. "We still have a third person of interest, too. Both of these people had their shoes."

"That, they did," Keith agreed.

"The person from the back seat—the killer—is about Emma's size."

"That, they are."

"Okay, Oz. Go back to when Herman left the house. Let's get a timeline established."

"Yep." He let out a profanity when the video jumped too far in a huge chunk, stopping about midday. A young female came into frame, standing in front of the house.

"That's Emma," she blurted. "The housekeeper said she came by sometimes."

"If you're going to murder someone, it's smart to do a dry run, right, Nik?"

True. Nikki's face turned hot. "We'll have to examine this whole thing back at the station."

"I'll make a copy." Oz spun around in the chair to face them. "We'll take the recorder with us."

"Why hide in the back," Keith asked, "When you could just wait for him on the property? Kill him when he gets out of the car like this second person planned?"

"It insures no one tracks you to the scene."

"That's premeditated."

"I would agree." Oz pulled the computer cables.

"What if she wasn't hiding? What if Napleton knew she was back there but didn't figure she'd release the back seat rest?"

Nikki's brow furrowed. "Odds are, he wouldn't bring her into his home."

"Also, he wouldn't leave her with a knife."

"No, he wouldn't." Nikki stopped to answer her cell as Aaron Neville sung the ringtone. "Hey Lan, did you dial the wrong number? Keith is right here reading his *Detecting for Dummies* book."

"Sounds like you two are getting along."

"We're watching surveillance. I'll put all this in my report."

"I'm not calling for an update. A deceased female was reported under the I-10 overpass on Claiborne."

"We're a bit busy here."

"I understand, Nik. But you'll want to get over there. Keith told me what Oz found in the car. This victim is missing a shoe."

10

Located on the border of the Quarter, the stretch of Claiborne Avenue that ran alongside the raised I-10 was depressing by day, sketchy by night. A wide concrete expanse sat under the interstate, interrupted only by massive columns. City vehicles and construction equipment were parked there, but the large area had been used for anything from a tent city to a car show.

Nikki arrived at the scene first, having suggested Keith stop at a P.J.'s for coffee. He volunteered without argument. The horns and revving engines of morning traffic echoed from every direction under the interstate.

A female cop stepped away from her conversation with three other officers to meet Nikki halfway. The nametag pinned to the responding officer's uniform read *L. "Jonesy" Jones.* She was close to six feet tall, with great facial symmetry. Her brunette hair was pulled back into a bun. She'd be cute after a salon day. Jonesy escorted Nikki to the dead girl's location.

"She was called in a half hour ago." The cop blew hot breath into her hands, stopping before a long row of jersey barriers, which were concrete dividers used to divert traffic.

Nikki picked up on her apprehension. "What's wrong, Jones?"

"Everyone calls me Jonesy." Her hand waved toward the body. "She has rat bites... I don't need that visual stuck in my head."

Nikki took a few more tentative steps until seeing a female body between the fifth and sixth barrier. The slope of each base next to each other acted as a cradle. A punch of rotten milk wafted by.

"Who found the body?" Nikki checked between other barricades.

"Dispatch didn't say. I'd guess a tipster."

"Someone who doesn't want to be involved. No bag or wallet? Any identification?"

"We didn't find anything. Did I hear right? Is Herman Napleton dead?"

Nikki pointed at her nametag. "What's the L?"

"Laura. I've been called Jonesy forever."

Nikki nodded. "You heard right, Jonesy."

"I don't like these gutter punks as much as the next cop, but this poor girl." Jonesy cringed.

Nikki kept eye contact with her. "She's wearing nice clothes. Her hair looks washed. Why do you assume she's a gutter punk?"

"I've seen her in the Quarter. Maybe she made it to a shower and Good Will. She begs on Royal."

Keith walked toward them with a P.J.'s cup in each hand. He frowned. "Jonesy!"

"You again?" Jonesy giggled. "Good morning."

"If I knew you were here, I would've got you a latte with the oat milk."

"What a memory." Her eyes fixed on his while she continued on to join the other cops.

Keith handed Nikki one of the cups. "Here you are, m'lady."

Nikki seductively repeated, "*What a memory, Detective*. Wow."

"Jonesy's cool. We've worked a few scenes together."

"She's *very cool*." She turned serious. "Take a look. Don't mind the rat bites. I see strangulation marks."

"Rat bites." Keith took in the victim. "Red lipstick. Smeared. We'll probably find some on Napleton's clothes."

"Not that we'll need to prove he killed her. And she isn't posed. He tossed her in there."

Jonesy shouted, "Can me and the boys help?"

Nikki projected back to her, "No one disturbed anything, right?"

"Nope. Above my pay grade."

Keith pointed to a few bystanders with their cells out to record. "Question everyone who stops. Get their info, if they're willing to give it. This ain't your first rodeo."

"I *do* like a good rodeo." Officer Jonesy backed away with a smile.

Nikki could've commented on that as well. Instead, she checked the body from top to bottom. The victim was young, early twenties. She had messy but clean blonde hair and pasty skin due to the cold and the blood pooling on her backside. Her clothes were twisted around, and as reported, she only had one shoe matching the other from Herman's car.

"She's lying on her coat. Cushion for the sex?"

Keith leaned in. "Why not just have sex in the car?"

"DNA. There's just enough room for them with total privacy." She takes a sip of the coffee. "He liked it down and dirty?"

Keith scanned the whole area with a cringe. "Yeah, but out here? In the cold? Herman could go to a motel. I'm willing to bet no sex."

"Not our job to psychoanalyze them."

"Two dead bodies, and it's not even eight yet."

"At what point did the killer enter the trunk—that's the question."

"You agree it's Emma?"

Nikki put her free hand in her coat pocket. "Look, Emma is first on my list, but I don't have to like it. How about we wait until Oz comes back with solid evidence before we name her for everything?"

"I can do that. Anything else you want to tell me?"

"Yeah, thank you for the coffee. Sugar and cream—*what a memory.*"

"Stop it." He winked.

"Don't do that." Walking past, she nudged his arm with her shoulder. "Let's look around all this crap for something that might've been discarded."

They each walked around the tow trucks, sprint vehicles, and bobcats, meeting back at the body. Keith spoke over the distant sirens. "Oz is going to have a busy morning."

"There's nothing to do here. Go back to the Lakeview scene and get into the GPS on Napleton's phone. Oz should let you. I'll see if Lan can send another forensics team."

"His cell has to be locked. We'll need a warrant. It'll take a week at least…but you know that. What did you do?"

"It's not locked."

Keith squinted at her. "You know it's not locked?"

"I do."

He smiled. "Facial recognition would've been difficult. You used his prints?"

"Some people don't lock their phones."

"Bullshit. You've been watching *Law & Order*."

"I'm going to try Emma." Nikki pulled out her cell.

"That's right. You have her number."

"I doubt she'll answer." She put the phone to her ear. "No, I get that stupid automated recording. She has it off, or the battery is dead." Nikki pointed at the uniforms milling about. "Is Jonesy a good cop?"

"Great cop. She's good people. Good *with* people, too. Why?"

"We can use her and Perez from the Lakeview scene. Start a task force."

"You're going to stay here and wait for Forensics and the coroner?"

"No, I'll make sure the cops out here can keep the scene secure. Jonesy can help me bring Emma in. If I can get past her father."

"Why would Jonesy's father care?"

"Emma's father, *dick*." She reared her hand back, but held it in midair. "Warren Courtland."

He laughed. "Serious question, though: Are you going to treat her like a suspect or your friend?"

"I'll treat Jonesy like a cop."

"*Emma*, asshole." He held his grin.

"I'm going to do my job."

11

Keith sensed Nikki wasn't herself—and she shouldn't be. Investigating this particular murder and working together was a lot for anyone. Underneath Nik's nerves, something was...*off.* He'd learned her tells and quirks. Her rude and gruff attitude were good signs, however. If being together was untenable, it'd be obvious.

He parked on the glimmering, wet street in front of the Napleton house again. A moment in the warmth was enjoyed before exiting the car. Oz and his team were still in the garage. News people were reporting from different vantage points. Details would have to wait for a press conference.

Roy Kent's voice yelled out of his cell. It was a restricted number. He started the recording app. "This is Detective Teague."

"Are you alone?" a female voice asked.

He pulled back the phone to look at the number again. "I'm alone. I figured you'd call."

"Napleton is dead? What the hell is going on?"

"It's too early to know anything. What do you expect me to tell you?"

"That you have his killer in custody."

"I can't tell you that. Give us time to sort through this, okay?" He leaned his head against the window.

"We don't have time. This has to end ASAP."

"We'll do our best."

"This investigation needs to be wrapped up without names in the press. Make sure that happens."

"Why don't you go ahead and destroy me."

"*Oh, boo hoo.* Word of advice? Focus on the killer, not the victim."

"I get it."

Keith ended the call and wiped his face. He yelled out like a madman.

He finished the tepid coffee and prepared himself with a calming breath. After slamming the wheel with his palms, he exited his car, facing the levee. *Should he walk over?* His shoes would sink in the mud without wading boots. But, all he had were the thin booties Oz gave him.

The hospital-type shoe sleeves would have to do. The flat ground leading to the levee might've absorbed most of the rain, but there were obvious pools of water. He headed toward the incline, keeping to the left side of the tape. Nikki had to know the storm would turn any footprints to slush. She'd made the call to rope it off.

Two steps in, and his shoes were toast. The cold hit his feet, but he couldn't tell if it was a false sensation or if they had gotten wet. Still, Keith climbed until reaching the top. His booties were like wet diapers, heavy with mud and slipping off his feet. They weren't meant to protect shoes. *Screw it.* He kicked them off, then descended the other side facing the lake.

The yellow tape stopped containment just before the top of the levee. This person of interest most likely parked right behind the rest area to avoid a visual from Lakeshore Drive. The rain and umbrella were extra cover. They had patience, waiting for this storm.

He walked the small parking area, stopping at a discolored mess. Vomit? *Maybe.* It was orange, like baby food—or mushed carrots.

Nikki? A moment of resignation passed. He checked over his shoulder, then stepped in it and spread it around.

If this was indeed Nikki, she had been nervous—never having murdered before. The video showed someone handling a weapon with skill and knew the location of Napleton's cameras. This person said something that gave the killer pause in the garage. Who else could?

Keith continued to track a possible foot path, not to collect evidence but to cover Nikki's tracks. The bathrooms of the rest area were locked, and there was nothing obvious left around the building. Where is the best place to toss evidence? Do you take it with you to another location? If he had fled the scene of a murder and had to nix something... Where would...? His eyes found Lake Pontchartrain.

Keith waited for a break in traffic before crossing Lakeshore drive, stopping at the top step of the sea wall. He scanned the length of concrete steps left and right. One dark object caught his attention on the last step, taking mild waves. He walked toward it, first thinking it looked like a stingray in trouble, but the skinny metal spokes sticking out made it easy to identify.

It was the umbrella. A generic, cheap common umbrella.

He straightened, looking around at the morning activity, which paid him no mind. No one else was ever going identify that as evidence. He turned and headed back toward the Napleton scene. Nikki covered her tracks well, *but cops were good at that.*

His *blackmailer* would probably appreciate pinning Herman's murder on Nikki.

No, he'd give his own life to make sure Nikki stayed in the clear.

12

THE COURTLAND ADDRESS was Uptown off St. Charles Avenue near Tulane University. Nikki loved the area brimming with majestic oaks. The Courtlands owned one of many historic homes in the Uptown area, handed down from generation to generation.

Living in such a place should have made Emma a little princess socialite, not a gutter punk. The 8,000 square foot mansion was built on raised earth, with a solid, decorative iron gate set in a three-foot-tall wall of concrete around the property. The house had a white exterior with impressive columns and a lovely porch with rocking chairs.

Nikki pulled next to the keypad mounted on the driveway with Jonesy's squad behind her. She announced herself on the intercom. Without an answer, the gates hummed to life, opening inward, allowing the two cars access on a slight incline until parking next to a shiny new Audi.

Jonesy and her partner, DeAndre Williams, a bald black man with muscles filling his uniform, caught up with Nikki on the way to the front door.

Jonesy whistled. "Nice pad."

Nikki turned to face them. "The family is comfortable with me, so I do all the talking. No commentary or opinions. Think before you act, because this guy will pull the *Superintendent* card."

"Rich white people. Got it." Williams made a face at the large fountain with a cherub dispensing water from his baby penis.

One of the large double doors opened. Instead of a housekeeper, Warren Courtland answered the door in a suit. "Nikki. If you're here about Herman, I've heard."

"What did you hear?"

"He's dead." He looked at the two officers. "You don't think I had something to do with it?"

"We don't, Warren. Is Emma home by chance?"

"*Emma*. Figures… my stepdaughter hasn't been here for days."

"Still won't say *daughter*? Mind if we talk inside?"

"I'm on my way out to meet with Mary."

"Give me a few minutes, please."

"Are you certain it's Emma, or is it a guess?"

Sharon Courtland appeared at Warren's side, wearing Lululemon sweatpants and a Tulane sweatshirt. Despite Emma being half-black on her biological father's side, she resembled Sharon in every aspect except shade of skin.

"Warren, this is *Nikki*," Sharon emphasized. "Of course she can come in."

"Fine, but *they* wait outside." Warren pointed at the uniformed officers.

"I got this," she told Jonesy. "Knock on the neighbor's door; maybe they've seen Emma coming or going."

Nikki was led to the parlor where she chose the same leather-studded chair used during the rape investigation. A white Roman bust hovered over her shoulder. Nothing had changed in the way of décor. Sharon took a seat on the *eggshell* sofa. Warren remained standing with his arms folded.

"Word travels fast. Who informed you?" Nikki asked.

"You know I'm connected. And you think it's Emma?"

"It can't be Emma," Sharon stated.

"So, you haven't seen Emma for days? Is someone out looking for her?"

"She's not missing." Warren lets his arms drop, exasperated. "She comes back."

"Can you contact her?"

"The cell Sharon gave her is turned off. She probably threw it in the river. Or one of those *gutter punks* stole it. I use every favor I can to keep her out of the system."

"No one ever called Social Services?"

"No need to involve them. She comes back." Warren hesitated. "As manager of Herman's hotel, I have calls to make."

"In a minute, Warren. Please. The press will contact you soon. Herman was just discovered hours ago. Did either of you engage with him last night?"

Warren checked his watch. "No, we were both home by eight last night. We've been here since."

"Video places Emma on Herman's property earlier in the day. We just want to question her."

He pointed toward the front lawn. "Do you always bring backup to take a statement?"

She stood to be at his level. "We're being careful."

Warren stepped in Nikki's face. "I said it before, I'll say it again. Emma lied about the rape."

"I saw the video. Herman Napleton raped Emma, along with three conspirators."

"The video that disappeared under your noses?" He backed away when she stood her ground. "The girl being raped was unconscious and you couldn't tell a 100 percent it was her. You said it yourself."

"It was Emma, and the mask was off Napleton's face for a few seconds." Nikki stayed even. "Don't tell me it's a fake or AI. I'm not rehashing this with you."

"Emma manipulates everyone. Sharon agrees."

His wife nodded without looking up.

"We're done here," Warren announced.

"Mary Napleton stands to inherit majority ownership of the hotel. Are you worried about keeping your stake in it?"

"Please." He adjusted his tie, collecting himself. "Mary must be beside herself. I have to go talk to her."

"I thought they were divorcing."

"They are—*were*. She's moved into the *river suite* at the Esplanade."

"You don't mind losing the revenue on that expensive room?"

He hiked an eyebrow. "Herman offered the suite in a show of generosity for the divorce lawyers. I support that decision. He never held resentment toward me for Emma's lie. He understood that girl is troubled."

"If Emma comes home, please call me."

"Sharon, see her out." He adjusted his pocket square, returning to a foyer mirror.

Sharon dabbed her eyes with an embroidered napkin. "Don't mind him. Would you like a coffee, Nikki?"

Warren huffed. "Coffee? Sharon, sometimes... Do what you want. I have calls to make."

After Warren left the room, Nikki said, "Coffee sounds nice."

Nikki followed Sharon into the kitchen where she selected a coffee cup from a cabinet with glass panes. This was another dream kitchen, with copper fixtures and amber accents. A large island with distressed copper under glass anchoring the space.

"Emma's in more danger out there on her own, Sharon."

She nodded on the way to the refrigerator. "I remember you like milk and sugar. I never told Warren, but I enjoyed your company during that whole ordeal."

"I did, too—when we spoke about other things."

"Look at this place. This is way too much house. A chef cooks our meals, and we have a girl who comes in twice a week to clean." She laughed in a bittersweet way. "Poor little bored wife, right?"

"No, that sounds lonely." Nikki's eyes found a large block of knives on the counter. One was missing. The handles looked to be the same as the one sticking from Napleton's groin. Nikki's entire body tensed. "You don't have to agree with your husband about Emma."

"Emma has always acted out. Always contrary. I wouldn't put it past her to accuse Herman of rape to have the platform." She looked down at the floor, speaking in a whisper. "It's easier to agree with him."

"I can't counsel you, Sharon, but you have to stand up for yourself—for your daughter."

"She is sixteen with issues and anger, and yet, look how close you are to her. That was by her design."

Warren poked his head in the kitchen. "Mary is waiting for me. *May I go, Detective?*" He didn't wait for an answer.

"I'm leaving, too." Nikki finished her coffee and walked to the dishwasher, opening it up. Not a dirty utensil to be found. "A knife is missing from your set." She stepped over to the block.

Sharon didn't miss a beat. "It got caught in the disposal. Threw it away."

"Those things happen." Nikki touched the empty slot. "Did Emma cook a lot when she was here?"

"Sure, on Sundays we used to make red beans and rice for Monday." She smiled with the memory.

"You will again. After this rebellious phase passes." She hoped Sharon took the hint. "Thanks for the coffee."

"I'll walk you out."

Nikki exited the house in time to see Warren leaving the property in his brand-new silver Audi. He had just enough room to get by Nikki's Accord and the squad.

She joined Jonesy and DeAndre at the car. "Okay, I have y'all for the day. Check in with Officer Perez and start patrolling the Quarter for Emma. I'll touch base later."

As the two uniformed officers backed out of the driveway, Nikki texted Keith to head over to the Grande Esplanade to keep Warren Courtland from meeting with Mary Napleton.

Then, she called Lan Tran. "Hey, I'm at the Courtlands'. We need to put a BOLO out on Emma. She's not at her house, and the Courtlands have no idea where she is."

"On it," he said.

"We need to get a warrant for the Courtland estate."

Lan paused. "Until we get forensics back with solid proof, no judge is going to sign that warrant—and considering who it is, I'm doubtful."

13

Nikki parked in standing water on Esplanade Avenue. The *neutral ground* stood between her and the Grande Esplanade Hotel. She spotted Keith's car under an oak tree not too far ahead. Her eyelids closed with fatigue, and it wasn't even noon. She needed glasses to hide her bloodshot eyes, but didn't want to appear cliché.

The five-story building had tiny balconies meant for two people max, which was fine as the street view on the eastern border of the Quarter was less than postcard-worthy. The façade wasn't very remarkable, either, relative to the architecture in the Quarter behind it. However, the inside of the hotel more than made up for it.

Nikki walked into a plush lobby described best as cozy luxury. Deep sofas, chairs, and plants created a nice flow where guests could relax without the annoyance of people checking in and out. Mardi Gras decorations had already gone up as purple, green, and gold would soon dominate the city.

Courteous, well-dressed staffers catered and laughed along with the guests. In the center of the lobby, Keith sat on a sofa opposite Warren Courtland, who leaned forward on the edge of a dark green chair. They both perked up right away. Keith showed instant relief, like the bomb squad had arrived. They each stood.

"Tell your watchdog I need to speak to Mary."

"I told Detective Teague to delay you."

"What law says I can't?"

"You got me. No legal reason. I need Mrs. Napleton's unfiltered, unbiased statement before you two compare stories."

Warren laughed, but without humor. "You think someone's going to *cover for Emma?* Just remember, I have the Superintendent on speed dial." His head swiveled between her and Keith. "I'll grant you a half hour." He tapped his Rolex.

They walked toward the elevator. Nikki said, "Lan's putting a BOLO on Emma. You find anything with Napleton's cell?"

Keith pushed the UP button. "You were right. As luck would have it, the bastard was trusting and had no security code."

"Amazing."

He stepped in the elevator, pulling out a notepad to read. "He gets a call from Mary Napleton at 7:32 p.m. At 8:17 p.m., he arrives at Harrah's Casino."

"Okay. We'll pull their video."

"At 8:45 p.m., he receives a call from an unrestricted number. Ten minutes later, he's on Frenchman Street—Marigny Triangle."

"Frenchman? Bars and boutique shops for artists. When did the storm come in?"

"Rain didn't start until about eleven. At 10:13 p.m., he arrives at the Claiborne overpass."

Nikki watched the digital numbers increase as they headed to the fifth floor. "So the victim is conceivably killed between 9:15 and 10:20?"

"I have him arriving here at the Esplanade about 10:30 p.m. From here, he gets home at 11:45-ish, as it matches with the video time stamp."

The elevator doors opened to a narrow table against the opposite wall with fruit and flowers. Ornate sconces were mounted above it. Nikki stepped out first. To the right was the cleaning cart loaded with towels and such, but the housekeeper wasn't around.

Nikki turned left to head to the *river suite*, meaning the one closest to the Mississippi. "We'll get the hotel security video before we leave. In case he spoke to someone."

"What's Mary Napleton like?"

"Started as a trophy wife, but turned out she was smart. Twenty years younger than Herman, but she learned the business under him, no pun intended. She either likes you or she doesn't. Turns out, we liked each other. I do believe she's going to like you, too."

"Why's that?"

"You'll see. Just don't get a big head."

"Okay." Keith straightened his clothes. "The Mercedes was unattended while Napleton was up here. The valet wasn't paying attention."

"Right. Emma slipped into Herman's car with the fob after it was parked."

The door to the suite was already open before they had a chance to knock. Keith announced their arrival. "Mrs. Napleton? It's Detectives Teague and Mayeaux."

"Come in," a richly feminine voice commanded as if she was in a 1950s film. "I was expecting housekeeping. They're late."

Mary Napleton sat with elegance, with one leg crossed over the other in the den of the suite. Her Irish red hair swept behind one shoulder. A hot-pink pantsuit came off as stylish instead of gawdy, like a picture out of *Vanity Fair*. She sipped from a crystal glass. "Nikki, good to see you."

"How are you, Mary?" Nikki walked closer.

"Considering my pervert husband is dead, I'm dandy. This was a better outcome than a conviction."

"I don't know," Nikki said. "I kind of wanted him to suffer."

Mary smiled with a light clapping of her hands. "Bravo."

"You're not upset," Keith said.

"After you've entertained dozens of scenarios where the outcome is his death, you don't really shed tears when it happens."

"On that note…" Keith pulled out his pad again. "… you wouldn't mind telling us where you were last night?"

She answered with charisma, "Oh, I was at Harrah's early in the evening where I talked with Herman."

Nikki glanced at Keith. "You planned to meet there?"

"Oh, no. I called to tell him about a piece a jewelry I left behind at the house. I had no idea he'd show at Harrah's. He brought me the earrings." The back of her hand displayed one on her earlobe. "Can you believe this man?"

"Why do you suppose he did that?"

"He wanted to butter me up to talk about the divorce. We both got heated, and thankfully, someone called him. He sapped my gambling mojo, so I came back here. About 9-ish."

Nikki moved around the spacious suite. "When you moved out of the Lakeview house, did you happen to take the spare key fob for the Mercedes?"

She groaned. "No. I hated that car."

"Did you see Herman again here at the hotel last night after Harrah's?"

"I did. He wanted to apologize for accosting me at the blackjack table. Didn't have a lick of jewelry to barter with that time."

"How'd he look?" Nikki asked. "Calm? Agitated?"

"It looked like he'd ran a mile." She flipped her hand.

"You let him in your suite."

"Yes. He teased me with bigger settlements and then reneged. I won't get lagniappe from that man. But I always reach for the carrot."

"Good thing you're still married," Nikki said. "No disputes."

"Tell me about it." She put her hand over a silver cross on a necklace. "God answers prayers."

"But without his demise in sight, why live in the hotel?"

"*Motivation*, Detective. Otherwise, I wouldn't piss on his grave."

"You understand he was killed after leaving here?"

"Most dead people were probably leaving from somewhere. If you want to hear me say *I didn't do it*—I didn't do it."

"Will you be handling his services?" Keith asked.

"He made his own arrangements. There won't be a wake. He didn't want his body on display. The arrogant bastard arranged a Jazz funeral."

"Not surprising." Nikki paused. "May I freshen up, Mary?"

"Of course, you look like you haven't slept in ages." She pointed at the bathroom, then looked Keith up and down. "Detective Teague and I will be just fine."

"Keith, please," he said.

Other than a vast selection of makeup peppering the vanity, the bathroom was clean yet lived in. A white towel with black and red smears had been left on the floor near the shower door. Nikki picked it up, running a finger over the waxy substance stuck to the threads. Could it be mascara and lipstick?

Nikki left the towel on the vanity. She prepared to ask Mary if Herman had taken a shower. Instead, she saw Keith scrolling through his cell while Mary had her back turned, looking out the window. Her cell was pressed against her ear.

"Warren Courtland called. I couldn't stop her." Keith shrugged.

Nikki lowered her voice to a whisper. "Let's go. I need to speak with the cleaning staff about collecting her towels for us. I think there's trace."

"Great, but if she now owns the hotel and lives here, wouldn't taking the towels be illegal search and seizure?"

Nikki took off her cap and adjusted her hair. "Ah...gray area."

14

Nikki and Keith assembled the murder boards with the collected evidence. An erasable whiteboard butted next to a corkboard about the same size. They were for tracking gang affiliations or theft patterns.

Emma's high school freshman picture was pinned at the top along with a candid shot snapped during the rape investigation. It made for a hell of a *before* and *after*. The pic of the murder weapon was placed to the right.

A box with four donuts waited for takers at the center of the long table. Lieutenant Lan Tran, Miguel Perez, and Laura *Jonesy* Jones listened at the far end as Nikki summed up the day.

Bringing Jonesy on board to help organize boots on the ground was a good idea. *Were Keith and Jonesy an item?* Jonesy was one of those *guy's girls*. At any rate, this operation needed trusted cops invested in the case.

Lan reached for a glazed donut. "I put out a feeler with a judge friend of mine. We can't serve a warrant until something concrete comes back pointing to Emma Courtland."

"Warren is probably circling the wagons." Nikki yawned and stretched. "We need lab results on the *five* written on Napleton's face."

"It was lipstick," Keith said with authority.

"We assume for now. And we're waiting on the head of security at the Esplanade to send over their video. CSU still needs to finish up with Napleton's car."

"And *our* job?" Perez referred to Jonesy and himself.

Keith said, "Find Emma Courtland. We informed the Eighth since they're ground zero in the Quarter. She's been hanging out with the gutter punks and living in abandoned houses and couch-surfing. Some stay on the West Bank. Tell the uniforms not to harass anyone. If things escalate, walk away. Intimidation doesn't work."

Jonesy agreed. "When they get shitty, I back off. Not worth it."

Lan said, "DA Collins already called me. Napleton and Courtland are friends of hers and the Super. They hold fundraisers for a lot of politicians. You know the deal."

"Great, let's focus on *her* career." Nikki shook her head. "If Simone had prosecuted Napleton without the video, win or lose, we might not be searching for a sixteen-year-old."

"You can't accuse Collins of that," Lan said. "Keep it professional."

"I'm fine." Nikki swiveled in the chair. "Just fine."

Jonesy spoke up. "So, will we have a picture of Emma Courtland to show around?"

"They're being printed," Keith answered.

"None of Napleton's neighbors heard or saw anything," Perez said. "He's neighborly, but not friendly. No help there."

Nikki stood to work out some kinks, pointing at Napleton's picture. "So, we have the murdered owner of the Grande Esplanade Hotel who employed Warren Courtland as manager of said hotel. Not only is Courtland the manager, he recently became a minority owner."

"That's crazy," Jonesy commented.

"Warren never supported Emma's claim of rape, and it was business as usual."

"Is that a *Dateline* episode?" Keith asked.

"Those family dynamics suck," Jonesy continued. "Is Courtland a *douche* because of the money, or because she's not his real daughter?"

"Both?" Nikki stepped back to view the board. "Warren takes out his wife's infidelity on Emma. And Emma's rebellious behavior doesn't ingratiate her to Warren."

"Would Emma being half-black be an issue?" Keith asked.

Nikki shrugged. "I never had any reason to believe he's racist. He's just a sack of shit."

Jonesy failed to stifle her laugh. "Sorry. Why didn't the District Attorney press charges against Napleton? The stolen evidence, right?"

"Simone Collins stands by her claim that the video would've been a tough sell to begin with. No video at all? Forget it. Plus, Emma had no memory of the rape. And to Jonesy's point, that stolen evidence was an inside job. Keep in mind, these people are connected so what we discuss in this room stays in this room. No water cooler talk, guys."

Lan added, "DA Collins wants the easiest target to prosecute, so don't let her pressure you."

"Not convicting an innocent should be a win, either way," Perez added.

Nikki put a check mark by *hotel employees* on the board. "Perez, before end of shift, can you and Jonesy interview the second-shift employees at the Esplanade about Herman Napleton's visit? Show Emma's picture, too. Nudge them to send us the security footage. I wouldn't put it past Warren to stonewall us."

"No problem." Perez nodded at Jonesy. "We can canvass Frenchman Street to ask if anyone remembers him."

Keith said, "Good idea. But, with all the tourists and pedestrian traffic, he would've had to stick out."

"Unless he shows up there on routine," Nikki countered.

Keith raised his eyebrows and nodded. "True."

"What about Harrah's?" Lan asked.

Nikki looked at the board. "That's me."

"I'll go with you. I know the head of security there."

Nikki nodded at Keith. "That's right. We'll get security video to corroborate Mary's story. No reason not to believe they had a public argument on the floor of the casino."

Lan gave an approving smile. "Good work, you two. I like it."

At that moment, an officer appeared in the doorway. "Warren and Sharon Courtland are downstairs and insist on seeing Detective Mayeaux."

Everyone turned to Nikki. "Interesting. Take them to Interview B. See if they want coffee or a Coke. Tell them I'll be right there."

The cop added, "They said to bring your laptop, too."

"They have something." Nikki glanced around the room. "Let the games begin."

15

NIKKI ENTERED INTERVIEW B with her laptop as requested by Warren. The team assembled to view the session from the adjacent room. There weren't two-way mirrors. Instead, a casino-style video camera was mounted to the discolored ceiling. On her own turf, she wouldn't let Warren bully her. Still, letting him win certain battles would gain the most returns.

Interview B was the nicest of the four interrogation rooms the homicide department used, with padded chairs, the newest table, and no whiffs of mold. Stark conditions worked wonders for confessions.

Sharon sat in the chair closest to the corner, having changed into jeans and a nice blouse, with a bit more makeup. Warren stood behind the empty chair.

"Is this really the best accommodations?" Warren asked.

"Do you want sarcasm, or was that a rhetorical question?" Nikki set down the laptop, then took a seat on the opposite side.

"These chairs are for criminals."

"I would've met you at the hotel." She waited a beat. "You came to poke around and learn some intel."

"A decent room is all I asked."

"You should've called the Superintendent. We could've used his office."

"Is that the sarcasm?" Warren frowned.

"You're right. I'm sorry. Let's start over. Warren... Sharon... What brings you by?"

"When I came home for lunch, Sharon and I had a nice, long talk about Emma and what to do with her."

"*Do with her?* She's not a pet." Nikki caught herself.

"You don't make it easy."

"I'm sorry. You're trying to help." Nikki turned to Sharon. "Can I get you something to drink?"

"No, thank you." Sharon checked her face in a compact. "We *do* want you to find Emma. That's why we came."

"Do you know something?"

Warren placed a thumb drive on the table, sliding it toward Nikki with one finger. "This has a video of Emma and a *pedophile* that came to the house. I did make my own copies."

"Don't blame you. Where did this come from?"

"My home security."

Nikki plugged the USB into the laptop, opening the drive. "So, who's the second person of interest? And when was it recorded?"

"Some character she called *Dread*." He waved his hand around his head. "He's got these dreadlocks like some Jamaican. Emma brought him to my house last month."

"*Our* house," Sharon mumbled.

"Yes, *our* house." Warren rolled his eyes.

"You talk like I'm not here."

"Then be here, dammit..."

Her body jerked like a tiny, contained explosion. "I can't when you're being *you*." Her eyes diverted to the table. "Sorry, Nikki."

His jaw clenched. "I apologize, dear." He turned toward Nikki. "We've been on edge."

"The video's starting," Nikki announced as a distraction.

"It doesn't have sound, but I can tell you what was said."

The video showed the Courtlands' empty foyer from above the entrance with a fishbowl effect. Emma walked through the front door first, with a second figure following. Warren's pedophile was a black man with long dreadlocks and dark sunglasses. He was built well, but his layered clothes were unwashed. A backpack drooped from his shoulder.

"Did he threaten you?"

"No. Keep watching." Warren puffed out his chest.

Emma reached for the alarm, but stopped before pressing the keypad. She called out. Dread touched a sculpture on a pedestal.

"See, the alarm was already off. She didn't think anyone was home."

A moment later, Warren appeared on video from the parlor area. He and Emma argued. Dread looked around the place like at a museum, not caring about the fight. Stepfather and stepdaughter were both animated, shouting in each other's faces. Seconds later, Dread and Emma left. Nikki spotted a good screen capture of Dread's face to isolate. The video ended with Warren running his fingers through his salt-and-pepper hair.

Warren sat next to his wife, but miles apart. "I threatened to send him to jail for having sex with a minor. You saw him, he didn't give a shit. They were high, too."

"What was Emma saying?"

"She claimed they weren't having sex. She told me to *chill*."

Nikki copied the video to her laptop. "You didn't believe her—like with Herman's rape."

"She just wants to hurt me."

"Wouldn't admitting to sex with an African-American hurt you?"

Warren slapped the table. "I'm not racist, Detective Mayeaux. That is a *man*. I don't give a shit about the color of his dick. Emma being mixed isn't the issue."

"Right. You're an elitist. You care about money and power."

"Emma would never admit to having sex because he'd be tossed in jail. She was only protecting him."

"Why did Emma bring Dread in the first place?"

"We're close to the streetcar. There are vacant houses Uptown—still. She probably wanted food or to shower. I've seen other videos from time to time of her sneaking in."

Sharon said, "If you find Dread, you might find Emma."

"And when you do find her, there will be no questioning without my lawyer."

"We can't question her without a guardian."

"I wouldn't doubt if that *Dread* killed Herman after hearing her sob story."

Nikki leaned back. "Now, that's a theory."

"Don't underestimate her feminine charms. Men look at her."

Sharon scolded him. "She's just sixteen, Warren."

Nikki handed over the thumb drive, but he refused. "Keep it."

"Do you mind if I come back to your home and look around Emma's room for something that might give us a clue to where Dread or Emma is?"

Warren's face grew dark. "I told you she'd ask to search our house, Sharon. That would be a firm *no*."

16

DREAD ENTERED THE Quarter by foot, after crossing over the Mississippi River on the ferry from the West Bank. He hit the hangouts, asking everyone about Emma. Along the many miles, he managed to beg for a total of seven dollars from tourists—not great considering the price of fast food.

He veered onto Bourbon from Canal Street just as the streets swelled with the lunch crowd. A sight-seeing family caught his eye. The meek dad was slouched, fair skinned, with thick glasses and thin hair. The mom doted on the two children. They appeared out of their element: perfect targets.

Dread gravitated into their orbit. Nothing like planting the tiny seed of fear in a man who wanted to protect his family. The trick to successful begging at his age was to appear unpredictable but to speak with kind words. The thing with white people was that they liked to pay money to make problems go away.

The father maneuvered in front of his wife and kids. Dread stopped just short of them.

"Dude, I'm hungry. A couple bucks would help me out." Dread learned from Rot not to sound pathetic. It's more like asking for a favor. Dread managed compassion in his eyes while searching the family for understanding.

"I don't have cash," the man proclaimed.

"No cash is the way to go. People get robbed here. Here's a free tip. Put your wallet in your front pocket. Someone asks you where you got your shoes, it's a trick. You got 'em on your feet, dig? You have a blessed day." Dread gave the kids a good look. "Beautiful kids."

As expected, the wife pulled out a ten-dollar bill, handing it to her husband. The man gave it to Dread with a forced smile.

Dread pointed a finger gun at the woman. "You have a fine wife there, sir. Enjoy yourselves."

Tourists parted as Dread meandered into the busiest part of Bourbon. A group of traveler kids had set up camp against a roped-off garage door. A large cardboard sign read: NEED MONEY FOR BOOZE. He recognized one of the girls.

"Hey Jinx, how's things?" Dread started.

The others scrutinized him as she answered, "The cops are looking for you."

"What?"

One of the guys spoke up. "Yeah, cops are shakin' us down. Looking for you and that girl."

"Emma?"

Jinx nodded. "Yeah. I mean, they were pretty cool about it, but they're asking us where Emma is and where you was. Shit, what you did?"

A punk spoke with his eyes closed against the wall. "That hotel dude was killed this morning."

"Hotel dude?"

"You know—the rapist. I'll bet she's the one he raped."

Dread made sure no cops were in sight. "Herman Napleton? He was killed this morning? Shit."

"They probably think you both did it," Jinx added. "You two are thick. She's a minor, you know. The cops might think you banging her." She gave him that look.

"We're friends. That's all."

"Calm down. We ain't a jury."

❦

Dread couldn't stay in the Quarter long if the cops were on his ass. He took the most populated route back to the ferry and then to the abandoned warehouse on the West Bank. He crossed the barren, cracked parking lot toward the temporary home. Boarded windows and graffiti tagged the walls. No one in the area complained as long as the traveler kids kept to themselves. He entered the side door.

Everyone had left or was close to leaving at this point. Someone was cooking pasta. One girl was painting a poem on a wall. Rot appeared at the top of the catwalk in a long flannel shirt and thick, beige work pants. His long, wavy brown hair hung over his face while bending over the railing like a 1970s rock star.

"Back so soon?"

Dread looked everywhere except up at him. "Herman Napleton was killed. Emma's missing."

"Napleton? Fuck me." He put his hands against his head. "Not good."

"I'm surprised you care."

"I don't. Not about her."

"Napleton? You knew him?"

"Don't worry about it."

"I won't. We need to find her."

"Right—yeah, you're right. We'll find her."

Dread continued to her section of the room, which she shared with two other females. He hovered over her mattress. Not much to collect. Emma came from a rich family and still had a home. She didn't need to hoard and protect her things like everyone else.

He reached into the slit in her mattress and pulled out the cell her parents still paid for. Location services were off, and she kept it on airplane mode. It was her net. She kept one foot in each world. He punched in her passcode, then scrolled through her gallery until finding a pic of Detective Nikki Mayeaux that she talked about so much.

He found her number. "Got you, Mayeaux."

17

"I ISOLATED THE video you're looking for," Lyle said. "Mary is a fixture here."

It took only minutes for Lyle Robicheaux, head of security at Harrah's to pull up the security footage. They stood in the middle of a futuristic command center, with several agents watching live feeds from different parts of the floor.

Nikki and Keith followed the first monitor as Herman valet parked, then walked into the casino. The next monitor showed Mary Napleton at a blackjack table while gambling. The feed was sped up a half hour until Herman Napleton appeared and they started an animated conversation.

"That looks contentious," Nikki commented.

"My team didn't intervene because we know who they are. We were ready if it escalated."

"What were they fighting about?"

"Divorce stuff. Lawyers."

"Any threats?" Nikki asked.

"Nothing beyond name-calling."

Mary excused herself from the table, and they continued to argue face-to-face. It turned calm for a few moments, but soon, just like Mary said, Herman took a call and stormed off, exiting the casino.

"Well, there you go," Keith said.

"And Mary leaves, too." Nikki pointed. "No more gambling mojo."

"Okay, then, Nik." Keith slapped his hands together. "I'm hungry."

Nikki and Keith broke for a late lunch. The Gumbo Shop was a personal favorite of Nikki's. The casual place enjoyed consistent business, being located near Jackson Square. She had wanted a bowl of gumbo, however changed her order to red beans and rice. *Second Line* by Stop, Inc. filtered overhead.

"Asking Warren to search his house was a risk." Keith followed that statement with a deep bite of his shrimp po'boy.

Nikki squeezed ketchup in a spiral on her red beans and rice. "Not really. You heard what he said when he first came in—*no cops in the house.*"

"He dared us to get a warrant."

"My heart goes out to Sharon. She's a smart woman and a single parent, if we're being real. Warren takes up so much space." She mixed the red beans and rice.

"You and Emma got close during the rape investigation."

"Is that a question?"

"Can you slap cuffs on her when the time comes?"

Nikki scooped another bite followed by sweet tea. "We're allowed to like victims. Emma…reminds me of Morgan."

"I know. I used to love it when she'd lip-sync…"

"Stop it." Nikki tried to keep eye contact. "I don't want to talk about my little sister."

"Okay." He looked around at the lunch crowd.

Her fork stirred. "Emma took to the gutter-punk lifestyle, but most are transplants from other states. They choose this. I always thought Emma would lose interest in transient life."

"Not a great support system at home when you're not believed."

"You got that right."

"Where do you want to start?"

A server walked by, and Nikki reached out to him. "Excuse me, can we get a shrimp basket to go, please?"

Keith smiled. "A little bribery?"

"Can't hurt. We can go where they like to beg for alcohol and drugs around the Square. We've hit the Canal Street side. We'll head toward Esplanade."

Keith ate loose shrimp from the plate. "They're pretty aggressive with the tourists."

"Not all of them. Many have that hippie mentality. It's how they want to live."

After paying their bill, Nikki carried the to-go bag to Jackson Square. In the center was a gated garden and walkway where Andrew Jackson's statue was reported to be tipping his hat at the Pontalba Buildings, due to the Baroness de Pontalba funding the statue. The Pontalba apartments were argued to be the first in America.

Jackson Square was walled off on three sides like a horseshoe, with the iconic St. Louis Cathedral facing the river. The other two sides had shops on the ground level, while artists and musicians lined the dark slate walkways. Art hung on the tall gates, with artists hoping for sales and tips.

Nikki encroached on a group of gutter punks enjoying cigarettes and beer. "Anyone hungry?"

A smiling punk took the bag and opened the container. He passed it around. "Thanks, lady."

She and Keith held up a photo of Emma and a screen capture of Dread, asking of the pair's whereabouts. They received the expected negative responses.

One skinny, frail girl balanced on a bucket with sunken eyes and a rat's nest for hair. She held an unattended cigarette, as well. "I love fried shrimp."

"You guys have a good day." Nikki threw a ten on their cardboard sign before they moved on.

Keith said, "There's thirty bucks down the drain."

"It's an investment."

The rest of the afternoon was much of the same. Some of the gutter punks had already been questioned by other cops about Emma. They walked Royal Street and back up Dauphine. Most of the tourist activity was closer to the river, so they skirted the French Market, which resembled a flea market with cheap jewelry and clothing. It happened to be a few blocks from the Grande Esplanade Hotel.

Just before ending their day of futility, Keith checked his cell. "Let's wrap it up. I have to run."

"What's going on?"

"Dinner plans. A friend."

"Jonesy?"

He blushed. "*No*. Don't worry about with *who*."

They made a lazy walk back down Decatur, turning before Jackson Square toward their vehicles. They had driven separately, knowing their day would end in the Quarter, not at Headquarters. Nikki checked her cell in her car after Keith had driven off with a salute.

As Nikki started the engine, a text alert startled her. It came from Emma's phone.

meet me at the absinthe house in fifteen minutes alone or i walk

18

Nikki had her doubts about the validity of the text. Not that it came from Emma, just that she wouldn't risk a meeting in public. Dread or another punk would most likely be her proxy to find out her options. At this rate, the day would never end.

She followed the note's instructions by not informing Keith or the team of this secret meeting at the Absinthe House. Transparency would come later. She arrived first, or so she assumed. Dr. John's *In the Right Place* was playing at a nice level.

The restrooms needed to be checked. It was an opportunity to splash water on her face. The stalls were clear. The end of the bar offered a segmented view of Bourbon through the windows. Another important thing in the bar's scouting report was to speak to the college-aged bartender about Emma or Dread ever being a patron, and to tell him to put on a pot of coffee. Her badge worked wonders.

The lanky boy with a full beard pulled out a bag of Community Coffee, then turned around to face her. "Nobody ever orders coffee. Anything else?"

"Can I have a clean cloth napkin back there?" She pointed, having spotted one.

He hesitated, but a *don't give a fuck* look crossed his face, and he handed it over.

Nikki made sure a stool was saved for her guest. She glanced between Bourbon and the entrance. Conversations blended around her, putting her to sleep. She wondered if anyone would show. No new texts came.

She yawned, hard. The coffee was about ready.

Dread emerged from the meandering crowd on the street wearing mismatched clothing and gloves with no fingers. His boots dragged. As he drew closer, she could see his light-brown skin was oily and his eyes twinkled. Dreadlocks flowed into his hoodie. He had a lot of character in his handsome face. Tattoos crawled up his neck, but stopped short. A few piercings displayed studs and loops.

"He's with me." Nikki waved away the bartender as the gutter punk entered.

"What can I get you?" the bartender asked him.

"I like that Abita Amber."

"ID?" The bartender pretended to hold a card.

Dread sat with a slacker attitude, pulling off the cap. "I also like that coffee and chicory."

"Two coffees, coming right up." The kid gave Dread an extra glance.

Nikki waited until the two sturdy white mugs were delivered. "No charge, Officer," the bartender said.

"Nice *mane*," Dread said to the guy.

He touched his beard. "Thanks. Nice locs."

"Cool. Appreciate you."

The bartender pulled out a small fan from the back and placed it where it blew on Dread toward the window behind them. "No offense."

Dread chuckled. "I don't blame him."

"Try sniffing a dead body after three days." Nikki picked up the cup. "You don't know the day I had."

"You not going to ask about Emma? You damn near asked the whole Quarter." He spun the mug by the handle, looking at it. His manner was lazy, but his speech hinted at an education.

"It's your meeting." She tested the coffee.

"You're looking for me, so here I am."

"I like Emma. Do you like her?"

He let a soft laugh escape his lips. "Let's get this out of the way. We are in no way having sex, Detective. I know what her *bitch-ass* father told you."

"I'm trying to be open-minded."

He waited a beat. "Let me restore your faith."

"Why be friends with a sixteen-year-old when most gutter punks are early twenties?"

"Can you call us *traveler kids?* That's what we like."

"So, you guys have a marketing team? *Traveler kids.* Not so gross. Sure."

"Gutter punks are those aggressive ass-bags I don't hang with. Emma is not like them. I got her back."

"It doesn't hurt she has access to a lot of money."

"I don't give a shit about that."

"Are you going to help me bring Emma in, so we can sort all this out?" She blew on the coffee and took a sip.

"Thing is, she doesn't trust you anymore."

Her stomach sank. "Did she tell you this?"

"Before the video disappeared, she'd talk about you all the time. She was angry. I think she blamed you for not preventing it from happening."

"I blame myself, too."

"All that is between you and Emma. The NOPD is giving the full court press around the Quarter for me. I want to put this shit to bed."

"Interesting choice of words."

"I didn't kill her rapist. I'm not hiding her."

Nikki rested her arm on the chair next to her. "We don't think you did. Emma's father showed us video of you at the Courtland house."

"We was hungry."

"Any idea where she'd go?"

"None. She got her shit from where we stay and made tracks. If I'm found, she's found. What is that saying you got? Plausible deniability?"

"What's your real name?"

"Jamal."

"Is it really?" Nikki shook out the cloth napkin and used it to reach out for Dread's coffee cup. She poured the remaining liquid into her own cup. "You don't mind, right?" She rolled it in the napkin.

"You gonna do that CSI shit?"

Nikki raised her cell and snapped a pic of his face. "I'll figure out who you are."

Dread raised his hands to his chest. "I said my piece. You can stop looking for me. I'm out of here."

He made for the exit, with Nikki following just a few yards behind. Once he was out on Bourbon, a row of gutter punks appeared, forming a cluster at the entrance. She ordered them to move out the way, but they were like peaceful protestors, not allowing a path.

By the time Nikki squeezed through, Dread was long gone.

19

DETECTIVE KEITH TEAGUE found it difficult to think when alone. A long day with Nik didn't help. A shot of whiskey was a temporary distraction. He paced his darkened house not quite ready for sleep. His late parents' dated furniture appeared like a collage in the muted light.

He turned on the television to a marathon of *The Simpsons*. They were always on, but that was fine. He enjoyed them to the point of memorization. The show was the closest thing to having company that didn't have to leave.

Keith fell into the recliner as if into an open grave, not caring if one day the backside would break off and he'd find himself flipping over. No, it held again like a champ. The cell in hand was propped upright at his belly button. He swiped through pictures of happier times with Nikki. The photos didn't lift his spirits.

He stopped scrolling when his vision blurred. Nikki's little sister Morgan had started getting into the selfie action as he and Nikki became more serious. A picture of a huge oak tree in Audubon Park ended the string of pictures with Nikki and Morgan. He closed his eyes to release a tear. The cell turned black through his eyelids. Lisa Simpson's voice let him believe he wasn't alone.

The cell rang, but it wasn't Nik.

The woman on the line spoke first. "We need to meet. Pick a place."

❧

The Tree of Life was a gigantic, centuries old sprawling oak located on the edge of Audubon Park. It was a famous spot for weddings and pictures for graduation or birthdays. The hauntingly beautiful oak required a picture in its presence. Gatherings had to be reserved. Keith visited this spot often.

He meandered under the Spanish moss, which was low enough to touch. The sun had set, and deep shadows fell. Moonlight filtered through as sunlight would. Thick branches defied gravity inches from the ground. Keith sat between two roots and rested against the trunk.

Why did he pick this spot, of all places?

"Why did you pick this of all places?" The voice startled him.

Keith waited for a figure to appear from the dark abyss, but she stayed in hiding. He twisted in a futile effort to get a vantage point. "You said somewhere private. You agreed."

"I was curious." The voice remained low. "You should have picked a quiet bar or café."

"Too many spy movies, I guess." Keith brushed off an imagined bug. "You don't even want me to see you."

"Not out here, genius. We can explain running into each other at a coffee shop. Under this tree, where everyone and their grand-mother takes a picture of it? Both of us here is not a coincidence."

"You pick the place next time."

"Let's plan on not having a next time."

"We came all the way out here for me to say we have nothing." Keith waited for the hammer to fall.

"No. We came out here because you need to be reminded of your place."

"I know my place. We think it's the girl. We're close."

"You need more incentive."

Keith inched his butt closer to the voice, leaning on an elbow. "I'm not lead."

"Everything you say is pessimistic. I need optimism."

"Rich people. Private lives. Got it."

"Do you? Count to three, then come around to this side."

Leaves shuffled and crushed under foot, before fading. Two joggers on a nearby path ran by. He stood and used the flashlight on his cell to walk around the tree. There was an envelope on the ground.

Inside the envelope was a bloodwork report from the River Bend Medical Institute. The Blood Alcohol Concentration was listed at .216. His name was at the top of the report. Behind that report was a still shot from the police evidence room, timestamped the day the cell phone went missing. That too, had mysteriously been erased. It was his face—that, he couldn't dispute.

20

WELL PAST DUSK, Nikki arrived at her condo in the Warehouse District, which buffered the Quarter and Uptown. The area was commonly referred to as the Art District after regentrification. The building had housed the Sugar Cane Confectionary Co. until the doors closed in the 1960s, where it sat abandoned until the 1980s.

Tired legs carried her through the fifth-floor hallway on the colorful, diamond-patterned rug. She had picked up a burger and caught a third wind. She shoved fries in her mouth as she made a casual game of stepping on the blue diamonds. The design was spaced for her stride.

Her neighbor, Major, opened the door of his condo with a bag of trash at the same time. He was a soft-spoken, forty-something black man with minimalist furnishings, and yet a great selection of wines. "Evening, Nikki. You look beat."

She spoke with a mouthful of fries. "I am. Heading to the garbage chute?"

"Can't fool the detective." The trash dropped at his feet. "I can throw this away later. Want a relaxing red with those fries?" He motioned to enter his place.

"Go throw your trash away. I'm a little tired."

Concerned wrinkles appeared. "In the months I've lived here, you never turned down a glass of wine. Besides, my bad knee just started acting up."

"Damn that bad knee."

"A little red will help."

"Why do I gravitate to friendly neighbors who stock wine?" She smiled. "Okay, okay. Twist my *knee*. One glass, and then I need to pass out."

"One glass."

Nikki followed him inside, shaking her head with a smile. At least once a week, she found herself sitting on Major's balcony with an inspiring view of the Crescent City Connection spanning the Mississippi.

The same view was offered from her place, but she appreciated it more with company. He lived alone, and she'd never seen his friends or family visit. Their condos were similar, except his was neat and clean while her condo was a place to sleep.

The bridge glowed like a spaceship on this crisp, clear night. It wasn't a horrible way to decompress after a grueling day of investigating—oh, and attempted murder.

Major placed down a glass of red after a light pour. "Don't worry if you don't finish it."

They sat side-by-side in cushioned rockers, angled into each other with a small, round table between them. In front of the table was a potent space heater near their feet. Without wind, radiating heat eased the chill.

He held up his glass for a light tap. "Cheers."

"Clink-clink."

He swirled and inhaled from the glass. "You didn't make any sound this morning."

Nikki pushed fries toward him. "I got the Napleton murder."

An eyebrow hiked. "Saw it on the news. That's yours?"

"All mine."

"No wonder you're draggin' ass. You can't tell me about it, but… *tell me what you can*," he said in a low register.

"You're right, I can't say. It's a knotted ball of mess."

"Is that girl involved? Emma? The one I saw staying in your place those few days?"

"I told you that wasn't her."

"Don't bullshit a bullshitter. Her name never came out in the media, but you were on the case. I can add that up."

"That shouldn't have happened, Major. I crossed a line letting her stay with me."

"Hey, my lips are sealed. You two looked chummy, like sisters."

Nikki froze.

Major sensed her apprehension. "Did I say something wrong?"

"No, you—I never told you, but my little sister died in a car accident. Her name was Morgan."

"What?" Major put down his wine. "Oh, I'm sorry. How recent?"

"About three years ago. Someone ran through a red light. T-boned the car."

"Shit." Major dipped his head and closed his eyes. "Shit. That's so hard."

"Emma is like Morgan in a way I can't explain." Nikki turned her head away.

"Well. I hope it's not her."

"Me too. Napleton had enemies. He's gotten threats. We'll look at everyone."

"Assholes online troll innocent people not knowing shit about them."

"*Troll?*" Nikki smiled. "You learned the lingo."

"I spend a lot of time doom-scrolling."

"*Doom-scrolling*—listen to you. I always told Emma social media would melt her brain."

"Napleton got what he deserved. Serves him right."

Nikki's head fell forward before catching herself. "Shit. I just had a *brown-out*. I'm sorry, Major. You were saying?"

"Thank you for being nice and keeping a lonely man company, but it's time for you to leave."

Major walked Nikki out of his condo and to her door. She fumbled with her keys, then bid Major farewell. He waited for her to enter, waving with a laugh. "Straight to bed, young lady."

21

Dread sat on the curb outside of The Crush strip club, leaning against a pole. His namesake dreadlocks were hidden under a large hoodie. Cheap plastic sunglasses completed the disguise. He drank from a plastic cup labeled *Big Ass Beer* while Bourbon Street hopped. The cops were more concerned with bar fights, robberies, and general peace than anything else.

Where the hell is Emma? he wondered.

"You got stones talking to that cop." Rot stood above Dread, leaning against the same pole wearing mismatched layers, topped with a cracked, leather-studded jacket.

"I told her I didn't kill Napleton, and Emma isn't calling me. I had to set her straight. Best way is to get in front of it."

"Damn straight. You gotta stand up for your rights with these fuckers. This ain't no police state."

"Either way, Emma is in trouble."

"Considering punks run from problems, your girl could be in Mexico."

"She's not in Mexico. Emma isn't done."

"Ain't done? Who else is she gonna kill?"

"Maybe you."

He laughed. "I had nothing to do with that."

"Who else you messing with besides Frank and Percy?"

"You'd be surprised." Rot's focus shifted to the façade of the Crush, decorated with large glam pictures of past dancers. "I should have sent Flower to try out at a different club."

"Are you a pimp now?"

"That's an ugly word, dude. I'm more of a manager."

"Marketing." Dread smiled.

Rot's scowl turned to a smile when Flower appeared across the way. Rot pushed off the pole to take a few steps toward her. She crossed over Bourbon wearing a full-length trench coat and gym shoes. In the middle of the street, she stopped and opened the coat, flashing a skimpy bikini.

Young male tourists clapped and whistled. She covered up with a laugh, running the rest of the way into his arms. Her face was minus the piercings, but she wore her charmed necklace. Flower reminded Dread of a puppy seeing its owner.

"I guess it went well?"

Flower pulled out a fold of bills from the trench coat with a wide grin, presenting it. "We did good. No one asked my age."

"Told you." Rot accepted the money. "We'll split this later. What'd Percy say?"

She clasped her hands together, leaning into him. "I only danced at the tables, but I made mad tips, and he wants me back."

"We need to celebrate. What do you think, Dread?"

Dread looked up at them from the curb. "I think next time you dance, he's going to want to fuck you or have you fuck someone else."

"Dude..."

"Really?" Flower lost her enthusiasm.

Rot pulled her close. "It's possible. It's your choice. You say no if you don't want."

The skin of her smooth brow wrinkled. *"If I don't want?* You... expect me to have sex with men in there?"

He sighed. "*Thanks, Dread.* Horny men are in there, babe. Their bank is our bank. All I'm saying is, it's your choice. Say no if you want to say no."

She stayed silent, in thought.

Dread slapped Rot's leg. "How about a Lucky Dog?"

Rot's eyes lit up with fake excitement. "How about *no*. Me and Flower are gonna get some H and celebrate the right way."

"Heroin." Dread huffed. "Don't start her on that shit."

She scoffed. "I'm not a baby."

"Fuck, you aren't."

Rot said, "I think a stop at Frank's is in order."

"Go without me. I want to look around for Emma. If she's out here, it's going to be now when it's jamming."

Rot shook his head. "Pussy."

"Give me a bill." Dread held out his hand.

Rot slouched. "You're begging from me?"

"Dude, pony up. I came out here and waited with you."

Rot ran a twenty under his nose, taking a big whiff before handing it over. "Don't wait up."

Dread waited until Rot and Flower disappeared in the Bourbon Street foot traffic before getting up, leaving his empty cup on the curb. He happened to look at the entrance to the Crush when Percy Fields appeared in the doorway with his bouncer. Dread crossed over where Flower had just come from.

"Percy." Dread stopped about five feet from his personal space. The bouncer grew in size.

"Jamal." Percy was dressed in a slick suit with a tight fade. A large diamond weighed on each ear. His timepiece was gold.

"We need to talk."

Percy's eyes darted to his bouncer. He patted the big man with an assuring word before motioning for Dread to step to the side where they could speak in private.

"Are you okay? I'm here for you."

"Don't blow smoke, *Dad*."

His father appeared hurt. "I'd rather you call me *Percy* then to hear you say *dad* like that."

"It's hard to say with affection."

He calmed, looking around. "You need money? What can I do?"

"It's about Emma."

"Is she okay?"

"She ran. I'm worried. They think she murdered your *masta.*"

"Funny." Percy's attitude changed. "We're all looking for her."

"The police talk to you?"

"Not yet. Look at you. When are you going clean up and work for me? Fuck that guy Rot."

"Sometimes you need a reminder you tossed my mom to the curb, then me."

"I want to connect. It's late, but not *too* late."

"It's way too late."

"Your mom was a drug addict who didn't want help. Look at you, you're clean."

"Right… I thought you should know, that girl Flower that just came out of your place. She's a minor." He folded his arms. "What would the cops think?"

Percy pushed Dread against the building, pressing against his chest with his forearm. "Now, you're threatening me?"

"That white friend of yours raped Emma, and you took his side, like a *Tom*. Now, you have Rot bringing underaged girls to you. And you want me to call you *Dad?*"

Percy shook his head. "We're done here."

Dread pulled down on his Aztec hoodie and backed away. His hands shot into his pockets as he walked toward Canal to find a Lucky Dog vendor. Percy was never a father to him, and he didn't need parenting now.

Soon, he spotted a big, colorful Lucky Dog umbrella on a busy corner. The tourists cleared, then the silhouette of the person he sought appeared. It had to be his imagination.

He crept closer from the side so as not to startle her. "Emma," he whispered.

"Fighting with *dear old dad* again?"

"You saw that?"

"I knew you'd come over here for a dog."

Lucky Dog, indeed.

THURSDAY

22

Lieutenant Lan Tran stood at the head of the table in the war room. His dark hair was slicked back. He wore prescription glasses, choosing to skip his contacts this morning. When Nikki had joined Homicide, Keith had briefed her that Lan was a rule follower, but knew how to play the game within those rules.

Lan started. "Okay, Harrah's checked out. Nikki dropped off Dread's coffee mug with Forensics as well as the towel collected from The Esplanade. Who wants to share? Perez? Jonesy?"

"Don't be shy." Nikki leaned back in the conference room chair while Keith stood at the board with an erasable marker.

Perez volunteered. "Dead end on Frenchman. Probably a rendezvous spot. But, I did end up buying a sculpture made with gears and cogs."

"I know that artist," Nikki said. "Bow tie, right?"

Jonesy added. "Uniforms hit some punk hangouts, but the freaks won't snitch. I'm proud to report no incidents, either."

Lan said, "I appreciate that. We don't need any viral videos."

Keith held up some printouts. "I reviewed the call logs on Napleton's phone this morning and nothing stands out, but there are a crap ton of numbers. Spent half of his life on calls. I figure a uniform can catalog them."

"Good." Lan opened his laptop. "The hotel surveillance arrived this morning." He grabbed one of the wires coming from a hole in the table and plugged it into a port. Miguel reached for the remote to turn on the large screen hanging from the opposite wall.

"I never can get those to connect," Nikki said.

Lan adjusted his glasses. "This thing senses fear. All right, there are three sets of videos: the front of the hotel, inside the lobby, and the elevator. We'll compare them side-by-side to track Napleton's movements."

The screen came to life, mirroring Lan's laptop. The three videos were positioned left to right. Lan scrolled forward to 10:25 p.m. The bird's-eye video on the left began with Herman leaving his Mercedes with the valet.

Perez said, "The valet is Tim Greer. Napleton didn't talk to him. Greer said they always park the car half a block up at his reserved spot."

"Was his statement *validated?*" Keith looked around the room with his arms open wide. "Validated? C'mon."

"You're so stupid." Nikki laughed under her breath.

"Eh, needs some work," Jonesy offered.

"Focus, people."

The valet was only gone a moment. The middle video started with Herman powerwalking through the lobby straight to the elevator. He didn't stop to engage with anyone. The right panel showed Herman on the elevator. It was the only video in black and white. He acted squirrelly until glancing up at the camera.

"He's trying to be calm," Nikki said. "He just killed that girl after the argument with Mary, and then he goes back to Mary after. Why?"

"For an alibi? For more arguing?" Keith finished.

Lan moved the videos forward to 11 p.m., showing Napleton leaving Mary's room calmer than when he had arrived, with wet, combed hair and a tucked shirt. Outside, Herman waited for the valet to circle back around to the hotel instead of just walking the half block. Herman passed a tip to the kid before climbing into his car.

"Emma had to have gotten in his car after the valet parked it. Play the outside video after Herman goes in the hotel. See if Emma walks by."

The key fob cabinet stayed in plain view of the camera. Two valets tag-teamed back and forth, grabbing keys and putting them back. They laughed and chatted between retrieving cars. No one fitting Emma's description appeared in frame.

"Emma used to visit the hotel. It's common knowledge they park Napleton's car in a reserved spot. She avoided the camera. So, we place her in the backseat at 10:35 p.m." Nikki looked at Lan.

Keith added, "We need to get Forensics in Mary's suite. If Herman took a shower, he could've left trace in the drain."

Nikki shook her head. "We know he killed the Claiborne victim. It'd be a waste of resources."

"Not that I agree, but too much time has passed, and we can tie Napleton to the victim with the shoes." Lan nodded. "The towel that cleaning services gave Nikki is the best evidence from the suite."

Nikki's cell rang. "Speak of the devil." She answered, "Oz, you're on speaker. What you got?"

"Hi, everyone. I thought you'd appreciate a quick update since the mayor wants my entire caseload set aside for this."

"Oz, this is Lieutenant Tran. We do appreciate you."

Nikki said, "Shoot."

"The five on Napleton's face was consistent with black lipstick. The brand, I couldn't tell you. I'll run the towel next to compare the samples."

"We figured it was lipstick."

"The extra key fob didn't have any prints. It was wiped clean. Nothing in or on the car other than Mary and Herman."

"Dead end," Lan grumbled.

"Ye of little faith. I found one print you're gonna like. The knife you took out of Napleton has a ten-point match to Emma Courtland."

23

"We got the warrant to search the Courtland estate." Nikki left Lan's office, waving the paper in the air. "The tech team will meet us there."

"That didn't take long."

"Ink's still wet. I'll drive."

Keith stood. "Let's take my car."

"Nope. I'm lead. I drive. Call Jonesy and Miguel."

"Just the four of us and the tech team?"

"I don't want a crowd in the Courtland house."

Keith didn't say much for the ride. It allowed Nikki time to think. Somewhere in the back of her mind, she hoped Sharon took the subtle warning about the knife set. Deep down, she regretted nothing.

"Are we waiting for the tech team?" Keith asked.

"We can start without them."

The impressive gate to the Courtland estate eased open after Nikki pushed the buzzer twice. "First time here?"

"It is." He shifted in the passenger seat as if sitting on a tack. "We mere mortals don't often get to see inside these houses."

"The kitchen alone forces you to re-evaluate your life choices."

After parking outside the two-car garage, Nikki and Keith led the way to the front door with Miguel and Jonesy. The fountain cherub forever relieved himself. Limbs from fantastic oaks growing outside the fence gave cover to the front lawn.

A white police SUV pulled into the driveway. Oz stepped out, waving to them. "Figured I should handle this, too."

"Welcome."

Sharon Courtland answered with her hair in a bun, wearing a simple floral-patterned dress. "Nikki, hello."

"Hi, Sharon. There's been a development." Nikki presented the warrant. "We need to search your house."

"Warren isn't home. Shouldn't I call him? Can I call our lawyer?" She stood aside, letting everyone into the foyer. Oz and another tech brought up the rear.

"Call whomever you like. I've instructed everyone to leave your house the way we found it."

Sharon waved everyone inside, then turned to get her cell.

Nikki huddled with the team to discuss the scope of the warrant, including the knife set and any material that may indicate Emma's whereabouts. Nikki and Oz found Sharon in the kitchen. She focused on the counter where a different set of knives in a wood block occupied the space.

"They're gone," Nikki whispered to Oz. "She replaced them."

"We'll search the trash bins, just in case." He started opening the cabinets.

Sharon slid into a seat at the island, dialing her cell. "What are you looking for, Nikki?"

"Anything that will help us find Emma." They shared a moment before Nikki asked, "What happened to the other knives?"

"What do you mean?"

"Last time I was here, this block was short a knife. Now, you have a brand-new set." Nikki pulled out the biggest one.

"Maybe Warren ordered them. One caught in the disposal. I think that's Williams Sonoma."

Nikki pushed the knife back into its slot, then glanced at Oz. "What did you do with the knives?"

"Maybe they were given away? Tossed in the dump? Recycled? I swear, we go through so much crap."

"We have a warrant for Emma's arrest. Her prints were found on the knife that killed Herman Napleton."

"Warren isn't answering."

"Why is Emma's home life so hard? You have money. The best schools. Therapists, if you need them. Why is Emma drawn to that lifestyle with the gutter punks?"

Sharon frowned at the cell screen. "Emma rejected therapy. After two sessions, the therapist believed her anger comes from being half-black and not knowing who her real father is. And then the bullying in school." She frowned and hung up. "Warren won't answer."

Nikki deflated a bit. "Children are hard. No matter how perfect you raise them, they end up being who they're going to be."

Her voice went deadpan. "You don't have children."

"I don't, but I do have years of personal experience with every type of family."

"Thank you for being kind, Nikki." Sharon stared in her lap. "Forgive me if I'm not."

Jonesy appeared at the kitchen entrance. "Nothing yet. Detective Teague asked me to stay with Mrs. Courtland so you can search Emma's room."

"Thanks. I'll be right back, Sharon."

Nikki walked the quiet hallway staged with impersonal furniture and derivative art. Loneliness came with spending day after day in such a large house. Sharon's husband and daughter abandoned her. She had no career and no respect.

Emma's room couldn't be called a shrine, but nothing changed since Nikki told her they weren't charging Herman Napleton. She never forgot the shock on Emma's face, and then the hurt. One tear rolled down Emma's cheek. It almost felled her. Her sister Morgan cried like that, seconds before her death.

As with the knives, Nikki hoped anything useful wouldn't be there anymore. The wrinkled cover on the bed indicated someone had been lying on it. The desk was clear of the everyday personal things. An easel in the corner held a partial sketch of a grim reaper. A table with a fancy printer for photographs stood ready for use.

Nikki opened the walk-in closet, entertaining the thought of Emma hiding under the hanging clothes that hadn't been worn since her dark phase started. She opened boxes, one after the other, finding old schoolwork, obsolete electronics, and toys she'd outgrown.

However, the final generic shoe box contained candid pictures on quality glossy paper, probably from the printer. She recognized her own face staring back. She and Emma had been together often during the rape investigation, and Emma liked taking selfies from time to time. The pictures were torn in half, separating her and Emma. Some pictures had an X over Nikki's face, written in black marker.

What the hell...?

Keith appeared behind her. She closed the lid on the box.

"What's that?" he asked.

"Old schoolwork. A dead end." She pushed the box back in the closet and stood to face him. "You find anything?"

"Nada."

Nikki nodded, but her thoughts were elsewhere. Dread was right about Emma being upset with her. If Warren and Sharon combed through Emma's things, why wasn't this box brought to her attention?

24

Nikki entertained the nightmare of Emma taking revenge on her. She'd have to check her trunk moving forward. Was that box of torn pictures a fleeting moment of anger? At times, Nikki had been the only one fighting for Emma. Defacing those pictures didn't make sense, but deeper psychological issues were in play.

Without the knife set, Nikki considered the search a success. To keep appearances, she voiced the opposite to Lan. Her shift ended at Headquarters with paperwork. The other detectives joked and wrapped up for the day. She focused on work and reports since nothing waited at home.

"Want to grab a bite somewhere, Nik?" Keith put his jacket on over his shoulder holster.

"You don't have plans?"

"Yes. Important man-stuff, but I'll cancel it for you."

"Your Scrabble tournament? They'll be pissed."

"Pissed is only a seven-point word."

"What would *shithead* get me?" She ended the exchange. "How about we work up our appetite first?"

"Bow-chicka-bow-wow." He sounded like a guitar.

"Keep dreaming. I want to walk the Quarter and look for Emma."

"No need for two cars. I'll drive."

"I'll drive, if you don't mind."

∽

Nikki cruised through the one-way Quarter streets. Again, Keith was reserved while riding shotgun. She pointed out the window while approaching Rampart. "You ever been to Queen of the South?"

Keith looked at the bar on the left as they passed. "No. Worth it?"

"Their cocktails are crazy good."

"Love a crazy good cocktail." He played along, but with no real enthusiasm.

Nikki let out a long sigh. "It doesn't surprise me we didn't find anything useful at Emma's house."

"They're not stupid enough to leave evidence out. That's good for Emma, right?"

"I suppose." Nikki took a right on Rampart Street. She pulled to the side where a few gutter punks were sitting on a stoop. "You think Emma blames me?"

"Are you kidding? You're the only one on her side."

"That might be how it looks on the outside, but I'm another adult that let her down."

"I can't even attempt to unpack what Emma went through, but you're the one person I'd want in my corner."

Nikki appreciated his answers. They approached three slackers on the Rampart stoop outside a vape store. One male was covered with tattoos extending onto his face. The two females had heavy eyeliner and piercings. Nikki recognized the woman that she assumed was on heroin. The other female had a squat face and body with protruding ears.

"You're the cop that gave us the shrimp," the girl said. "Next time, I want an oyster sandwich." Calling a po'boy a sandwich meant she wasn't local.

"You're Sparkle, right?"

"Right." She smiled with closed lips.

"Have you seen this girl since the last time I asked?" Nikki presented a physical photo.

"The Punisher," the heroin girl said with flourish.

"Shut up, Sparkle," the male commanded.

"Chill. She's cool, man."

"The Punisher?" Nikki questioned. "That's what you call her?"

"That's her new street name." Sparkle had dark rings under her eyes and a wide grin. "I heard she stabbed three frat boys. Bad-ass. Love her."

The male threw a bottle top at her. "She makes shit up, Officer. If that girl stabbed three dudes, you'd know about it."

"You've seen her around, Sparkle?"

"I've seen her at Tips. On the neutral ground."

"Tips?" Keith asked.

"Tipitina's. Tips. You got more shrimp?"

The male hung his head. "A lot of people hang at Tips. That's no secret."

"Yeah, go to Tips." The other female handed Sparkle a bottle of water. "Drink."

With no more information coming from Sparkle, Nikki and Keith agreed to abandon the Quarter for the new lead. Keith remained quiet while Nikki steered through evening traffic. They made their way across a bustling Canal Street and cut over to St. Charles Avenue. He glanced at her several times. "We're not going to mention it?"

Nikki smiled, exhaling. "Yes, our first date was at Tipitina's. The Rebirth Brass Band."

"One of my best first dates."

"Come to think of it, I remember there were some people hanging out on the neutral ground then too, like a big picnic."

"It's Thursday, so probably won't have a huge crowd there tonight. I'll check their site."

They pulled up to the curb alongside an oak growing from a square of dirt cut out of the sidewalk. The iconic club was a two-story building with different shades of yellow siding that received repair in sections. An attached awning hung over the entrance next to a large Tipitina's logo bolted into the wall. A bike rack sat by a light pole near the rear. Across the street, the neutral ground was deserted.

"Hmm, opens at nine. Dead end?" Keith asked. "Get some food and come back later?"

Nikki spotted a rusted beat-up white van slowing down. "Wait, look at this."

The van stopped in the middle of the street, causing two cars behind to tap their horns before going around. The side door opened with a painful screech, letting four people pour out with a cloud of smoke. They were stoned, drinking alcohol and stumbling onto the neutral ground.

"Old-school weed smokers. Good. Let's go ask…"

"No, I'm going to follow the van. We'll get the same shit answers from those guys."

"I'm with you."

Nikki crept onto the road and stayed a good distance behind the ancient van that had one brake light. Suspicious drivers could tell if they were being followed on the Uptown side streets, so Nikki stayed as far back as possible. The driver was too high or drunk to check.

Not a mile away, the van pulled next to a tall chain-link fence wrapped around an abandoned Greek Revival-style house with an uncut lawn and boarded windows. Nikki crept under an oak on the one-way street, just next door. The van shut off, but no one exited yet. She turned off her engine, too.

"It's your show. Do we call for backup?" Keith stared at the house.

"You scared?"

"Of them? Yes. You don't know what the hell is going on in that house. They're like rats."

"Don't want to corner a rat. Call in a squad to assist. No crime in progress. Tell them to roll up quiet. And no storming the castle. They wait outside. I don't want to surprise anyone in there."

Keith made the call with the proper radio codes, but still explained there were two detectives on the scene.

Moments later, the van doors opened, and two traveler kids stood in the street, laughing about something. One turned and looked right at them. She read his lips, which included the F word.

"Shit." Nikki reached for the door handle.

The two young men slipped through the chain-link curtain. Nikki and Keith ran after them, yelling at them to stop. The boys shouted a bird call to the house that was an obvious warning. Nikki squeezed through the fence first, with Keith right behind. She unbuttoned her holster for quick access.

Nikki and Keith jumped up the steps to the small porch, stopping on both sides of the door. Nikki could hear the commotion and voices bouncing off the inside walls.

"So much for surprise," Keith said.

"Still use diplomacy, okay?" Nikki reached over and opened the unlocked door to a dark room. She nodded once and then shouted, "NOPD, we're coming in! We just want to talk."

25

DREAD INWARDLY LAUGHED at Rot relaxing in the plush, green high-back chair as if it were a throne. Rot appeared as a king with the weight of the world on his shoulders—a ruler of the transient sub-culture. To Dread, he looked like a joke. Silly or not, the traveler kids in their circle feared him, and they listened.

A few candles on the coffee table illuminated half of Rot's face. Dread had to concede that Rot's build was impressive. With a hidden bank account, he could provide creature comforts, food and supplies to the traveler kids, which in turn inspired loyalty.

Besides the West Bank warehouse, Rot had also found and claimed this abandoned house in the Uptown area near the river. No electricity was challenging, but somehow Rot knew that the owner of the property lived in California, and no one would be back until summer to continue renovations. At least, that's what he said. Won't the owner be surprised to find their beautiful home had been trans-formed into this smelly nest of art, drugs, and stained squalor?

Dread sat on the ruined sofa, with a beer, facing Rot. The others had given them privacy in the large house. Flower pulled a Coors Light from a cooler of ice sitting at Rot's feet. She twisted the cap off and handed it to her *manager* with a kiss. The initial affection Flower showered on Rot had been replaced with uncertainty. Rot fed on that. Flower ushered a random chicken out of the room as she left.

"How many girls you have dancing at these clubs?" Dread asked.

"Four." He took a long pull from the bottle.

"Are they on payroll at any clubs?"

Rot laughed. "They're like contract workers. They show up and do lap dances, whatever, and they split their tips with the house." Another big swig.

"And you get a cut."

"Everyone makes good money."

"Your pal Frank, too?"

"Frank." Rot stared forward. "He insists on having my girls go through him. I don't need him."

"What'r you gonna do?"

"Squeeze him out?" He swirled the remaining swallow, then finished it.

"Nothing is perfect."

"We boys, right?" Rot moved hair from his eyes.

"Sure."

"I'm going to need your help soon."

"Sure."

"The punks respect you, Dread."

"Because I hang with you."

"No, you're a leader. You're my right-hand man. We won't be traveler kids forever."

"I won't pimp."

He threw his bottle across the room, but not in a hostile way. "I have more than that going on. You, on the other hand, have nothing going on—except for searching for your little girlfriend." He turned toward the kitchen and yelled, "Beer!"

"Dude, just reach down and get it yourself."

"She has to *learn*."

Flower appeared from the darkness, pulling out a beer for both of them. She waited a moment in the silence, then left.

Dread shook his head. "You're such a dick."

"It's human nature to exploit human nature." He held up his bottle. "Thank her sometime, okay?"

Rot smiled. "Oh, I thank her."

"I found Emma." Dread waited through Rot's silence.

"Where is she?" Rot leaned forward. "I need to talk to her about the problems she's causing."

"Her trauma is all about *you*."

"Where is she, dude?"

"She was posing by the Lucky Dog vendor, knowing I'd go there. Believe that shit?"

"You, at a Lucky Dog stand? *Noooooo*. You're still not telling me where she's parked."

"I have no idea." Dread regretted telling Emma to meet him at the Uptown house. Rot never said if he was staying there tonight. "She'll be in touch. That's it."

"You told her to turn herself in, right?"

"What do you care?"

"I told you. She needs to chill. Percy is asking me questions about her. I think Emma has dirt."

"Percy's in Napleton's circle. Tight with Warren. He's fishing for info."

A sharp bird call echoed through the house from outside. Rot's eyes squeeze shut. "Shit, this place is off-limits."

Dread shot off the couch and started for the back door. "You coming?"

"I'm not running from these assholes. You shouldn't, either."

"I don't need a night in OPP. Good luck." Dread ran from the room to the back of the house with the other traveler kids, escaping as the bird call had signaled a police raid. Emma would see the police presence and know to stay away. He had to trust that.

Defying the cops in the Quarter was one thing, trespassing was another. A night in the Third-World hell called Orleans Parish Prison was not on anyone's agenda.

26

Nikki and Keith used small flashlights to clear each room in the abandoned Georgian home, but the punks had fled. A gamey stink hung in the uncirculated air. She imagined this place had many hiding places. The backup squad had yet to arrive.

Scented candles were lit in strategic spots; however, they couldn't mask the body odor. Battery-powered lamps also illuminated the kitchen and common areas. A little can of Sterno heated an aluminum pan of pasta.

"Look at this." Keith pulled a rag from his jacket to hold up a machete lying in the kitchen sink. "There's blood on it."

Nikki pointed at the table. "My paycheck that isn't an insulin needle."

Keith swung his gun toward a live chicken scooting through the room. "Are you kidding me?"

"Don't shoot the chicken, Keith."

"He might be dangerous."

"Chickens are female."

"I don't see gender."

"*Oh, my God.*" A male voice projected from the corner of the living room. "Are you two for real?"

Nikki and Keith both crouched and aimed while assessing the

danger. A tall gutter punk in overalls materialized from behind a tall chair. He held his arms like Jesus on the cross. The torches flashed on his long and curly hair. He plopped in the highback chair. A studded collar adorned his neck.

Nikki patted him down, then holstered her weapon. "I'm Detective Mayeaux, and this Detective Teague. Are you the Vampire Lestat?"

One side of his face caught the light. "You can call me Rot."

"Because you don't bathe?"

He smirked. "Short for *Rottweiler*."

Keith moved closer. "Why didn't you run?"

"Simple. I know my rights."

Keith stressed, "You're breaking the law just being here."

"I'm squatting, not trespassing. Check the law."

"Oh, you're one of *those*. The only rights you have are your Miranda Rights."

"That heroin isn't mine. The place was like this when I got here."

"Those are all good answers," Nikki admitted.

"You're looking for Emma." He sat, crossing one leg over the other.

"Right," Nikki said. "Punisher."

The corners of his lips turned up in a smile. "I gave her that name. She's a legend with the traveler kids. Even I can't find her."

Keith moved about the room. "You underestimate us."

"You don't understand the gutter-punk network. The Punisher united everyone."

"For what cause?" She stood firm.

"Injustice. Us against you."

Nikki let a pair of cuffs dangle in his line of sight. "Stop doing that."

"What am I doing?"

"Distracting us with Emma so we don't look at you. Classic magic trick."

"I'm not hiding from the police. I'm around on any given day."

"Are you going to resist arrest?"

"No. I've seen what resisting gets." Rot stood again, putting his hands out in front of him. "You have nothing. Any lawyer will eat you alive."

"You're under the impression public defenders care." Keith gravitated back to Nikki.

"We can hold you for seventy-two hours." Nikki placed him in cuffs. "We have the heroin, trespassing, and the machete. You're going to be processed and spend the night in jail while we go home and sleep."

"The machete is chicken blood. We have coops in the back."

"Doesn't matter," Keith said. "Unless you give us something, you're going to OPP. Have you ever been in Orleans Parish Prison?" Keith sucked air through his teeth. "One big human rights violation."

Nikki joined in. "You think you're the *shit* out here? Wait until they throw you in a cell with bangers."

"New Orleans cops understand Bourbon and the Mardi Gras spirit. They will arrest a nice white boy who got too drunk and put them in a cell by themselves or with non-violent offenders. But you add nothing good to the New Orleans experience. Those overworked, underpaid, agitated guards hate gutter punks. So do the bangers. Just wait until they see you."

Rot swallowed. "If I give you something, my cred will be shot. I'll have nothing."

Nikki circled him. "You might think cops are a lot of things, but we don't give up our sources. In fact, everyone will think you told us to *fuck off*. Spill it."

"It might surprise you, but I want Emma caught."

"Then, help us." Nikki put her hands on her hips.

"I got something that can help you find her."

Nikki held up the key to the cuffs. "Go on."

"I have info on the phone with the rape video."

27

"Frank Brehm mailed that phone to you." Rot's eyes were wide. He pulled back his hair several times. "You can't say it was me. He'll seriously kill me."

"That name is familiar." Nikki glanced at Keith.

Rot continued. "Frank was head chef of the Grand Esplanade Hotel. He was fired for having a heroin party with traveler kids in one of the rooms. I wasn't there."

"Of course not."

"He owns Elysian Snowballs on Tchoupitoulas for a few years now. He's more hands-on with that place since he's been fired."

Nikki cocked her head. "What you're saying doesn't make sense. Having that video would get his job back with Herman."

"Those dudes go way back. Frank was betrayed like a little bitch. Pissed him off more than anything. Plus, blackmailing that dude isn't a good life decision, dig? An anonymous video sent to the cops? Sweet revenge."

"Did he record the video?"

"He didn't say. Frank *hated* Herman. Turns out, Herman took care of that cell like some kind of mob boss. Cell phone *gone*."

"Frank confided in you with all this?" Keith asked.

"The dude vents while on drugs. Like a truth serum."

"Did he say anything about a party?"

"What party? The Midas Ball?" He looked between them.

Nikki said, "We'll check it out."

"What's your relationship with Frank other than consumer of product?" Keith asked.

"We hang. Frank's not uppity like those rich ass-clowns."

"You ever bring females by?"

"Frank likes the occasional walk on the wild side. Nothing wrong with legal sex." His lip curled like Elvis.

Nikki snapped a picture of Rot. "You did good, Rot. Don't worry, we won't bust the house or reveal your treason. It's way too much paperwork, and you guys will only find a new spot."

Rot reclaimed his arrogance. "You won't tell Frank?"

"Lips sealed. We may need to talk again."

As Nikki and Keith stepped out of the house and onto the decaying porch, a figure started climbing the steps. This small person wore loose jeans and a huge Army jacket, as well as a hoodie with the drawstring pulled tightly over their face.

Emma.

Two squad cars pulled up to the curb just as the threesome saw each other. She had one escape path. Emma bolted around the side of the house toward the back. "It's Emma! Go through the house," Nikki commanded as she leapt off the porch in pursuit.

Large bushes scraped at her while ducking to protect her face. Trash and debris made for unsure footing. A distant rattling of the fence told her to sprint into the unknown darkness, or Emma would be gone.

Without seeing it, Nikki's shin connected with something hard, and she stumbled onto stacked cages of chicken wire. The sound of clucking and feathers attacked from all sides. She landed in something wet.

Chicken shit.

Keith ran up, cringing. "Are you okay?"

"Not hurt, but…"

Four uniformed officers appeared with their guns drawn and their torches lit. They stopped in a circle, with Nikki dead center in the spotlight. They looked at each other and the chickens scrambling around in the yard. One cop chuckled.

Keith said, "What the hell are you guys standing around for? Call in for more cars and go canvass the area. Emma Courtland is out there on foot. Set up a perimeter!"

The cops rushed toward the front of the house, leaving Keith to help Nikki to her feet.

She looked at her clothes. "I'm never going to live this down. You know how cops are."

"We can hose you off."

"I'm not a five-year-old that dove in a mud puddle. I need a change of clothes."

"*You sound like a five-year-old,*" Keith mumbled.

Nikki shot lasers at him.

He struggled not to grin. "You going to let me drive now?"

"I'm not getting chicken shit in my car." She handed over the key fob. "Drive it back to Headquarters and park it, *please.* One of the squads can take me back to my place. I'll have Jonesy pick me up in the morning."

"I'll come get you."

"You don't have to."

Keith's expression was as serious as she'd ever seen. "Damn it, Nik. I'll pick you up."

28

KEITH ARRIVED BACK at his house, standing inside his open doorway. The quiet was eerie. Nikki had breathed life into the home when she lived with him for that short period. He didn't want to take a step forward into the isolation. As much as he wanted to blame the house for his funk, he couldn't.

He closed the door and pulled a seldom-used lamp string. Disturbed dust particles floated like a tiny expanding universe. Nikki would never condone being this lazy. No more self-pity. He criticized the punks, yet he was living with the same apathy, minus digging in trash for food.

No Simpsons played tonight. He blasted a playlist named *battles*, consisting of alternating Beatles and Stones tunes.

The smelly garbage can was emptied and disinfected. Bugs from the sink drain drowned in bleach spray. The dishes collected in the dishwasher, which also needed the filters and rubber seams cleaned as muck had built up in the corners. A list started.

All his scattered clothes were balled up in his arms and brought to the bedroom hamper. The extra weight caused it to tip over. The vacuum cleaner came out of the closet for the first time in a month, collecting debris in the old, puffy bag.

Taking a piss prompted him to clean the yellow stains off the toilet. Thank God he hadn't entertained in months. The punch of bleach to his nose offered a glimmer of hope. With or without Nikki, his outlook needed a jump start.

The hour grew late, and he stopped the playlist on "Hey Jude." He'd earned a beer on the couch with a *Family Guy* episode to change things up. Just when he released a full breath, Roy Kent yelled through his cell. His first thought was Nikki. He didn't recognize the number and assumed who it would be. "Yeah."

"You let Emma get away?" she said.

He leaned forward in his recliner. "Yeah. She ran. We'll find her."

"I don't like your cavalier attitude."

"I told you…"

"Tell me everything that happened."

When Keith finished explaining, he waited for a threat that didn't come. He said, "You'll always have this over me."

"There are worse things, much worse things."

The call ended without warning. Calls from this person were never bookended with a greeting and farewell. He opened the recording app on his phone and listened to the conversation again.

FRIDAY

29

KEITH'S CAR AGGRESSIVELY pulled next to Nikki with a hard stop. She had already parked in the lot of the Coroner's Office, but it wouldn't open for five more minutes. He appeared agitated and rough around the edges. Anger looked like a clown suit on him. Even when Keith handled criminals, it was like bad acting. She summoned him inside of her car.

The passenger door opened, and he fell inside. "We have to get past this."

"Past what?"

"I told you I'd pick you up. You didn't text me."

"Sorry."

"We're not good, are we?"

The question struck her hard. She paused before answering. "I don't blame you. I swear I don't."

"What is it, then?"

She twisted to face him. "Every time I look at you, for the first few seconds, I see Morgan covered in blood."

"Christ." Keith wiped at his face.

"Just for a second. It goes away. It *will* go away with time."

They sat in silence. "I miss her too."

"She adored you." Nikki laughed. "Sometimes, I think she

wished I was out of the way so she could have you all to herself. That's another reason this is so hard."

He slapped his thighs, rubbing them. "Yeah, I...I can take myself off the case."

"No, you won't. Despite everything, you're comfortable. Don't worry about what I said with Morgan and the blood. A lot of things trigger me."

"I get it." Keith reached over and moved hair off her cheek. "Here's the thing. I need you to let me drive, or we can't work together."

She moved his hand from her hair. "Really, Keith? Don't be a dick."

"Don't be an asshole."

Her mouth opened, but nothing came out. She almost laughed. "My sister died in a crash while *you* were driving. *I'm an asshole?*"

"The woman had a seizure. Morgan never wore her seat belt. A fucking horrible cocktail."

"I know the details," she blurted.

"I'm sorry it wasn't me that died." He punched the roof. "I'm sorry!"

That wasn't acting. "Don't abuse my car." Nikki snatched a tissue from the middle console. "Both of us would've switched places with her."

"In a heartbeat." He opened and closed his fist.

"That's what you get for hitting my roof. How's your girlie fingers?"

"My girlie fingers are sad."

"Let's go inside." She slipped out of the car before he said anything else.

Keith caught up with her. "So, that's it? Did we resolve anything?"

"That's all I can take for now...okay?"

Keith closed his eyes to regroup. "So, we're here because Meachum found something?"

"You don't have to come in. I can meet you back at Headquarters."

"Hey." He caught up to her, holding her shoulders. "I'm here. No matter if you hate me, like me, or don't care about me. Dick—asshole—whatever. I am *here*."

She stared into his eyes. "You're a good guy, Keith. I never said otherwise."

He opened the coroner's front door. "When I said you're an asshole, I didn't mean you're the swampy truck driver kind of asshole. You're more the clean, bleached kind." He kept a straight face.

A grin appeared. "Oh, I'm the porno kind of asshole. Thanks."

Keith pulled her hand over his heart. She let her palm remain there a moment, but she couldn't lose herself. Nikki let her hand slide off as she walked ahead of him, using her tissue again.

"It's cold in here," Keith said.

She looked around reception. "Suck it up."

Nikki and Keith signed in and met Dr. Meachum in the hallway, outside the autopsy room. The entire place reeked of antiseptic. After a pleasant greeting, they walked through the double doors into air that felt colder inside than out.

The white tiled walls had sporadic blue squares designed to be densely populated near the floor. They saw two bodies on the stainless-steel tables. Herman Napleton and the Jane Doe had been cut open with the standard *Y* pattern. Both lay side by side, adding insult to fatal injury.

"Oh, that's god-awful. I'd rather roll in chicken shit," Nikki commented.

Dr. Meachum interrupted them. "You're early, but I've been here for an hour. I was just getting ready to sew them up." He was an older, balding man with pointy features like a bird. He was casual in his mannerisms, like a mechanic that worked on cars.

"Got something beyond the obvious?" Nikki asked.

"The female victim was strangled by a set of strong hands. No ejaculate, but latex and spermicidal jelly consistent with condoms were found."

"And Napleton?"

"His wounds are consistent with your account, having been attacked from behind. The throat slice wasn't deep, but the jugular was perforated, so it didn't take long for him to exsanguinate, bleed out. That determined the cause of death."

Nikki pointed at Napleton's naked pelvic region. "The stab to the groin?"

"The penis and right testicle were severed. Oz took lots of pictures of the wound before the knife was removed."

"Not the typical dick pic."

"Tox come back?" Keith asked.

"Not yet. I'll send it when it does."

"What's so special you had us come in, then?"

"I found something unusual." Meachum walked to the counter and retrieved a folder, opening it on his return. "This made me think of three other cases I've come across in the past five years, so I dug these up from the archives."

Nikki and Keith stood close to look in the folder. Keith commented, "You must have a good memory."

"This victim had an odd characteristic common to a few other cases."

"What?"

"These three were unidentified females. They were all strangled, and each has a fingernail indention on the back of their neck." Meachum had circled a short, dark line in each photo. "I would hazard to say the index finger. I pointed it out to the detectives in each case, and one said they'd submit it to VICAP, but no one has ever compared them. They're a match to Napleton. Nobody caught it."

"Doesn't surprise me. Different detectives. Different districts. Lazy. I want the names of the detectives on each case."

Keith said, "It won't do any good to stir up trouble when the suspect is dead."

"They need to know they could've had a high-profile collar." Nikki walked over to the female lying on the table. She leaned in to see the same tiny cut. "He was a serial killer."

"Nikki, you might want to consider the detectives on the case protected Napleton." His eyebrow hiked. "You wouldn't want to kick that ant pile."

"You got a point. Do we arrest Emma or give her the key to the city?"

Keith put his hand on her shoulder. "We arrest her."

30

NIKKI SHOOK A rubber chicken in the air. "Okay, who left this on my desk?"

Sam and Lawrence, two detectives in the squad, took off their jackets with exaggerated flare. They approached wearing tee shirts with Foghorn Leghorn and Chicken Little over their normal button-downs. "Why-why-why, that's outrageous, *Chick*."

The other agreed. "Don't worry, the sky isn't falling, Chick."

"*Chick?* You geniuses figured out it rhymes with Nik? That's how it's going to be?"

One spoke with a high-pitched, British accent. "You will hence-forth be known as *Chick* by the royal court."

Nikki slapped both on the shoulder with the rubber chicken. "Where the hell did you buy the shirts so fast?"

"Target," they said in unison.

Keith walked onto the floor with a bag of Popeye's Chicken. "Got lunch."

"*Et tu, Brute?*"

The laughter roared. Nikki took it with good humor, letting them get it out of their system. The detectives broke off to their respective desks. Nikki and Keith sat down with the chicken, biscuits, and sides.

Nikki could make out her name still being used in other conversations with laughter. She said, "I've been thinking about Emma's prints on the knife, and her wearing gloves."

"Strange, but not too strange. What are you thinking?"

She chose her lunch items. "Warren Courtland could have hired someone and passed off the knife. The hotel is motive."

"Hire someone *and* supply their murder weapon? No."

"Any staff had access to the knife. Dread could have taken it, having been inside the house."

"That's true, not likely. Try again." Keith pulled the crispy skin off the breast. "You have to think like Collins on this one."

"Yikes. Take that back." An e-mail appeared on her laptop from the Forensics team. She used another clean napkin to tap her keyboard. "Oz says Dread's fingerprints are a dead end. Not in the system."

"Doesn't matter. He's only a connection."

As lunch ended, Lan walked by with a huge grin. "Chicken? You guys are funny."

"What you got there, Lan?" Nikki asked.

He set down a folder off to the side. "That's a file on Frank Brehm. After lunch, go visit his snoball stand on Tchoupitoulas."

Keith said, "That was next on our list. It's open year-round. Not many stands are."

"Those things can pull in some serious cash."

"May I?" Lan reached for the extra biscuit. "Frank has been clean. I wouldn't be surprised if his house and business will be clean too."

"Rot." Nikki groaned.

Lan pointed his biscuit at her. "Frank supplies heroin, Rot wouldn't want him busted."

"I dunno," Keith said. "Rot seemed pretty eager to flip on him."

Nikki let her hands fall and rolled her eyes. "Rot played us like we'd protect him as a source. We've waited too long."

"Still, go find out what he has to say." Lan backed away with a mouthful.

Nikki gave Keith a lingering gaze.

"What? I got something on my face?" He wiped at his lips.

Nikki smiled, pulling her hair into a new ponytail. "I'd like you to drive."

⋘

Nikki climbed into Keith's Acura, putting the seatbelt on. She looked in the back seat on reflex. Morgan had been so excited to visit Audubon Park that day.

Keith started the engine. "You sure, Nik?"

"I'm good. So, dealer's choice." She turned to him. "Elysian Sno-balls is upriver on *Tchoup*, pretty close to Tipitina's coincidently, and Frank's home address is in the Treme—opposite direction."

"Let's go to his house first. Treme is closer."

"Don't drive like a maw maw. That'll make it worse."

A quick and safe eight-minute drive took them to Frank Brehm's doorstep. Nikki felt relieved, another hurdle in her healing cleared. Keith turned off the engine with a slight grin.

Frank lived in a light-blue shotgun home, raised a couple of feet, as most were. The bricked sidewalk led to five steps and a narrow porch. The bright-blue door was on the right, with two tall windows resembling entrances on the left.

Nikki knocked. "Frank Brehm, police!"

A man in an undershirt and boxers opened the door long enough for Nikki to see inside where a young female was lain out in an odd position on the couch in her underwear.

"What's this about?" he asked.

"Is she okay?" Nikki pushed Frank aside to check on the girl. "What's she on?"

"You can't barge in here."

A full-grown Golden Retriever with a large cone around its neck bounced behind Frank with a wagging tail. Keith kept Frank and the dog from interfering. "Imminent danger, Mr. Brehm. Is anyone else in your house?"

"*Imminent...?* No, just me, the lady, and Shrimp here." He patted the dog's head.

"Whaz gon on?" the female slurred. "Who er you?"

"I'm Detective Mayeaux. Are you okay? You need help?"

She laughed, still not forming her words. "Ged out of my face, *biatch.*"

"She's tripping." Nikki put a pillow behind the girl's head and covered her with a throw blanket. "How old is she?"

"She's not a minor." Frank gave off a Stanley Kowalski vibe from *A Streetcar Named Desire.* He put on a robe that had been draped over a chair. "She's twenty-two, maybe. She showed up like that, needing a place to crash. I told her to take the couch. Again...what is this about?"

"Emma Courtland."

"Warren's daughter?" He scratched the back of head. "I have no idea where she is."

"How do you know she's missing?" Nikki asked.

"I hear things."

"You two friends?" Keith asked, peering down the shotgun's hallway.

"Friends with her?" He broke into a laugh. "I met her a few times...years ago, when he'd bring her by the hotel."

"Never as a gutter punk?"

"Nah, she knows better than to come here."

Nikki scrolled to the Claiborne victim. "Seen her before?"

"Is she dead? No, sorry."

"What was your relationship like with Herman Napleton?"

"Since he fired me?" He shrugged. "I don't blame him for that. We haven't really spoke since."

Keith said, "Even though you got him laid with gutter punks?"

"That's ridiculous. And sex is not illegal." He laughed, taking a seat on the sofa at the feet of his guest. "Don't know who you've been talking to."

Nikki pet the dog while talking. "Apparently, you like to talk while on a bender."

His face twisted. "What do you mean?"

"A punk came forward. She said—I mean, they said you were rattling on about how you sent the phone to me with Emma's rape video."

"What? I said no such thing because I didn't do it."

"Whether you did or didn't, you had no idea Herman's connections would destroy the video, and now he's dead. I'm no math teacher, but two and two…"

Frank stood again. "And you think I equal four? As you can see, no one is in *imminent danger*. If you'd kindly leave."

"Where were you Thursday night between nine and midnight?" Nikki asked.

"Here. Alone with Shrimp. Ask him." He grumbled. "Arrest me, or get out of my house."

Nikki stepped onto the porch, with Keith following close behind. Frank locked the door. She held the railing on the way down to the bricked sidewalk, stepping on sprouts of weeds trying to grow through the seams.

"Do we believe Rot's story?"

Nikki frowned. "We have a new suspect, either way. His place was clean."

Keith glanced at the unassuming house. "I don't think Rot told him."

"I don't think so, either. Wait for his guest to leave?"

"That might be tomorrow."

"So, Frank, Napleton, Warren and Rot are connected, probably providing a local pipeline of drugs and girls."

"How does that help us find Emma?"

Nikki exhaled, walking in a tight circle. "Not sure. Have we stumbled onto something bigger than just a vigilante murder?"

31

Nikki walked through the common hallway to her condo with a bag of New Orleans Hamburger and Seafood. She stopped at Major's door, debating if she wanted to eat alone. Before even facing the peephole, her arm reached out like a phantom limb and knocked.

Major answered in a Saints sweatshirt and jeans. "Nikki, how are you?"

"Thirsty. Split an oyster po'boy?" She shook the bag.

"I have a nice white that will pair beautifully."

"*I'm* a nice white that pairs beautifully."

He belly laughed. "*True dat.* C'mon in, crazy."

"I promise I'll stay awake this time."

❧

Nikki and Major sipped chardonnay as they relaxed on the balcony with the empty fast-food bag crushed into a ball. After the fried chicken at lunch, she was glad Major shared the dinner calories. New Orleans wasn't the best place to maintain a figure.

A bite hung in the air, but Major adjusted the space heater to waft up between them. "The news reported a young girl found under the Claiborne overpass. Related to Napleton?"

"Shame." Nikki swirled her wine.

"Ah, I'm learning to read you. Can't talk about it, right?" Major smiled. "You know what else is a shame? You ever see pictures of Claiborne before they built the I-10?"

"Yeah, in the Louisiana History class I took at UNO. You don't recognize it."

Major stared forward. "My paw paw owned a business on Claiborne. Cigars. It was an up-and-coming black neighborhood. Then, like overnight, it was all undone." He turned to her. "The white man came."

"Words said after every country's theft or downfall."

"I can't say it was a black-white thing, but it was about money and access to the Quarter. Anyone would've been screwed in that neighborhood—white, black, or Vietnamese. They never had a say."

"Or a chance."

"Remember the sink hole at the foot of Canal Street?"

"I read about it. Caused by the tunnel."

"Part of the same initiative back in the '60s. Those crazy bastards dug a tunnel from Canal to Poydras for traffic. We can't bury people here, and they build a goddamn tunnel. Giant sump pumps and shit."

"Harrah's still uses it for valet parking, right?"

"I think so."

"Why wasn't it ever used?"

"The project got pulled after they damn near had it finished. Typical government waste."

"All that *is* a shame. Sorry about your paw paw's business."

"There's a point somewhere. I just lost my train of thought."

Nikki looked at him. "Is there a lesson?"

He dipped his head to look up at her. "Not a lesson or moral, but advice… when all else fails, follow the money."

"Words of wisdom." They tapped glasses. "Can I ask you something?"

"Anything."

"You like snoballs?"

"On a hot day, I love 'em. Can't say I seek 'em out on the regular."

"Would you buy a snoball in the winter?"

He laughed. "Maybe if it was spiked with a little vodka, but that's a frozen daiquiri, isn't it?"

Damn, he's not far off.

SATURDAY

32

DESPITE HALF A bottle of wine with Major, Nikki started fresh on her supposed day off. She called Keith who had approval from Lan to use his Saturday catching up on his caseload, paperwork, and whatnot. Nikki volunteered to help, but Lan denied her overtime. She couldn't sit home alone doing nothing.

Nikki waited in her car on the Tchoupitoulas curb in the sunny, 55-degree weather. The late morning sun magnifying through the glass had the temperature rising in the car. She cracked the window. Her free afternoon had turned into an unpaid, unofficial stakeout.

The line for Elysian Snoballs grew to seven deep. She couldn't believe these people would pay for shaved ice and syrup on a chilly day like this. However, people did crazy things. On her third date with Keith, he had a convertible loaner while his car was in the shop and they barhopped in forty-degree weather with the top down, so she couldn't criticize.

The structure was the size of a large shed, built on a quarter-acre lot of ugly, pocked land. It looked solid, constructed with two-by-fours, planks, plywood, and siding on a four-foot-high foundation with bowing stairs from constant customers. A blue porta-potty stood behind it along with a pallet of plywood and two-by-fours.

He had electricity, as well as a generator. The signage and menus were hand-painted in fun, colorful letters.

Two of the people in line were *traveler kids*, as Dread corrected. Nikki got out of her car after they received their order. Both the kids looked confused and pissed. She met them on their way out. "What flavor you got?"

"What?" One guy looked at it.

She took it from his hand, turning the cup upside down to empty its contents on the ground. Her foot smashed the red ice into the grass. "Huh. Just ice."

"C'mon!"

"Take this for your trouble." She placed a five-dollar bill in his hand.

Both boys glanced back at Frank in the window, then continued walking. *Bitch* was said in a mumbled sentence.

Nikki held up her badge to the line as she climbed the stairs. "Sorry, folks, the stand is closed for the next half-hour."

Frank's arms flew up. His torso framed in the window in a black-and-gold Saints jacket and knit cap. "What are you doing to me?"

"I'll take a chocolate cream." Nikki rested her arm on the ledge as she looked inside the shack at the ice shaver and a folding table of different-colored syrups in condiment containers. Stacks of cups were wrapped in plastic in the corner. Vents near the ceiling let in sunlight.

Frank grudgingly made the snoball. "What else do you want?"

"Do you miss being a chef? The city was your oyster, and you royally assed it up."

He shrugged. "I do a pretty good living out here."

"Cash business. Low overhead. Heroin on demand. But where is the culinary challenge?"

"Less pressure with this."

"Less pressure selling heroin?"

He stared at her, frozen with the snoball in hand.

"Look, you tried to help Emma in my book. You may have sent the phone to fuck Herman, but there is good in that act."

"I didn't send that damn phone."

"Either way, you don't have to beg Herman for your job anymore. Maybe Warren and Mary will give you your job back as chef."

"You sure you're not on crack? I don't understand why you're harassing me into losing my cool."

"The chocolate cream is my fav. I have to admit…heroin and snoballs, that's a good operation. But if you're not selling your special flavor, why open? You're just pissing off your clientele."

He folded his arms, aggravated but silent.

"Oh, I get it. You can get the new business model out to the others. You found another way to distribute, and this is how you spread the word."

"Who's your boss? I'm calling to complain."

"Bottom line, I'm looking for Emma. You tell me where Emma is, and I go away."

"I. Don't. Know."

"You're tense. Yeah, I'd be pretty anxious about ever keeping drugs here again."

"I'm filing a complaint."

"My boss is Lieutenant Lan Tran. Headquarters."

He made a show of writing it down. "Vietnamese?"

"Good guy. Explain to him how buying a snoball is harassment. This is good, by the way. Wasting your talent."

"Mind the plywood." Frank reached for the diagonal bar propping up the awning, releasing it, so that came down to cover the window. Nikki had a second to move before the plywood would've knocked her torso into the open window.

The outside read *Sorry—Closed!* She heard it latch from the inside.

"See you at Herman's funeral tomorrow," she said to herself.

33

Dread had finished eating a bowl of Frank's cereal when the homeowner himself came through the door with a big box. Rot looked up from porn playing on Frank's flatscreen, using the remote to mute the fake moaning. Shrimp ran out of his giant cage with a wagging tail.

Frank shook his head, closing the door behind him. He squatted to drop the box and scratch at Shrimp's neck under the cone. "Make yourselves at home."

"We don't have homes." Rot adjusted his crotch, throwing one leg over the other.

"What's in the box?" Dread asked.

"Syrup. Thanks to Mayeaux, I had to close early."

"*Bitches*, right?" Rot smirked.

"At least you ain't banging each other on my couch." Frank reached in the box for something. His hand came out with a gun.

"Frank...?" Dread started, but then shut up.

Frank stepped behind Rot, placing the barrel against his head. "Hey, fucker?"

"What the hell is that, Frank?"

"Did you tell those two detectives that I sent the cell phone?"

Rot's hands rose to head level. "No, the hell I did."

"How would you suppose they know?" Frank pulled the weapon back to load the chamber. He pressed it back against his neck.

"I swear, Frank. You talk, dude. Do you know how much shit you say when you high?"

"I've heard you," Dread said.

"Shut it. I don't like you."

"Why the fuck would I do that, man? Why?"

Frank put the gun in his waistband. "I'm going to kill whoever told them."

Rot rubbed his neck while Frank headed for the box again and picked it up.

Dread asked, "The cops know anything about Emma?"

"They think I know where the little bitch is, thanks to this anonymous punk."

"I'll ask around." Rot watched the porn. "Could be a punk told another punk. If the cops had something, you'd know it."

Frank looked ready to jump on top of Rot. He carried the box of syrup to the back of the house. Dread and Rot shared a curious shrug. Frank came back with a Coke. "I got another issue with you. You brought a girl to Percy?"

"Yeah. He say something?"

"Girls go through me. That's the deal." Frank eyed Shrimp, trotting back into his open cage where a bed and blankets welcomed him.

"Our deal is heroin. Girls I introduce to you are a bonus. What do you care about a side piece?"

Frank snatched the remote, turning off the television. He then threw it back at Rot, bouncing it off his head. "It *all* goes through me. Warren and Percy will try to squeeze me out now that Herman is dead. They won't play well with you."

"You trying to be a big dick?" Rot rubbed his head. "That's not you, man. You're mid-level all the way."

"Look in the mirror next time you give an opinion. You're a bottom rung. I'm your handler."

"Handler?"

Dread jumped in. "Like a boss. But what he really said is you his bitch."

Frank pointed at him. "Yes. I'm your boss. Don't go around me again."

"Whatever you say, boss. You want me to bring Flower by for you?"

"I do. But in the meantime, can't one of you deliver Emma to the cops? Get her off my back?"

"Shit, I want her caught as much as you."

Frank gazed at Dread. "What about your boyfriend here?"

Dread answered, "I want her to turn herself in. There's no other way out for her."

Frank wiped hard at his face, then scrubbed his hair with a final exhale. He sat on the coffee table, facing Rot. "Herman controlled a lot, boys. With this shake-up, we need to take advantage. I can't give Warren any reason to cut me off. And you can't give the cops any reason to fuck with me."

"You're just paranoid," Dread offered. "The whole operation depends on you."

"I like him." Frank pointed at Dread again. "If the girls go through me, then they need us."

"Warren is the new Herman?" Rot folded his arms.

"I'll talk with Warren at the funeral, and we'll make arrangements. Once I give them a scenario without me involved, he'll change his tune."

"Warren Courtland is a dickhead. How will you do that?" Dread spoke up.

"Let the adults talk." Frank glanced at him.

"Just want to be on the same page."

"It's simple. I'm a problem-solver."

"Problem-solver? What's the problem?" Rot brushed away hair from his face.

Frank stared at Dread. "Can I speak in front of Lenny Kravitz?"

"We're together on this," Rot assured.

"Mayeaux and Teague. They're a problem. Can you handle it, if needed?"

Rot sat back. "If the price is right. What about the party?"

"What about it?"

"Herman killed those girls, right? Who's gonna do it now?"

"You volunteering?"

Rot lit a joint from his jacket. "You guys wear masks, and these girls will be doped. No cop in their right mind would believe anything they say. Why take it there?"

"You heard of Epstein? That movie guy, Weinstein? One accusation is easy to discredit. But, for those of you punks that don't die on the street, you either go home or you go straight. So, after years of having these parties, if multiple women came forward with accusations about rich, white men…with these fuck-head lawyers out there, *shit*."

"Whatever you need, Dread and I got it." Rot looked at him. "Dude, I never knew a black dude could go pale like that. What up?"

"Nothing. Lactose intolerant."

"That's what you get for eating my cereal." Frank ignored him. "Talk to any cop in this city, they'll say killing these punks—no offense—is doing the city a service."

34

A 40-PERCENT CHANCE of showers appeared on Keith's weather app. How silly that a threat of rain could instill such anxiety. He understood the trauma behind the storms. His father had taken his life during a rainstorm. At fourteen years of age, Keith found his body. He never accepted help from his mother in processing his grief. And then she died of an aneurysm the day after he turned seventeen, while she entered the house with a bag of groceries. It was raining.

Instead of staying home to chance a session of gun therapy, he found himself driving without direction in the Quarter under gray clouds. Unless you worked there, the Quarter was someplace the locals tended to avoid. However, he couldn't deny the sense of pride in being homegrown amongst the tourists.

He parked in the lot by the river, stopping to admire the bridge hovering over the expansive current. An umbrella came along just in case he got some of the 40 percent. Barges and tugs moved slowly while a riverboat docked nearby.

Jackson Square was a short walk across Decatur. A few gutter punks were loitering, but not as many as in years past. They wouldn't rat out Emma even if they knew where she was.

If New Orleans were a garden, Bourbon Street was the fertilizer. The economy relied on the outside dollars. The lax liquor laws laid the foundation for excitement, and so the reputation became legendary. It was America's *hall pass*.

Keith found himself at The Crush as if he'd happened upon it. Nikki wouldn't mind if he scoped things out before their official visit—if he even told her. The club was high-end, yet came off as seedy on purpose, like a haunted house. It offered safe danger.

Keith showed his license to the bouncer, then followed a barrier around a short wall where he paid the cover. Sturdy, wide-seated chairs surrounded little tables. The chairs also butted up against raised islands meant for a single dancer. Most of the clientele were straight men, but it wasn't uncommon to see all walks of life.

"Abita Amber." Keith pulled out ten for the clean-cut bartender.

The older man poured the beer into a tall glass. "Enjoy, Officer."

"What gave me away?"

The bartender gave a sly smile. "You're here alone. Haven't been drinking yet. You checked out the customers before the dancers. It's a vibe."

"Percy doesn't pay you enough."

"True dat. Should I get him for you?"

"Let me guess. Mr. Fields is sitting in his office upstairs, watching a feed from a camera." Keith pointed at one. "You just pressed a button near the register alerting him to focus on the bar area. You give him a nod, and he'll come down."

The bartender faced the overhead dome camera, tilting his head at Keith. He came back with a smile. "That's accurate."

A forty-something black man in a designer sweater and slacks stepped up to the bar with a pleasant smile. "May I help you, Mr....?"

"*Detective* Teague, as your man here figured out. But, call me Keith." He held his hand out to shake.

It was welcomed. "Call me Percy." He clasped his fingers in front of his belt. "How can I help you? Does this involve Herman Napleton?"

"This isn't an official visit, but I wanted us to talk before that happens."

"Off the record? How does *that* work?" He leaned on the bar, mocking interest.

Keith took a healthy sip of beer. "The way this works, Percy, is up to you."

"Up to me?"

"You associate with a lot of powerful people."

He turned to the bartender, motioning for a drink, probably having a *usual*.

"These influential friends keep you out of trouble, right? They make sure your business has all its permits, zoning, health code—makes sure it runs smooth."

"Nothing underhanded." Percy accepted a bottle of Barq's root beer. "It's good to have friends. I'm busy, Keith. What's the point here?"

"Detective Nikki Mayeaux isn't one of those friends who looks out for your interests."

An eyebrow raised. "Detective Mayeaux and I spoke during the unpleasant business between Herman and Emma. She's legit."

"*Legit* is a good word for her. And she's tenacious."

"That's admirable."

"Is there anything you know about Emma that you might hold back under questioning?"

"Why would I lie about Emma Courtland? I'm confused. What are you here for?"

"I'm not so sure, anymore. Look…the more time it takes us to find Emma, the more likely something else in this little orbit will come to light. Dirt on people in high places. I'm sure you understand."

"I understand you have as much to lose as anyone."

"So, I can put you in *that* column. I really didn't have to come here."

"Sucks when you don't know who to trust."

"Finding Emma could put all that to rest."

"I have no idea where she is. And the fact that a sixteen-year-old can elude the police doesn't instill me with confidence."

"Okay." Keith finished the beer, then threw a five on the bar. "Good meeting you."

"I do appreciate your visit. Stay for a dance. On the house."

"I'd rather spend that money on a nice dinner and conversation."

Percy couldn't contain a deep laugh. "Have a good night, Detective Teague."

When Keith stepped out onto Bourbon, it was pouring.

SUNDAY

35

EVEN THOUGH KEITH would volunteer to accompany Nikki to Herman Napleton's funeral, she decided not to invite him along to play the *unofficial* angle for anyone who'd ask. Lan had officers posted at every street corner of the cemetery in case Emma made an appearance.

In most cases, Jazz funerals were reserved for musicians, but local figures and prominent members of society sometimes received such treatment. Anyone with enough money could have one, but it didn't mean they deserved one. Herman thought he did.

Six members of a brass band played "Down by the Riverside" as a *second line* progressed toward St. Louis Cemetery No. 1, New Orleans's oldest cemetery, where Herman Napleton would be interred in his family tomb. About a hundred people surrounded the ornate, black-and-gold carriage as it carried the body to its final resting place. Most laughed and danced at the lively trumpeting through puddles from last night's rain.

Located near the old red-light district called Storyville, the cemetery was beautiful in its decay. Some tombs had been painted white by loved ones as the yearly tradition dictated. The gates weren't open to the public anymore, except for guided tours. Nikki had seen the

Voodoo queen Marie Laveau's tomb a few years back, and something about it stayed with her like a ghost.

Nikki hung back on Conti Street at a respectful distance under a clear sky. The pathways inside the cemetery were too narrow to have everyone file in, so the procession meandered about on the sidewalk. She felt a twinge of guilt for not telling Keith her intentions, but she wanted a clear head. What better place to scrutinize how these people interacted?

Frank danced in the second line with a flask and an umbrella. His tailored suit presented a gentleman, not your typical dealer. Not caring about unwanted attention, he moved with white-man rhythm. Most avoided him.

As the dancing subsided outside the gate, most of the crowd hung back, not allowed to enter. The carriage parked as close as it could for the body to be carried inside where the caretakers would slide Napleton onto a shelf in the family tomb for a year and a day, after which the bones of the decomposed body would be swept into an opening in the floor. Leaving room for the next in line.

The music stopped and the quiet jarred Nikki. As friends and family settled into conversation, she crept closer to Frank. "I'm sorry for your loss."

"Shit. I can't get away from you."

"Calm down. I'm not here to harass you at a funeral. Just observing."

"Don't do that near me, okay?"

"C'mon, Frank. Let's be friends."

Frank hurried off, weaving his way closer to the crowd as Sharon Courtland walked up in an elegant lavender dress and pearls. She also had an umbrella decorated with tassels and glitter used for spinning and joisting. It was an uncomfortable prop in her hands. "Any closer to finding my daughter?"

"Officially, we're still tracking leads. Unofficially...no."

She nodded. "I only took this ridiculous umbrella for shade."

"A burial at St. Louis No. 1 is a rare occasion. It's not every day someone goes into one of those ovens."

"Oven?"

"These tombs reach 300 degrees in the summer."

"That's fitting."

"Fitting? I thought you agreed with Warren that Herman was innocent."

"It's easier to agree. Herman was evil." Sharon spoke her mind, as if she was liberated. "Mary won't show. She decided Harrah's was the best way to mourn. I don't think she'll ever forgive him."

"Will she be interred with him?"

"Not anymore. She used to brag about having a tomb here. Her family is in Metairie Cemetery. She'll go there."

"Do you know that Herman visited Mary the night he was murdered?"

"Not surprising." Sharon kept an eye on Warren, who was petting the horse that drew the carriage as if he'd bet on it. "When that much wealth is shared in a marriage, you learn to make communication work. Herman was a monster, but he was a rich monster. I'm sure they had things to discuss that couldn't end in a fight."

"I recognize some of those men that Frank just walked up to."

"You probably questioned them." She frowned. "Saul Green, the cheese-ball in the gray suit, is owner of Rue Paradise on Bourbon. Percy Fields, the black gentleman, is owner of the Marquis Hotel and a strip club on Bourbon."

"The Crush. I remember. A lot of money is here."

"With Herman dead, Warren is taking over his duties as president of the Krewe of Midas. Percy Fields is supposed to be king this year, but Warren thinks in honor of Herman, that Mary should ride solo as queen, no king. This close to Mardi Gras, not everyone agrees."

"Does Mary want to ride?"

"She does. It's her *coronation* as hotel owner. She is not liked by everyone in the industry, much less the krewe."

The band struck up again, playing "When the Saints go Marching in." Nikki and Sharon were both alerted to a commotion in the procession. Strained voices overpowered the crowd's chatter. Nikki spotted Saul Green grabbing Frank by the lapels. He shoved Frank against the wall. Percy squeezed between them, but was thrown to the ground. Other attendees pulled out their cells to film.

"What's going on there?" Nikki thought better than to intervene.

"You know."

Nikki smiled. "I do?"

"Rumor has it Frank sent Emma's video to the police."

"There's no proof of that."

"Right. I won't react to rumors. But those guys…?"

"Should I separate them?"

"No need. That's not *real* fighting. Frank came up with them like the *rat pack*. He might be the black sheep, but he's tolerated."

As quickly as the skirmish started, it ended with Percy Fields leaving down Conti Street in a huff. Saul Green trekked over to Frank and pointed in his face while scolding him, then turned his shoulders around and pushed him to leave. Frank stumbled forward and left. Warren stayed by the carriage, letting Saul Green handle things.

Sharon shook her head. "I don't know why I came."

36

NIKKI BROKE FROM the funeral attendees to trail Saul Green up the block. After the man sat in it for a while, his charcoal-gray Mustang came to life. *He's going back to his hotel,* she thought. She then backtracked to her own car, figuring after his little skirmish at the funeral, she could meet Saul Green back at his work.

She found parking a block away on Dumaine. She had been inside the Rue Paradise Hotel once to take an innocuous statement from Saul Green about the rape. The address was located near the residential end of Bourbon Street, a block beyond where the party-goers stopped venturing and homes began. If anyone walked past the hotel late at night, then they either lived in the Quarter or were lost.

The lobby wasn't as roomy as the Grande Esplanade, but it wasn't meant to be a gathering place. To the left of reception, Nikki spotted the sign for the *Oui Bar*, written in a fancy script with an arrow indicating where to go.

She entered the classy extension of the hotel which showed off brass fixtures, artsy stools, and a lady bartender in a tuxedo shirt and Mardi Gras beads. "I'll take an Abita Amber and a water. Can you call Mr. Green? Tell him Detective Mayeaux is here."

"Detective?" The bartender hesitated with the beer in hand.

"I'm off duty, but thanks for your concern."

"None of my business—understood." She picked up the courtesy phone, whispering into the receiver. "He's coming." The beer flowed into a frosted glass.

The young lady had green-and-gold eyeshadow, with purple streaks in her hair. Nikki admired the commitment. "You must do well during carnival."

She leaned close. "I hate Mardi Gras. No, let me rephrase that. I hate drunk tourists who can't control themselves. Like it's their first experience with alcohol."

"Preach." She pretended to toast with the beer. "I'm Nikki."

"I'm Tilly."

"Accent?"

"South Carolina." She pointed at a tattoo of a paw print on her wrist.

"Clemson grad. How'd you end up here?"

"Love for the city."

"There's a saying," Nikki started.

Tilly cut in. "If you love New Orleans, it will love you back. If you hate New Orleans…"

Nikki finished. "It will hate you back."

"The locals respect the city. These tourists are like idiots in Las Vegas. No self-control. My beef is with them, not Mardi Gras." One corner of her mouth turned up in a smile as Saul Green walked through.

"Detective Mayeaux." Saul Green held out his hand, noticing the beer.

"Call me Nikki." She held up her glass. "Not on duty."

"It's been a while. You attended Herman's funeral?"

"*Attended* is a strong word."

He started to say something, but thought better of it. "It's been a day. We're going to do a shot."

"Do I look like I'm still in college? An afternoon beer is all I need." Nikki's hair fell over the left side of her face. She traced it behind her ear.

He leaned on the bar, looking at Tilly. "Give me what Nikki is having."

"Relax, Saul. Come down to street level."

"I'm relaxed."

"If that's relaxed, you're going to die of a heart attack. Were you like this when we last spoke?"

"Probably." He made a Zen pose with hands out, closing his eyes and breathing deep. It wasn't a joke. When settled, he put one butt cheek on the barstool. "You want to ask about that little tête-á-tête at the funeral."

"You think that's why I'm here?"

"Isn't it?"

She sampled the beer. "Everyone looked upset with Frank."

He laughed without concern. "That idiocy is the result of decades of friendship."

"That didn't look like friendship."

"Sometimes that's how business is handled. We're all friends afterwards."

"Krewe of Midas pals?"

"You ever come to our parades? Lots of fun."

"I can't say I have. And Frank? Is he the odd man out?"

"Frank is a wasted talent." He drank half the bottle in one pull.

"Are you even enjoying the beer? Slow down. Savor."

"I savor in large quantities." He wiped his lips with a napkin. "Word on the street…"

"Word on the street?" Nikki mocked.

He smiled. "Emma Courtland is evading police."

"Yes, there is a warrant for Emma's arrest. So, think twice about protecting your friend's stepdaughter."

He kept a poker face. "Warren wants her found. We all do."

"You know the rumors about Frank and the video. When you learned the NOPD received the video, did you think it was real?"

"I was worried the cops were manufacturing evidence. Then, it went away just as fast."

"Your gang was upset earlier. Was that about learning Frank sent it?"

"The video wasn't real. Those things are easy to fake nowadays. Did Frank deepfake the video, then send it? He has that mentality."

"He does strike me as the needy type."

"Frank is like the little brother who wants to play football with the older boys."

"Did Frank introduce young girls to Herman? That's the word on the street."

Saul reared his head back, looking like he hadn't heard right. "Wow. What a question. Who is your source?"

"Is it true?"

"I have no idea. I mean, no. How could he have done that under our noses? No."

"Have you ever seen Frank and Emma together?"

"When he was Warren's chef, maybe. I can't believe the problems she's causing that family. Such a beautiful girl, too. It's like she's making herself unattractive."

"All things being equal. You'd believe Herman over Emma?"

"I knew Herman well. Warren is like a brother. I didn't know Emma beyond the sneer."

"You found her attractive, you said."

"Don't say it like that, Detective. There's nothing unseemly about thinking a young girl will grow to be an attractive woman."

"It doesn't sound good, Saul."

"Because you're cynical. It's ingrained in men to see the beauty in young girls throughout evolution, when survival of the human race was imperative. Since the dawn of civilized man, we seek attractive mates. Children were expected early in marriage. Thinking a sixteen-year-old is pretty is no different than finding beauty in a painting or music or a classic car."

"Keep digging, Saul."

"You can't shame me. I'm a student of psychology."

"No, you're a creep," she said with a smile. "It's official."

"I'm a deep thinker, not a perv. That's what's wrong with today's society. No one can have a discussion anymore. Either you're right or wrong. Let me record you on social media so my generation can cancel you. Individual thinking is lost when someone is part of a larger group with cultlike beliefs. Instead of learning from each other, we want to take a bat to the other person's head."

"You're something else, Saul." She sipped.

"You bet your ass."

"Is your pal Percy Fields upset he's not king of your krewe this year?"

"This murder has the whole krewe in upheaval. If that's the vote, he'll be fine."

"Besides the Marquis Hotel, Fields also owns the Crush strip club. That's a candy store of young women, drugs, and cash." Nikki finished the last of her beer.

"You described every strip club everywhere. What's your point?"

"I don't blame you for being defensive. I expected it."

"Not defensive, annoyed." Saul glanced at Tilly, who stood off to the side, waiting to be needed. His cell went off with an alert. "I just remembered I have an engagement to attend. The detective's tab is on me."

"No thanks, Saul. I'll pay my bill. We'll talk again soon."

Tilly inched over to Nikki as Saul left the room to give her a high-five. "Slay."

37

FRANK BREHM CLIMBED backwards off the foot of his bed, stepping on his discarded suit he had worn to Herman's funeral. Flower moaned with the shaking mattress. He put his Jockeys back on. Flower was indifferent to his hairy potbelly, but he didn't like his junk to be exposed.

The drunk gutter punk posed naked on her stomach, feet in the air. Her thighs had a few small bruises, but were silky smooth. The contour from the small of her back rising up the hills of her ass made him pause with envy.

Her head shifted to catch him staring. "What?"

"You kill me." He grabbed a pair of beads off his dresser from the Krewe of Midas. They dangled in front of him.

She rolled onto her side, waving one hand. *"Throw me somethin', mister!"*

He tossed them. "Put them on."

She sat upright while placing them over her head, flipping up her hair like a 1950s pinup. They hung over her chest. Her eyes glazed over. "How do they look?"

"No words." *Flower* was a perfect name. At fifteen years old, Rot had found another rose in a garden of weeds. "You ever ride on a float?"

"Nope." Her torso swayed.

"We'll have to change that. Pretend the bed's a float." Frank waved his arms. *"Throw me something, sister."*

Flower's hair caught in the beads while struggling to pull them off. She tossed them with a soft touch, missing wide.

Frank caught them low before landing on the floor. "Oh, we have to work on your technique."

"I'm so drunk."

"I need to send a text, but when I come back, I'll show you a whole new use for these." His eyebrows popped up and down.

She appeared confused. "Oh, God. I'm going to throw up."

"Bathroom—go!"

Flower put her hand over her mouth and stumbled forward. She vanished toward the back of the shotgun house. He walked with the beads through the front room to find his cell. Flower's moans and gagging echoed from the bathroom.

Shrimp looked up at him from the open cage, then lay his head back down on the cone. First, Frank checked messages, but none of the guys had reached out. They will be sorry when he trots this show pony in front of them. He had a thriving business and all the pussy he could handle. Maybe they were holding *him* back.

He heard Flower approaching from behind, but didn't turn to acknowledge her. "Feel better, dahlin? Give me a sec."

No response came, but Flower's cold hands rubbed his back.

His eyes grew as something stung his neck. He pulled a syringe hanging from his jugular. Before he turned to face the intruder, their weight attached to his back. Legs wrapped around his waist and arms grappled his head, covering his mouth. He stumbled forward, but caught himself. He didn't have much time. This person on his back had a death grip.

The walls moved on their own. The weight fell off, but that didn't matter.

He tried to land on the sofa, but he collapsed to the floor in an utter state of confusion where his muscles refused to work, yet he was aware of everything happening around him.

Shrimp's tail wagged inside the cage as Frank tried to call out.

⤬

Frank came to as water splashed on his face. His head could move, but the rest of his body was immobile. He was sitting, bound tight to a chair with duct tape covering his bare skin everywhere. Shrimp's dog cone was around his neck. "What's going on? You!"

"I have some questions." She held up one of the containers used to squirt flavored syrup onto snoballs. The box from the refrigerator was on the floor. She twisted off the cap and poured the liquid coconut into the cone.

Frank felt the cold, sticky mess collect around his neck. "I don't know anything. Shrimp, what have you done with Shrimp?"

"Dog's in his cage. He's fine. You sent the phone to Nikki, didn't you?" She picked up another container from the floor.

His eyes darted to the back room.

"Looking for your underaged date? She's passed out in the bathroom." The strawberry flavor was squeezed onto his head like ketchup. "Did you make copies of that video?"

The syrup coated his face. "I couldn't. It wasn't my phone. I knew the video was there, but I couldn't get to it without the passcode. So, I sent Mayeaux the whole thing."

"I don't know if you're unlucky or just stupid." She poured yet another on his head. The cone was filling up. "I can see why people like working at snoball stands. This is fun."

"Let me go, and we'll go to the police together. I'll give them everyone involved!"

"You have nothing positive to offer this world." She used both hands to compress a container until it unloaded into the cone.

The syrup was up to his mouth. Frank tried to rock and lean his head forward to drain the syrup, but it was useless. He strained for one last gasp. "Don't kill me. I'll do anything..."

She held the container upside down over his head as it drained. "Pretty pedestrian. I thought I'd enjoy your begging a little more than this."

38

Nikki had stayed at the Rue Paradise bar to share a plate of calamari, trying to extract insight from the opinionated bartender named Tilly. A glass of water balanced out the beer. When Nikki determined the Clemson alum had nothing else to offer on Saul, she paid the tab with a nice tip and her cop card.

No call or text from Keith. She shouldn't need him to check in...but *she wanted him to*.

Instead of heading home, Nikki pointed her car to Frank's address, a mile away from the hotel. She circled the block, but spotted no activity. The six-foot-tall windows on his home were dark. She parked and attempted to peek inside. No peep from the dog. The long curtains were closed tight. Frank was right; this verged on harassment, but he deserved no less.

"Frank," she shouted, rapping on the glass. "You in there?"

Nikki moved to the side of the door in case someone answered with a shotgun. However, the entrance wasn't closed all the way. The screen door hid that fact from the street view. She released the retention strap on her holster, retrieving her Glock. An officer of the law brandishing their weapon after a beer was never a good thing, but she'd take that chance.

"Frank?" She pulled open the screen door, letting it rest against her back. With her gun at the ready, she pushed the main door open. "NOPD! Anyone home?"

A sweet fragrance hit her nose. Maybe he took the dog for a walk. Shrimp didn't seem like a barker. The house was dark with no light sources. She used the flashlight on her phone. In front of her was a man sitting in a chair with something large around his head. It looked like Shrimp's dog cone. He was in the threshold of the second room.

"Frank?" She found the light switch for the small chandelier above.

To her left, Shrimp lay in his locked cage licking his hind leg, no cone.

Nikki started forward, shifting her cell to dial for assistance, but never got the chance. Both feet slipped forward, falling back with no control, not aware how close the coffee table was. The base of her skull smacked the edge. An instant, bright white light flashed behind her eyes, and with that, she found herself incapacitated.

Shadows blurred on the ceiling, and she could've sworn her head lifted before settling back down. The shadow disappeared like a ghost, and the light faded to nothing.

39

Nikki came back to consciousness in a state of confusion. The pain in her head coincided with opening her eyes. *Where was she?* Frank Brehm's place? The ceiling's light fixture came into view, somewhat blinding her. She lay flat on the floor in his front room. Her head rested on a pillow.

Her right arm swung out to push off the floor, but planted on something slippery yet sticky at the same time. It was very much the consistency of blood. The pieces came together. She twisted and crawled for a better look at the man duct-taped to the chair. The cone around his neck looked like an upside-down lampshade.

"Frank?"

Nikki checked up and down her own body for injuries. A knot on the base of her skull drew a touch of blood on her fingertips. The pillow showed smatterings, but the dark material made it hard to tell. Her hand found her holster in a panic, then she drew a breath of relief. Emma put her gun back.

Her ears perked when a conversation outside on the street filtered inside. She struggled to rise. Equilibrium returned... She needed focus, clarity. The deep, crimson-black texture of Frank's blood became vibrant, like a high-definition television. Wait—a *sweet* aroma filled her lungs.

On the floor by the bloodstained pillow, her cell phone pinged with an alert next to the splatter. She touched the smear she slipped on. This wasn't blood.

Snoball syrup.

The discarded containers lying on the floor came into focus. None of it was blood. She dialed 911 while stepping around the wet spots and containers to get a better look at Frank. The sight was jarring.

He drowned in his own creation.

His entire head had been submersed at one point. Only his nose to the top of his head was visible but stained, as drips leaked onto his naked body. The number four started on his forehead.

"This is Detective Nikki Mayeaux out of Headquarters, badge number 2014. I have a dead body at 86324 Dumaine in the Treme. Drowned or asphyxiated is the best way to put it. I need a CSU team and the coroner."

"Thank you, Detective. Is there need for an ambo?"

She searched the house, lowering her voice. "Send one. I might need a stitch or two. I'm getting off the line to secure the scene."

Nikki kept her gun to her chest as she cleared each room. The soles of her shoes stuck to the floor as she walked. *Oz will love that.* The bedsheets were a tangled mess, yet he was killed near the front room. Someone had vomited in the bathroom.

Deep down, she figured with the pillow she woke on, and still having her gun and cell, that Emma had struck again. Did Emma throw up like she did herself with Napleton? Herman had a *five*, and Frank had the *four*. The pictures of her own face marked with an *X* came to mind, but if she was on the list, that would've been the perfect time to kill her as well. However, Emma took care of her instead. Who would be number *three?*

40

Two squads had arrived with sirens blaring. Nikki told the responding officers to string up the tape and not enter the premises. Nikki put off immediate medical attention, asking if the medics could wait while she dealt with the scene. Thanks to Rot's warning and the visit to the snoball stand, there weren't any drugs. Turned out Frank kept a Luger under his mattress.

Keith arrived an hour after CSU started processing the scene, wearing jeans, an LSU sweatshirt, and a North Face jacket. He embraced Nikki feet away from Frank's body. "You okay? What happened?"

"I'm fine." She touched the spot on her head.

"This has to be the craziest shit I've ever seen. Start from the beginning."

"I went to Napleton's funeral…" Nikki started.

"Figures you would." Keith folded his arms like a parent. "Is this Emma's work?"

"Can't say for sure."

Nikki briefed Keith on the events leading up to slipping backwards onto her head. She stared at Frank's tinted face as the photographer documented the scene. "So, now we have a countdown on our hands."

"All right, let the medics look at you. You really need to stop falling in shit."

"*Right?* While they do that, go through the house again in case I missed something. Oz is back in the kitchen."

"Where's Shrimp?"

"Animal Control took him."

Keith left for the back of the house. Nikki walked out the front, making the straightest line she could on the uneven sidewalk to the ambo. She sat on the rear bumper. After the medic inspected the abrasion, he performed a short concussion protocol. There was no need for stitches, but they cleaned it and instructed her to let it scab.

Keith came out of the house as the coroner's vehicle pulled up to collect the body. "There's nothing more to do here. Oz wants your clothes."

"Why my clothes?"

"You were lying in that mess. Any trace would be in the syrup."

"I'm not undressing here."

"We'll go back to your place. I already gave Oz that option, and he said to just keep the chain of custody. I have the evidence bags."

Keith stayed quiet for the drive, listening to a playlist of Mardi Gras music on low volume. Dr. John's funky, distinct tone calmed her. Keith reached over at some point and had taken her sticky hand, although she didn't remember when. Her eyes closed, and she replayed the whole scene again.

Nikki snapped from her fog in front of her condo building. Keith had already opened the door to help her out on the other side. As she started walking beside him, her hand went in her jacket pockets only to find something odd.

She pulled out a folded piece of paper. Keith didn't see she had stopped. In simple block was the phrase JUSTICE IS COMING on Grande Esplanade stationery.

"What you got there?" he asked.

Nikki hesitated, thinking of a quick lie, but instead, handed it over at the corner. "A note. Probably from Emma."

He accepted it at the opposite corner. "Hotel stationery. Is it poetic, or is it all she had to write on? I'll call Oz and tell him to collect any writing material he finds. Put it back in the pocket you found it."

"She has three more victims to kill. Weird—she put it in my pocket instead of on Frank's body."

By the time they stepped off the elevator, Keith had ended the call. "Okay, Oz said he found an Esplanade notepad they're going to bag."

They walked side by side in the hall until stopping at Nikki's door, where she inserted her key.

Major stuck his head out of his condo. "Everything good here, Nikki?"

"Hey, Major. We're good. This is Keith."

His head nodded in recognition. "Ah, this is Keith."

"You talk about me?"

"We talk about our day," Nikki returned. "You come up."

"Is that blood on you, Nikki?"

She opened her door, but didn't step in. "No, had a fight with a snoball. Long story. We'll talk later, okay?"

They stepped inside, and Keith brushed past her. "Let's get you out of your clothes."

"Just like our first date."

"That's so funny."

She walked to her bedroom, pulling out a long nightshirt from a drawer.

Keith appeared in the doorway. "Your neighbor looks out for you?"

"Major? He's my wine buddy." She slipped off her jacket, placing it in a bag Keith held open.

Keith placed the sealed bag on the dresser and marked the necessary information on the label. "That's good, I guess."

She unbuttoned her blouse. "Jealous?"

"Curious. Seemed he was waiting for you."

"Sound travels in that hallway, and he's lonely." She placed the blouse in the second bag. Her shoes came off for the next bag. Keith wrote on each one.

His eyes found hers. "Are you really okay?"

"I'm good." Her pants slipped off one leg at a time while sitting on the bed, until handing them over for the last bag. "You are trying so hard not to look."

"I didn't expect you in your underwear tonight."

"Tonight? So, you expected to see me in my underwear at some point?"

"You know what I mean."

"Don't be weird. You've seen me naked."

"Different context." He finally took her entire body in.

"I'm going to shower. You don't need my underwear, right? For police business, I mean."

"You're hilarious. You should knock yourself out more often. I'll be right out here."

The exchange she just had with Keith comforted her. The shower calmed her nerves, as well, but the abrasion on her head stung under the hot water. She came out half expecting him in her bed—but no. Keith stayed in the living room, looking out of the sliding glass door that led to the balcony.

"Nice view, right?" She wore a long nightshirt, not caring about her wet hair.

Keith turned, taking her in. "It is."

"Can you put a little dab of this ointment on my cut?" She handed over the tube and dipped her head for him. She felt his gentle fingers search for the bump.

He finished, then blew on it. "There you are."

Nikki felt her thighs turn hot for no apparent reason. That was a lie; she knew the reason. "I should go to bed."

"I'll sleep on the couch."

"No."

"I should stay."

"I'm fine. I passed the protocol. Besides, you should get that evidence to Oz tonight. You can't keep it with you overnight. Wouldn't look good in court."

"Yeah, Collins would have something to say about that." He headed for the door where he had placed the bags of clothes. "I'll swing by to check on you in the morning."

"Sounds good."

He opened the door, letting out a breath. "I'm glad you're okay."

41

DREAD DECLINED TO party on Bourbon. He returned to the West Bank warehouse a little past midnight. Their shelter was due to be raided by the cops, yet Rot was never concerned. Would it be crazy to think Rot was connected? He worked for Frank in that rich white-boy circle.

A single rat in the empty warehouse scooted into the shadows. He sat with a Checkers burger and a can of beer by candlelight— so much better than discarded food from a trash bin. A noise at the entrance caught his attention, but he didn't stop chewing. This person would reveal themselves in a few seconds.

A silhouette formed on the other side of the room. The female sniffled as she got closer. Flower meandered through the common area in a daze. Dread remained silent for a few seconds. A plastic grocery bag stayed clutched to her chest. She appeared lost.

"Rot!" she screeched up at the catwalk like an animal in a trap.

"He's not here," Dread said.

Her head snapped to his corner. Her voice quivered. "Where is he?"

"In the Quarter with everyone else. What's wrong?"

"I'm in trouble." She stepped toward him.

"Will knowing get me in trouble?"

She shrugged.

Dread smiled, trying to calm her. "I'm kidding. What's wrong?"

Her mouth opened to speak, but only a light moan escaped. "Frank…"

"I know you were with Frank. What's the *main* problem?" He chewed.

A tear rolled down her face. She barely got the words out. "Frank was murdered."

Dread froze. "Murdered? Okay, here's where you explain."

"I was there." She doubled over, then fell onto a mattress.

He threw his food to the side to kneel in front of her. "From the beginning."

"I didn't do it."

"I know. Start from the beginning."

"I drank so much. He gave me pills. I threw up. I passed out."

"Who killed him?"

She shrugged again. "A woman was there, too. Dead, I think."

"A woman? What woman?"

"She was on the floor. I think she was dead, too."

Dread took a beat. "You think they were murdered while you were passed out?"

"I woke up in the bathroom. I called for him. He was in the chair…" Fingers wrapped around her neck. "He had the dog cone…"

"You didn't see anyone? He didn't answer the door? Anything?"

"No." She wiped at her nose. "The beads."

"Beads?"

She held up the plastic grocery bag. Her voice rose and fell. "These beads were in his lap after he died."

"Why'd you take them? You took evidence."

She sobbed harder. "They were on me! My hair might be on them, or my fingerprints. My DNA!"

"That's good thinking." Dread scratched his chin in thought.

"Frank dealt in some bad shit. A lot of people wanted him dead." He reached for the bag. "I'll toss them for you."

"Is Rot going to be mad?"

"Fuck Rot. You need out of this situation."

She stopped crying. "And go where? My life was hell."

"Is this paradise?" Dread presented the entire warehouse. "Rot is nothing. Just another fucking guy that'll let you down."

"He's all I got."

Dread petted her head before taking the beads back to his chair. "Fuck it. I tried. Do what you want. He'll be in late. You might as well try to sleep."

"How can I sleep?"

"I have a gummy." He handed it to her.

"Will you sit with me?"

"If you don't mind me finishing my burger, sure."

MONDAY

42

THE DREAM OF knocking on Keith's bedroom door transitioned to the sound of someone knocking on her condo door in real life. It took a moment for her brain to come back online. *Was that going to be a sex dream?* Her eyes squinted, adjusting to the morning light. The rush of blood also woke the stinging in the back of her head. She glanced at the clean towel she had lain over her pillow.

The knocking continued, not hurried nor excited. *What did Major want?*

She kicked the covers off, then checked her phone, which had been set to vibrate. Keith called twice and had texted that he was out front five minutes ago. *Who the hell buzzed him in?* She crossed her living floor barefoot, greeting her ex-boyfriend, who held a large bag from P.J.'s Coffee.

"*Wakey wakey,* sleepyhead. Coffee's getting cold."

"I forgot to take my cell off vibrate."

"I almost called in a well-being check." He walked inside.

"I'd destroy everything you hold dear if twenty cops showed up here. How'd you break into the building?"

"Showed my badge to someone leaving. I should have a key, in case of emergency." Keith placed the bag down, pulling out two coffees and two large cinnamon rolls. "Ten second nuke?"

"Always." She picked up her coffee. "There's a key behind the painting in the hallway. For emergencies."

"Behind the Pirate's Alley painting? At least mine isn't obvious. You're not worried how easy that is to find?"

"First, you need to be buzzed in—*or not.*"

Keith placed both rolls on a plate and put them in the microwave. It started humming.

Nikki wiped at her face, clearing hair at the same time. "Strange how Frank is killed right after the funeral, around the time I questioned Saul Green."

The microwave dinged. Keith placed the roll in front of her. "Well, we know Green didn't kill Frank. Eat your breakfast. I checked with Lan. You can take the day. He's bringing in an FBI agent to help."

"I figured that might happen. He loves the feds."

"It has nothing to do with you."

"Easy for you to say." Nikki gazed at him in his work attire while she stood before him in only a nightshirt, showing details a bra might hide.

"It's just to assist. These decisions have to be fluid."

"Good to be in the loop." She reevaluated the entire dynamic. He had tucked her in last night and came back this morning. Was he still operating on guilt? "You could have just called to check on me."

"Your cell needs to ring for that to work. Besides, you'd lie over the phone."

She stepped closer, inches away from him. "You know I nuke my pastries. You know I'd lie. You held my hand last night in the car. I undressed in front of you."

"You liked that I was uncomfortable."

"Why am I fighting this?" Nikki reached for the back of his neck, pulling his lips down to hers. She kissed him hard. Her other hand gripped his butt, pressing herself against him, but he pulled away.

"What the hell are you doing, Nik?"

"I'm doing what you want. What we both want. What do you mean, what am I doing?"

"Yeah, this is what I want, but not like this."

"I'm throwing myself at you, Keith. I might as well be naked. You've been pushing for this since the night of the murder."

"I shouldn't have to push!" He sat on the sofa, putting his head in his hands. "We're skipping too many check points, things we need to get past first."

"Did you e-mail me this schedule?"

"Let's talk about this, okay?"

"I don't have time for a checklist. Thanks for the coffee. I'll see you at Headquarters."

He exhaled. "Nik, I do want this—we *will* do this."

"But only after we cross items off an Excel spreadsheet?"

"I'm not rejecting you. This isn't how it's supposed to go."

"How about *you* go." She folded her arms, looking away.

"We can't talk while you're pissed. I *should* go."

Nikki's phone chimed with a text message. She swiped at her cell to read it. "Unknown number. Says to meet in Championship Square. Has to be Dread."

"He wants to meet at the Superdome?"

"Alone."

"You can't go alone after whacking your head."

"He won't show otherwise. You said this case is fluid, right? This is as fluid as it gets."

"I'll stay close, and we'll put some uniforms on Poydras. We're still going to take precautions. Why would he want to risk meeting instead of telling you over the phone?"

"Funny, I asked you the same thing about coming here… I think he needs the face-to-face. Someone to *trust*."

"Can we just…shelve what just happened?"

"Shelved."

He gave a slight nod. "Make sure Dread doesn't shank you."

"Dread is harmless."

"Until he's not."

43

LAN AND JONESY had texted to check up on Nikki minutes after Dread's message. As far as they were concerned, she was watching television in bed. The meeting with Dread would be revealed if something came from it. She returned a thumbs-up emoji. Lan would understand.

Nikki had thrown herself at Keith like a psychopath. His rejection made it that much worse. She forced her embarrassment onto the back burner. Keith wasn't one to assert himself unless he felt strongly about it. It infuriated her that he might be right.

Dread would be at the Dome in a few minutes, and she needed a clear head.

She drove up Poydras, passing Keith's car parked on a side street. They wouldn't be in communication, but she'd use her cell to call for pursuit if needed. Dread wasn't dangerous, still…Keith had a point about not knowing someone. She threw her police placard on the dash after stopping in a no-parking zone.

She avoided a good amount of foot traffic on Poydras. Championship Square offered an open-air venue attached to the Superdome for fans to congregate and cheer at a giant screen when the Saints played. Without a concert or event, the Dome was deserted, creating an odd sensation to be alone in a place built for the masses.

After several minutes of strolling around the perimeter, Dread arrived, climbing up the stairs from Poydras Avenue. That Aztec hoodie announced him from any distance. He didn't say anything as they ended up just feet apart. He gave her a slight smile, reaching out with a Rouse's plastic grocery bag.

Before taking it, she asked, "What's this?"

"Evidence."

She took the bag by the handles. "Evidence from where?"

"From Frank Brehm's house."

She hesitated, but looked inside. "Mardi Gras beads? Is that blood or syrup?"

"Could be both." He sat on a step. "They were in his lap."

"Were you there?"

"Hell, no. A traveler kid was passed out in Frank's bathroom when it happened."

"She's the one that vomited. I need to talk to them."

"I told her I'd get rid of the beads, not set up a sting with a cop. Were you the second person she saw on the floor?"

Nikki sat on a step. "No offense, Dread. What the F are you up to?"

"I messed up." He pivoted toward her. "I'm all about protecting Emma, but that's the last thing I did."

"You wouldn't be betraying her."

"Do what you want with the beads. That's all I came here for."

"You can still help this one out. Is this traveler kid underage?" She leaned back to rest her elbows on the steps. "She won't be arrested if she's a minor."

"This girl and Emma are different. This one is naïve and doesn't know the world she's in. She was face down in a toilet. Out cold, dig?"

"That's the story she told you." Nikki closed the bag. "She might be lying."

"She wasn't. She put her trust in me. I won't be like her father."

"That's not how it works, Dread." She lifted the bag of beads with a laugh. "A lawyer would have a field day with these. No chain of custody. Handled by several people. These might have come off a tourist in the Quarter. If DNA came back with a hit, it creates more speculation than fact."

He shook his head. "Then throw them away."

"There's helping and there's interfering. Stop the bullshit."

"Bullshit?" Dread appeared hurt. "Good luck, Detective." He got up to leave.

"Dread. Don't be a bitch."

He stopped cold. His shoulders bounced in a perceived laugh. He turned with a big smile on his face. "No one's ever called me a bitch."

"I thought you'd like that. You're connected to two female minors now."

His eyelids dropped. "I'm not attracted to them. Something in me just wants to protect them."

She cocked her head. "Oh, wow. Are you gay?"

He didn't react. His Adam's apple bobbed. "What's it matter?"

"It doesn't. But it makes your intentions more believable."

"Shit, the biggest threat to children are straight white men. That's what I think, anyways."

"I believe you're right."

"Why did you become a cop? To protect people or make a paycheck?"

"As a child, I kept a bat by my door. I kept pepper spray in my purse. I avoided plain, white vans and stereotypes on the street."

"We all scared."

"But it's a small leap to terrified. I became a cop so I wouldn't be. Do me a favor. Talk to this traveler kid about coming forward. She can help prevent more murders. Nothing will happen to her."

"If she was dancing at Percy Fields's club, what would happen to Fields?"

"Depends on how good his lawyer is. It could range from a fine to jail time. Charges would be brought. A plea would be made. Is that your plan?"

"Hypothetical."

"What's your relationship with Fields?"

"Next question."

"Did you know Emma was going to show at that house Uptown?"

"The day you rolled in chicken shit. I ran, thinking she'd avoid the place when she saw the cops. But you weren't in a squad. She got there early."

"She has resources most don't."

He indicated the stairs. "I gotta go."

Nikki started to walk with him. "Promise me you won't put a minor in danger. We'll get Percy Fields along with everyone involved."

Dread dropped onto the first step. "We'll see, *Chick*."

"You know, that's kind of growing on me."

However, Dread was already descending the staircase, tapping his rings on the rail along the way.

44

BACK AT HEADQUARTERS, Keith sat pensive next to Nikki while holding his closed laptop.

Nikki ignored him, snacking on baby carrots. She searched the Internet while using her peripheral on him once and while. She figured Keith wanted to talk about their last exchange before Dread's welcomed interruption.

Keith said, "Those beads was a message to you from Emma, right? We should dig deeper into the Krewe of Midas. The victims have that connection."

"She left me a handwritten note already. Why would beads be a clue for us?"

"She left an additional clue?"

She crunched on a carrot. "Maybe we call Herman and Frank *targets* instead of victims. The females are victims. And I'm way ahead of you, Detective Teague."

"I hope you can appreciate the restraint it takes to not come back with something sarcastically hilarious."

Her tone stayed dry. "Krewe of Midas is a definite connection, which means they have money and power behind them."

"Being a private organization, we can't demand their membership list. It's like the friggin' Skull and Bones."

"Hmm." Nikki continued to research the Midas parade organization on the Internet and social media.

Keith sat like a bored child. "What are you reading?"

"Articles."

"What kind of articles? Tell me."

She closed her eyes. "Fine. Midas was formed in 2002 as a walking group handing out chocolate coins in gold foil."

"Love those."

"They started adding floats after Katrina. Like other popular krewes, it had the funding to grow."

"Must have a high membership fee."

"Yeah, most of these pics show people wearing gold outfits and glittery masks, throwing beads and doubloons."

"What about the ball?"

"You got ball jokes loaded in the chamber?"

"That's beneath me." His smile grew wide. "I think I'll sit on those."

Somehow, she managed a straight face. "The ball is held after the parade on *Lunde Gras*, Monday night. It looks like most of them are at the Convention Center. Some hotel ballrooms." She took another carrot.

"It's there again this year. I looked it up."

"Mardi Gras looks like one big celebration from the outside, but the whole enchilada is serious business involving big money."

"Did Oz say anything about the beads?"

"They'll be inadmissible, but may offer information." She stifled a yawn and stretched in her seat. The endless paragraphs about the krewe began to blur.

"Why don't you go home?" Keith flipped his laptop over for no reason.

"You're pretty good at acting like this morning never happened."

"Dread?"

"Us." Her mouth worked like a rabbit on the carrot.

"I have something I need to tell you."

Her eyes drop to his computer. "What is it?"

"It was you," Keith whispered.

"What was me?" Nikki's heart pounded.

"I suspected it was you when Emma was in Napleton's garage. In my mind, it always came back to one person."

Her voice lowered to a whisper. "That person was *not* me."

He matched her volume. "I saw the hill of fresh carrot mush at the rest area."

"You're crazy."

"I don't expect you to admit it. Hell, I don't want you to admit it."

"You didn't see that video, Keith. It was horrific. Naked masked men walking around her with their dicks…you don't want to fucking know. Thank God she was unconscious." She rubbed the bridge of her nose. "So, you're not going to bring your *opinion* to the team?"

"I'm not going to open my mouth." He reached out to take her hand. "You're a mama bear. You took to Emma, and Herman hurt Emma."

"All speculation, Detective Teague."

"When I said I'll be there for you no matter what, that wasn't bullshit."

She pulled her hand from his. "Why even tell me? To show me what a great catch you are? Because your mom said so?"

"My mom's dead."

"She is. She is dead." She cupped her hands over a smile. "She said it a long time ago?" She sucked in her lips, trying to look cute.

He checked for people around them. "I'm going to walk away. Imagine that I just kissed your forehead and palmed your cheek." He started for his desk.

"Is this one of our steps?"

He turned back with a small grin, then whacked his knee into a file cabinet. After the initial grimace, they both wanted to laugh but didn't. He then bowed out with style.

Nikki's smile faded. Someone else figured out she was at the Napleton house. A wave of panic turned her stomach. She made a beeline to the unisex bathroom, entering a stall to her right as the tears started falling.

45

THE REST OF the day was useless. Nikki couldn't concentrate on anything other than Keith's most recent revelation. Was she her own worst enemy? Most people lived in denial about their own faults and weaknesses. She was defensive and stubborn, and some people have said exhausting.

Nikki did her best not to make a sound while walking her condo's hallway. Her eyes stayed on Major's door on approach. *Don't open.* It was so hard to turn him down. The man was persuasive, like a combination car salesman and Willy Wonka and the Cabernet Factory. The handle on his door unlocked and turned.

Stay strong, Nik.

Major wore an Ole Miss cap and sunglasses. "Oh, Nikki. I'm heading out for supper. Maybe Lucy's. You want to join me?"

"I have a headache. I'm sorry, Major. Next time."

"Is it the case? How's that going?"

"I can't say."

"Of course. Take something for your headache and get some rest. Want me to bring back some jambalaya?"

"No, but thanks." She almost shut her mouth, *almost.* "You're going to eat alone?"

"I eat at the bar. Don't bother me none."

"How come family never comes by? Friends?"

He looked confused. "I told you. I'm…"

"From Pearl River. Managed a convenience store. Right."

"You think I'm lying?" For the first time, an *edge* crept into his tone.

"I don't. My job is…"

"I never planned on speaking of this outside of therapy."

"Then, don't."

"No—something's under your skin."

"You're right. It's work…"

Major stopped her. "I came out of deployment with PTSD."

"Deployment? You were in the military? A major?"

"No, that's an ironic nickname. I was a sergeant. When I came back, my wife and kids left me. I hurt one of my kids, Nikki. Rumors circulated with supposed friends and family. I moved here alone so I don't hurt anyone else. And I haven't… until now."

"I've been told I'm a porno asshole. I'm sorry, Major." Nikki reached out to touch his arm. "I had no right to question you like that. I've had a horrible day."

"I get it."

"I have a witness yanking my chain and Keith is… Keith is calling me out on my shit. And Emma is wanted for another murder. The stress just got to me." She gave him soft eyes.

He took off his glasses. "I'm not mad at you, Nikki. We all have our darkness, you know? You're one of the few lights in my life."

"That's so Hallmark."

"That's me. A softy." He leaned against the wall. "My therapist wants me to express myself. I've took to poetry. He said I can't have a relationship with someone else until I have a good relationship with myself."

"Good advice."

"So, I do things alone. Eat. Have a cocktail at a bar. Mardi Gras parades."

"Don't talk to me about parades. I'm up to my tits." She laughed. "Sorry, I said tits."

"You just said *porno asshole*. That sounds a lot worse than a regular asshole."

"Yeah." She laughed with a breath.

"Sounds ladylike, coming from you."

"Bullshit." She stared at him. He didn't appear to want to leave. She asked, "You ever go to the Krewe of Midas?"

"No. I like Endymion, Bacchus, and Zulu."

"The big guns. Where's your spot?"

"Neutral ground side of St. Charles near the overpass. Used to drive in from Pearl River every year. Now I can walk there."

"How is that? Being by yourself?"

"That was my family's spot. When I was at my best. Past few years, I hoped that Trina would show. You stand in your spot every year and catch up with the same people every year. Hell, you see other people's kids grow up without even knowing their names."

"Yeah, you do."

"So, I still go…alone. But, while I'm there, I'm not alone anymore. They chat with me. Accept me, like you accept me."

"You're sweeter than a praline." Nikki kissed his cheek. "Come out and eat."

"I'm not good company. Thank you for opening up, Major. Go enjoy your dinner. I have a couple of Ibuprofen with my name on them."

"I'll knock twice and leave a small order of jambalaya at your door."

TUESDAY

46

THE NEIGHBORHOOD STAPLE Port of Call was a bar/restaurant located down the block from the Grande Esplanade. It was famous for gigantic burgers and loaded baked potatoes. A few picnic tables were set up on the sidewalk, and the place often had gutter punks hanging nearby like strays.

The weather kept Nikki and Keith inside. They enjoyed an early lunch bellied up to the bar. So far, their conversation had avoided personal issues.

"You don't seem too concerned with finding this witness to Frank's murder." Keith took a bite of his burger.

"What more can I do?" Nikki sipped the straw. "I got no ID. DNA's a bust. How many people do you think wore those beads before this girl?"

"How did she get Frank taped to the chair?"

"Maybe drugged. He'd be pretty pliable."

"Or Dread helped her."

"I don't get that vibe from him. Even if they find his DNA, he admitted to being there a few times."

"So, is Dread your unofficial CI now?" Keith's burger was almost all devoured.

"Sort of. He'll reveal something if we filter through his bullshit. We gotta let him breathe."

"Has he talked about Rot?"

"Not yet. What's bugging me is this witness he won't reveal is another minor."

"That's a red flag with this guy."

"He's gay."

"Oh. Wouldn't have guessed."

"He's worried about this underaged girl dancing at Percy's club."

"Okay, let me ask you this, and I'm only playing devil's advocate here. I'm not being pervy."

"That ship has sailed."

"What would be the difference between a sixteen-year-old dancing at a club or bussing tables at a restaurant?"

Her eyes widened. "Dancing at a place that serves alcohol to your fellow pervs?"

"Not stripping. *Dancing.* I bartended when I was sixteen."

"Individual circumstances."

"Double standards. If this minor doesn't undress and she's up on a stage, not being touched." He held up his hands. *"Devil's advocate."*

"Oh, my God, Keith. It's sexualizing a minor."

"The same sixteen-year-old twerking on Bourbon wearing dental floss isn't? These pop stars? These social media influencers?"

"That's a choice."

"So's a job. All I'm saying is they're so self-centered, they don't realize it's wrong. We need to protect them from themselves."

She pushed her plate away. "I've been in Vice. I see the argument. In legal terms, what's the difference other than perception? The pervs watching is what's wrong, not the act of dancing."

"Yeah."

"But!" She smacked her fist in her hand. "You cannot be employed at a strip club under the age of twenty-one. That's the law."

"That's why I waited to work the pole." Keith made a stupid dance move. "Stage name Nine Millimeter."

She stifled her laugh. "That's about right. Oh, wait until you talk to Saul Green. You should partake in his wisdom. If he had his way, girls would still be married off at twelve."

"Sounds like he'd make a great senator. What do you want to do now?"

"We question Saul Green. You two can compare high schools you have to stay a hundred yards from."

"I just have the *two*." Keith collected his garbage. "We're going unannounced?"

"I'm not sure where he is. Let me call the bartender at his hotel I made nice with." Nikki pulled out her cell.

A friendly voice came over the speaker. "Rue Paradise, how may I help you?"

"Hi, is Tilly bartending?"

"Sure is, who should I say is calling?"

"Nikki."

"Sure. Hold, please."

After a moment, the young lady answered with the familiar accent. "Nikki?"

"Hey Clemson, how are you?"

"This is a surprise."

"I want to make sure Saul is there before I head over. I figured you wouldn't give me the runaround."

"He left over an hour ago, but you're in luck. Mr. Green said he was meeting someone at the Crush, the strip club."

"It's closed now."

"I wouldn't know, don't wanna know."

"Did he say who he's meeting?"

"Didn't say. I caught a snippet. He was on his phone being all high-energy. Everyone in the room overheard his plans."

"Okay, thanks, Clemson. Appreciate you." Nikki looked at Keith. "We're going to a strip club."

47

SAUL PACED THE floor of the empty strip club. His blood pressure rose whenever someone gave him an ultimatum. How dare that psycho make demands without a leg to stand on? He took deep breaths and counted to ten.

How do Buddhists do this shit?

The counting didn't help. Thank God she stormed out or he would've strangled her. He bent to grab the overturned chair, setting it upright again with effort. Physical displays of power didn't make any difference with twats like her. He'd have to change his strategy. Percy's cleaning staff could sweep up the shattered glass by the wall.

He fell back in the same chair he'd upended, clenching his fists. He chuckled. She needed an angry fuck, and he'd give her one. A sliver of shame pierced his heart. He'd turned his back on Judaism and depended on his online Buddhist course to calm himself. He'd certainly end *her* suffering.

Screw meditation. A shot was in order. He stood again to go locate the Woodford Reserve behind the bar. It was within reach on the higher shelf. He drank straight from the bottle, using his sleeve for a napkin.

Percy hadn't come downstairs to see the argument. He was inconsequential in those matters. Warren was going to get an earful. He put the bottle back and his bladder woke. The urge to piss became a priority. Bathroom, then up to see Percy. With Frank gone, they had much to discuss.

He stood before the urinal, tugging at his *schmeckle*, having to wait a moment. Everything had clenched. The bathroom door opened, subconsciously bringing back the fear from high school bullying for wearing his *yarmulke*.

He focused on letting the stream out. "Sorry about the glass, Percy. I tend to throw things."

As his flow started, he assumed Percy would step up to use the next urinal. That was when the wasp stung the back of his thigh along with the crackling of electricity. His muscles contracted and he seized, falling onto the tiled floor. Piss sprayed up like a water gun. He'd lost all perspective as the room blurred and body convulsed.

The crackling stopped.

His hand tried to reach for his thigh, but they wouldn't follow his commands as the seizures came again. It took all he had just to lift his leg. "What…are…you…" He lost his breath. His heart hurt.

A brick-like grating sound came from the stall. The movement behind Saul's head grew closer. His eyes found her hovering above with something rectangular in both hands. Then, the ceramic lid from the toilet's water tank came down on his face. In his mind, he begged for his life. He'd never seen that much rage.

48

THE CRUSH DIDN'T open until 4 p.m., so knocking on the entrance was a waste of time. Nikki and Keith entered the side alley, which led to the courtyard shared by multiple buildings. The walkway had red brick pavers transitioning to the same slate used in Jackson Square. Iron patio furniture and lush Amazon-like foliage surrounded them, hanging from balconies and a tasteful fountain at the center.

"Wow, so beautiful back here," she commented.

"Like traveling back in time, yet the public will never have the opportunity to piss or puke on it."

Nikki held up her badge to the mounted video and rang the buzzer on the rear entrance. A full minute later, Percy Fields answered, wearing designer jeans and a trim-fit button-down with one side untucked as a fashion statement.

He stared at Keith. "Sorry, you caught me upstairs. I'm a bit busy, detectives."

"I'm Detective Mayeaux, and this is Detective Teague. Can you take a short break?"

"Sure. Anything for New Orleans' finest. Are you here to question me about Herman?"

"Do you have anything to offer on Mr. Napleton?" Nikki asked.

"My last encounter with Herman was a week before his death. I was here, running my club the night he died."

"You're not a suspect, Mr. Fields. Can you tell us if Saul Green is here?"

"He was here a while ago. He wanted a private meeting, so I let him use the floor."

"Can we check inside?" Nikki asked.

"Sure. He probably left." Percy stepped aside and allowed them to pass.

Keith looked around the kitchen area. "Any staff here?"

"No, my cleaning service left at about ten. The bartenders show for three. I was the only one here, upstairs, like I said."

Nikki took a quick peek in the cooler and in the freezer. "Who was he meeting with?"

"I don't know, *like I said.*" Percy stepped through the entrance to the main room.

Nikki scanned a brighter interior than during business hours. "He never reached out? No good-bye text?"

"He's rather rude that way."

"Why not meet this person in his own office at the hotel?"

"Saul likes my club for certain VIPs. He believes there's a certain...*exclusivity* to a closed strip club—like being privy to something secret. Thinks it gives him an advantage."

"Your surveillance will show who he met with. Can we see that?"

"Saul had me turn off the cameras. And the outside camera doesn't record. It's a live feed." Percy took a few steps toward the front before noticing something. "Huh."

"What?"

"Glass on the floor. Saul's a lot of things, but he wouldn't just leave without telling me about this."

"The wall got wet, too." Nikki pointed out. "Someone was upset."

Percy shook his head. "I'm going to ring his neck."

"Why would he look to impress someone he'd only fight with?" Nikki pondered. "Let's check the bathroom and upstairs…if you don't mind, Mr. Fields."

"I should say no without a warrant, but go ahead."

She led the charge to a small, dark hallway seeing two doors painted black. One sign read *Janes* and the other read *Dicks*. Nikki pushed open the one meant for males to find Saul Green sprawled on the floor, next to a floor drain. His head had been bashed in with a ceramic toilet lid stained red, discarded under the sink. His button-down shirt had been pulled open, exposing the number three across his stomach.

Nikki jumped to Saul's side to feel for a pulse. "He's gone."

"Sweet Jesus," Percy mumbled. He turned away, shaking his head. "Damn."

Nikki followed him out while Keith called it in. "You're not too upset, Mr. Fields."

"I was raised in the East off Chef Highway. I've seen dead bodies. Nothing like this, though."

"Do you want to stick with your story about the surveillance cameras?"

Percy's eyes bulged. "I'm not lying. They aren't on."

"Who else was here, Percy?" Nikki stressed.

"I swear, I don't know." He swallowed. Nikki could tell the gears were spinning in his head. "Was this Emma?"

Keith came out of the bathroom. "Stay with him. I'm going upstairs."

After he left, Nikki asked, "You hold out on us, it's only going to be worse for you."

"Do I need a lawyer?"

Nikki looked between him and the door to the restroom. "I don't believe you did this, Percy. I need information."

"Your partner, shouldn't he be here, too?"

"Not for a statement. I'm more than capable."

Percy regained some composure. "Of course."

"Are you okay to answer questions? You need to take some time?"

He cleared his throat and pounded his chest once. "I'm good. Let's get this over with."

"Good. Okay. If you had to guess, who do you think Saul was meeting?"

"Maybe a gutter punk named Rot?"

"Rot's on our radar. What's your take on him."

"He was tight with Frank. They used to bring girls here to dance. Saul was looking to take over Frank's…business."

"Managing dancing girls isn't that lucrative, at least by hotel owner standards. Did he want Frank's heroin business?"

"People like Saul never settle. As soon as his hotel is successful, he needs the next adrenaline rush. It wouldn't surprise me."

"You have a camera feed upstairs, right? You didn't glance at the person? You weren't curious?"

"My head was in a clutter of paperwork on my desk. With Green, I'm better off not knowing."

"Did Frank bring his drug business here?" Nikki ignored the noises upstairs, nodding to continue.

He glanced at the stairs. "No. That's part of the reason we didn't get along."

"Has Emma ever danced here?"

"No. Christ. Why would she dance here?"

"To piss Warren off."

"And have him mad at me? He sends too many VIPs here. I need to stay on his good side."

Nikki received a text from Keith. *Nothing here. Need more time?*

She responded. *Yes, please.* "Did you ever visit with Warren during off hours? Lunch? In any capacity?"

Percy's neck pulsed with a big swallow. "Sure. We don't invite each other to crawfish boils, but we're cordial."

"I heard you guys started out as friends. That's not the case anymore?"

He thought on it. "It's complicated. Since we came up together, we understand each other. We've discussed each other's portfolio." Percy palmed the back of his neck. "That being said, Warren tries to alpha-dog Saul, Frank—me."

"You let him?"

"I'm not an egomaniac. I just want to run a successful business. As Uncle Tom as that sounds, I keep a smile on my face when I'm around them."

"So, you wouldn't be friends otherwise."

"Industry workaholics are only friends with others in the industry. We're competitors. Sure. Who isn't in the business world? Herman was a mentor. Warren, too. Our circle was like NATO in the tourism industry. We're stronger together."

"And formed a krewe. Like you wanted a frat."

"That started with Herman before Katrina. It was inevitable with these guys. It was another way to be..."

"Exclusive?" Nikki finished.

Percy's face relaxed. "If not beholden. Herman and Warren imagined us to be the Masons or Illuminati."

"Your alliance is decimated. So now there's you, and Warren left."

"And Mary and Sharon."

Nikki tilted her head. "Sharon?"

"Don't discount her. She has more influence with Warren than you'd think. There's the king, then there's the *king-maker*."

"Sharon made Warren?"

"Sharon was top in her class at Tulane. She was friends with Mary. Mary married Herman. Herman brought Warren aboard."

"Why does Sharon shrink so much in that marriage?"

"Behind closed doors? I can't speak of that." He checked his phone on reflex. "I've seen Sharon step up, and I've seen Warren change his mind in some business decisions because of her."

"What's your relationship like with Sharon? You ever use her to maybe influence Warren?"

He laughed under his breath. "This isn't some reality show where we scheme against each other. We lift each other, not tear each other down."

"I really appreciate your cooperation. This helps me get a better understanding of your relationships."

"Will any of this help you find Emma?"

"Every detail matters. Can you expand on the argument you and Saul had at Herman's funeral?"

"That was nothing. King of Midas stuff. At this point, the parade shouldn't even happen."

"It wasn't about the sex video?"

"That was part of it. Frank denied it. Herman convinced everyone it was fake. With AI, he made a good argument."

"Has Emma ever crashed any of these sex parties? As a guest, I mean."

"We're done."

"Not quite."

49

"Is this necessary?" Percy Fields complained at Oz as the CSU tech scraped under his manicured fingernails. He stayed seated at one of the tables near the soon-to-be-defiled pole. "I was never in the bathroom."

Oz returned, "Then, you'll have nothing to worry about."

"You're helping, Percy," Keith said.

"This is overkill."

Nikki sat. "It's to eliminate you, Percy. We don't want the lawyer for the defense to say we didn't do it and raise doubt."

"It's humiliating." Percy kept glancing at Keith.

"Would you rather be zipped up?" Nikki motioned at Saul in the bag being placed on a gurney.

"That was crass." He looked away.

"He's all yours." Oz walked away with the samples.

The coroner wheeled the body bag toward the front entrance. Oz nodded at Nikki while directing the circus.

"They're taking him right out the front door?" Percy sat back in dismay.

"Worried about bad press? The police have the block cleared. If anything, a murder might add to the mystique." Keith eyed him.

"Murder is not the image I want to portray."

"You said you were an Eastie-boy?" Nikki questioned.

"*Eastie-boy*. That's a blast from the past. New Orleans East was never the same after *the storm*. I was raised in a gangland area with no law. I've seen friends and family murdered. I was lucky and got out."

"That's sad."

"That's my past. I'm 24/7 thinking about my business. And my business needs to open tomorrow."

"Needs to?"

"My employees count on their wages. I still have bills, Nikki."

Keith jumped in. "We'll need to hold the scene indefinitely."

"Why?" Percy perked up.

"All due respect, the body isn't even cold, Mr. Fields." Keith sat, leaning forward.

"I had nothing against Saul, but I won't throw myself on his coffin. He'd understand."

"I understand, too." Nikki nodded. "What do you think, Keith? Do we really need to shut the club down? It's a small crime scene. All evidence was collected. Fingerprints are being taken."

Keith considered it. "I suppose there'd be no reason to come back."

"I don't see a reason to hold the scene, but I have to run it up the flagpole with my boss. You'll need a professional cleanup crew."

"I have a certified company on speed dial. They come in once in a while for a deep cleaning."

"Have them give me a call when they're done and notify every employee by phone—no texts. And then, you can open."

"Of course."

"You said Saul might've been meeting Rot. Do you know a punk named Dread?"

"I've seen Dread around." Percy folded his arms, leaning back. "I see them outside the club sometimes, but I don't engage."

Nikki recognized that was a closed-off, defensive position.

"So, one more question; can you explain how this dancing arrangement works?"

Percy leaned forward again. "Some gutter punks show up wanting to dance for tips. Once they're showered and dressed, it's all good. Sometimes, I give them a shot."

Oz stopped by. "Mr. Fields. Do you own a taser?"

"Taser?" Nikki questioned. "We didn't find one."

"My tech discovered a little singe on Mr. Green's pants. There are puncture marks on thigh. We'll have confirmation once the ME gets done with him."

Nikki looked from Oz to Percy.

"I do *not* own a taser. But, Mary Napleton has one."

50

"I'M DRIVING TO Headquarters now." Keith used Bluetooth as he pulled away from the strip club. "We don't know a damn thing yet."

"You're the only one in the car, right?" The emotionless voice said over the speaker.

"No, Nikki's right here. Say hi, Nikki. *Jesus Christ*, of course, I'm alone."

"Three prominent white businessmen are dead. This will garner national attention."

"Yes, it will."

"What's the takeaway from Saul's murder?"

"One less scumbag? I'm sorry, *alleged* scumbag."

"This banter might work with your girlfriend, but cut the shit with me, Teague."

He scowled at the phone. "We're not any closer to finding Emma. None of your friends are suspects."

"What did Fields have to say?"

"He didn't offer anything. I had a private chat with him the other day."

"That's brilliant."

"Give me some credit. He's aware you got me by the balls."

"All the feds need is a jurisdiction loophole to take over. Most gutter punks crossed state lines to come here. The hint of trafficking is enough for them to start their own investigation."

"I'm doing what I can."

"Do more. I'd hate for your bloodwork report to come out."

"What's that called? Mutual annihilation?"

"I'm bullet proof, Teague."

"What's more dangerous: having nothing to lose, or everything to lose?"

"Get Nikki to slow her roll with the boys from Midas and focus on the killer, or something may happen to her, too."

"That would be your biggest mistake."

"Aw…you love her."

Just as Keith started to respond with his own threat, the call dropped. Nikki had been all set to kill someone in the name of justice. So could he.

51

THE TASK FORCE assembled to discuss Saul's murder. The war room included DA Simone Collins, Perez, and Jonesy. Tran was flipping through news stations on the television when Nikki and Keith entered. The monitor had Herman, Frank, and Saul on the screen. The reporter repeated public knowledge of each murder, minus the countdown numbers.

"One station says it's a serial killer," Lan started. "Another says *spree* killer."

Simone put it on mute. "Is it a good idea to let Percy Fields open the day after a murder?"

Nikki said, "We need him open and doing business as usual."

Lan sighed. "I approved it, Simone. Next complaint...?"

Simone Collins continued. "The mayor is on my ass. He's getting calls from news affiliates across the country. I've already had three press conferences saying we can't answer questions regarding the investigation. We're going live in an hour. Any monkey can take notes and collect evidence. Is anyone trying to solve this?"

Nikki studied the board. "Your cheerleading leaves something to be desired."

"So does your investigating. Any closer to proving this sex party is real?"

"Still working that angle," Nikki said.

Simone tapped her lips with her manicured finger. "That would be huge. Although, what's worse: a serial killer or a trafficking ring?"

"We have both. That's why I called the FBI for assistance. They'll be sending someone from the Lakefront office."

"And that makes this an inch away from becoming a federal case." Simone scowled.

"You love hating this, Simone. Prosecuting these guys will cement your career." Lan wrote in a pad while speaking. "Top priority is finding Emma. We'll prove the trafficking in the collateral damage. Everything else will shake itself out."

"I need something to tell the mayor."

Nikki nudged Keith. "We should check out the snoball stand again after this."

Simone glared at Nikki. "That's been searched and boarded up. Emma isn't at the snoball stand. What the hell are you doing?"

"They're following up on related leads, Simone. Give us a break."

"I understand, Lan. How is it you can't find a sixteen-year-old in the Quarter?"

"Gutter punks live off the grid." Perez jumped in. "Even the West Bank. We're utilizing all our resources."

Nikki said, "Not charging Herman Napleton is a good reason for her to go rogue."

"That's uncalled for." Simone looked away.

"Some women's rights advocate you are," Nikki finished.

Lan slapped the table. "Nikki, you're doing the same thing Simone's doing to us. You don't understand what she goes through at the DA's Office."

"Thank you, Lan. You're the voice of reason. We need to trust each other to do our jobs. I apologize."

Lan explained. "Emma made herself a needle in the haystack. A substantial number of gutter punks are helping her stay hidden."

"Emma's gutter punk friend named Dread is a source. He's looking for her, too. Thing is, we have to wait for contact."

"Despite my not charging Herman Napleton for a case I couldn't win..." Simone paced the room. "...I have two prominent hotel owners murdered. An ex-chef turned snoball stand owner, too."

Keith said, "The public isn't in danger. We'll find her."

Simone rubbed each temple. "It's time we put Emma's face on the news."

"She's a minor," Nikki shot back.

"A minor with an arrest warrant for a murder spree that isn't over. We have that discretion."

"She's already a cult hero. They love her," Jonesy said.

"Who are you?" Simone asked.

"I'm Jonesy." She pointed at her nametag.

"Jonesy brings up a good point." Nikki glared at Simone. "You want this minor to end up dead at the hands of some vigilante or social media star looking for fame?"

Lan stared at the table's surface. "It might be time to cast a wider net, Nikki."

Keith said, "We're just one raid from finding her."

"Fine, but she's going to be on the evening news."

Lan nodded. "In the meantime, we're going to put eyes on Warren Courtland and Percy Fields, who might be next in line."

Simone stopped on her way out the door. "Why wouldn't Emma kill Warren first if he's a target?"

"I've wondered the same thing," Nikki said. "Is she saving him for last? If she killed Napleton for the rape, then Saul and Frank Brehm must have been the other masked men in the video."

"That's secondary to finding Emma," Lan said. "There are two more targets. Has to be Fields and Courtland."

Nikki swiveled in her chair. "She had the chance to kill Percy at the club. They were alone, no cameras. Why wait?"

"Get in, get out. Percy was upstairs. Avoid risk?" Keith offered. "Her plan was to do the lone kill. She stuck to the plan."

"Could they be working together?" Nikki pondered. "We need to find out if Mary still has her taser. Just Percy saying she has one isn't enough for a warrant."

Lan thought for a quick second. "Mary helping might explain how she's eluding us."

"Dig deeper into Fields." Simone Collins took another step in her red heels, but turned to Nikki. "I had reservations about letting you lead this case. Don't make me regret it."

Nikki did a double take. "*You* let me take this? Lan? What the hell is she talking about?"

Simone motioned for him not to answer. "I advised Lieutenant Tran not to assign you as lead. I wanted your partner, Teague."

"Thanks?" Keith said.

"Wait, Simone. Are you going to let Warren and Sharon know their daughter is about to be plastered on all the channels?"

Simone raised an eyebrow. "It was their idea. Along with a fifty-thousand-dollar reward. Let's see how loyal these punks will be now."

52

DREAD TAPPED HIS rings on the railing of the catwalk to announce his arrival. When he came to Rot's private room, he witnessed him consoling Flower. The annoyance on Rot's face said it all. Her nose was buried in his chest.

"You okay, Flower? Is she okay?"

"She's cool."

"We need to talk in private."

Rot caressed Flower's hair while her face migrated to the crook of his neck. "She's worried the police are after her."

"They think Emma did it. They have no idea who you are."

Flower didn't respond.

Rot asked, "So, you here to tell me about Saul?"

"I was about to. You heard?"

"Dude, they carried his body out the front door of the club. I'm going to kill Emma myself. She's going to ruin everything." Rot looked uncomfortable.

Dread's tone turned soft. "Hey… Flower?"

Rot tapped the top of her head to get her attention. "Listen up, girl." He rolled his eyes at Dread. "I'm trying to convince her it'll be okay to dance."

"She's traumatized."

Flower pulled her red, wet face away from him. "No, I'm ready."

"That's my girl. Percy loves her."

"Percy is going to tighten up with the cops watching."

"We'll see."

"Why would he risk it?"

Rot showed his teeth. "I have a fake ID for her. He'll be in the clear. Flower will have her shit together. She's fire."

"She's freaking out."

"*I'm fire*, Dread." A smile appeared. "I'll be okay."

"I guess we'll see. Tell me when she's dancing. I'll look out for Mayeaux."

"That's more like it, but I don't think we're going to have to worry about those two anymore."

"Why?"

"Things are in the works." A cell went off on the old, beat-to-shit desk in the corner, but Rot didn't move. "Throw that to me."

Dread tossed it, seeing an unknown caller. Rot caught it and answered, responding a couple times. He finished by saying, "I'm on it." Rot pulled away from Flower. "See, no more trouble from the coppers. I gotta go. You're good?"

Flower nodded, pulling the covers over her legs.

Rot scooted off the bed, collecting a few things. He stopped at the door. "You two can have the room. Wait, no...you have morals." He cackled.

Dread gazed at him with all the self-control he could muster. Instead of beating him to death, he hissed, "I'll hang with her."

"We're all pigs." Rot's eyes squinted. "Pigs roll in slop, Dread. Not sure I trust one who don't."

"If I haven't proven you can trust me, then fuck you. What do mean the coppers won't be trouble? Where are you going?"

"To fuck your mother again."

Dread ignored him, taking a few steps toward Flower. "If you don't want to go back to the Crush..."

"Rot said I'm fine."

"Rot doesn't decide that." Dread eased his tone so not to make her cry again. "You pick up anything the caller said to Rot just now?"

She shook her head. "Barely." She shrugged. "Something about cops and snoballs on Tchoupitoulas?"

"They boarded that up. Shit." Dread patted his clothes for Emma's phone that wasn't there. "Damn!" He ran after Rot, but he'd already exited the building, taking the van. He had to get to the Quarter by foot.

53

"DON'T LET SIMONE get to you." Keith drove onto the Elysian Snoballs lot. Compacted oyster shells crushed under the tires. "She can give a shit about the low-profile cases. If she doesn't have an airtight case, she won't prosecute."

"I've experienced that firsthand. It's frustrating. Going to trial is a major production."

Keith shut off the engine. The vacant snoball stand looked like a decaying relic. Some people left candles, cards, and flowers. "So, you think the first team missed something searching this place?"

"No, I trust Jonesy and Perez, but they're not detectives."

"They were only searching for drugs."

"That's my point. They might've missed something related to the case. It doesn't hurt to look again."

The small doorway had plywood nailed over it. Next to it, an official police seal had been taped across the seam with Perez's initials. Keith used a crowbar from his trunk to pull the plywood away from the entrance.

The door opened outward, exposing thin, cheap cardboard boxes strewn about. Different sized cups and plastic spoons were all over the floor. The ice shaver was on its side.

Nikki used her foot to move debris around. "Okay, I have to talk with them two. I'll never understand why cops think total destruction is the best way to do a search. It's a mess."

"Saves time."

"That's how you miss things, by throwing shit all over the floor."

Keith countered, "When drugs are the only thing you're looking for, it's hard to miss them. You can't blame Perez and Jonesy."

Nikki gave him a shove. "Will you friggin' take my side instead of Jonesy's?"

"Oh, snap. Are we dating again?"

"Not with that attitude."

"Jonesy's an ugly bitch."

"That's sweet. You're lying." They stared into each other's eyes, forced to stand so close. This time Nikki held back. "Is this a check box?"

"Check."

"Now?"

Keith smiled. "Now would be good."

Nikki leaned in and selected his bottom lip with hers. The kiss grew passionate.

When they eased apart, Nikki closed her eyes and rested her head on his shoulder. "I see what you mean about the right time." She spotted an odd seam on the floor. "What's that?"

"Just a biological reaction to…"

"No, not *that*. On the floor."

Keith stepped back. "Oh, yeah."

"They covered a break in the flooring."

"Trap door? A crawl space makes sense."

"I didn't read about this in Perez's report." Nikki cleared the debris blocking a well-hidden trapdoor. A recessed metal loop was used to lift the hatch until it rested against the wall. Activating the flashlight app, she lowered her cell and peered into the opening. "Sleeping bag, water. Food wrappers."

"Let's get down there."

With care, Keith helped Nikki drop into the four-foot space first, getting on her hands and knees to move around. Her partner eased down next. The flooring was plywood on the cement foundation.

"No drugs," Keith said, crouching over.

"Either Frank used this as his love shack, or he set Emma up here." Nikki's inspection ended as quickly as it started.

"Nothing proves Emma was here. We need Oz."

"If this was Frank's secret bang-space, I'd rather be in chicken shit."

A loud thump rattled the structure, with rapid pounding. Shadows passed the small vents on the wall where sunlight seeped inside.

"Who's that?" Keith asked. "Hello?"

Nikki pounded the wall. "Hey, who's there?"

Noises echoed through the structure. "Sounds like a hammer hitting wood."

"Is that gasoline?" Nikki duck-walked in the crawl space until she could stand in the opening. Gray smoke filtered in from the crevices. "It's on fire!"

"I'm calling 911."

"Let's get out of here!"

They each climbed out and banged against the door. As flimsy as it appeared, it didn't budge. Heat and the crackling fire grew intense.

Nikki jumped to the serving window. "We're boarded in!"

She grabbed for the latch, but it was like touching a hot stove. A nearby rag was used to unlock the plywood. When she pushed, a rush of flames knocked her back into Keith's arms. "Mother...*shit.*"

"Help's coming. This place is a tinderbox." Keith coughed. He rammed the door to no avail.

"Don't panic. Back into the crawlspace!" Nikki yelled.

As the snoball stand filled with smoke, they dropped into the cool space not yet contaminated with smoke. Small, slated vents were inches from the ground, proving the flames were higher up on the walls.

"Fire department better hurry." Nikki kept her shirt over her nose and mouth.

"There's no exit from down here."

They both lay flat on their backs with their noses next to the vent as Nikki pulled the sleeping bag over their bodies. Keith reached out and secured Nikki's hand. She squeezed tightly, inhaling the oxygen coming from the narrow opening while the heat intensified above.

54

THE FIRE'S HEAT grew unbearable.

Most people will never experience the fear of an unnatural, impending death. A rock climber in a free fall has that fear—a driver stuck on the tracks with the unstoppable train bearing down—a shipwreck victim whose muscles are about to give out in the open sea.

Nikki squeezed Keith's hand, still hot, as if she'd have gotten way too close to a bonfire. It would only be moments before the floor above them caught and minutes before smoke inhalation. Her closed eyes burned and watered. She couldn't even see Keith lying right next to her.

"Nikki, if this is our last moment..." Keith stopped in a coughing fit.

"Sirens. Fire department." She choked.

"I need to confess something," he whispered.

"Listen." Nikki stretched her neck to the vent and yelled between coughs. "Hey, we're in here! Help!"

Sirens overcame the roaring flames as Nikki and Keith smacked the wall. A deep voice told them to take cover. Seconds later, the slats exploded inward, and more light shone inside. Then, the water rushed in, dousing them with a heavy onslaught.

The deluge stopped. A hurricane had hit the snoball stand, chaos and yelling surrounded them. The sleeping bag and everything else was drenched, but they weren't out of harm's way. The water came in from the vent hole again.

They heard a massive crack, like a branch breaking from a tree. Despite hiding under the covers, Nikki could tell that they were exposed to a bright light. The fire department had pried open one side of the crawl space. Hands grabbed under her armpits as forces unseen dragged her backwards, into the sunlight.

⁓

Medics from two ambos on the scene had been quick to administer oxygen while Nikki and Keith each sat on the edge of a gurney with dry blankets and crimson eyes. It reminded Nikki of Napleton's murder.

Several squad cars kept traffic moving on Tchoupitoulas, not letting anyone else near. The firefighters put away their equipment, joyous in the outcome. The snoball stand was a charred husk. Nikki pulled the oxygen off when Lieutenant Tran powerwalked toward them.

"Uh-oh, we're in trouble," Nikki wheezed.

Lan stopped short of knocking Keith's gurney over. "Are you two okay?"

Nikki pinched her forearm with a finger. "Extra crispy?"

"Not funny!" Lan shouted.

"We're fine, Lan. A little smoke."

Keith cleared his throat. "It's like I went through a carton of cigs, but I'm good."

"Someone tried to kill us, and I don't believe for a minute it was Emma."

"I agree," Keith said. "Several people had to have done this."

One of the medics stepped up. "We need to get you to the hospital to get checked out."

Nikki shook her head. "I'm refusing treatment. I'm fine."

"Me too." Keith stretched and twisted while sitting on the gurney. "No injuries. Only cold from the soaking."

"That's your choice. Change your wet clothes. Don't do anything strenuous. Any shortness of breath, go to the hospital." The medic nodded, backing away.

"What happened?" Lan asked.

Nikki and Keith gave him the condensed version, skipping the kiss, explaining they didn't encounter anything strange after entering, except the crawl space.

Lan put his hand on Nikki's shoulder. "I can't force you to go to the hospital, but you're done for the day. I'll arrange a ride home for both of you. Fill out your reports in the morning."

"We can drive back to Headquarters and decompress there. I have gym clothes in my trunk."

"So do I," Keith said.

"For your walks of shame?"

"Are you two always on?" Lan shook his head. "At least you're okay."

Nikki tapped her chest. "I just need a little time for my adrenaline to come down."

His finger couldn't decide who to point at. "A squad will ride you back. Perez will follow in your car. Give me your key."

"You're sexy when you're demanding." Nikki winked.

Lan walked away with the keys, shaking his head.

Nikki and Keith moved away from the ambulances with the blankets still around them, almost parallel to the burned structure. A slight breeze felt good after almost dying, despite being cold. They stopped, then turned toward each other. Nikki continued to look past him.

"Who tried to kill us, Keith?"

"We're investigating some wealthy people who traffic girls. We must be close."

"Warren?"

"Wouldn't doubt it."

"I've been meaning to ask, do you know Percy personally?"

"No. Why?" Keith thought about it while his eyes darted.

"Ah, he acted squirrelly around you."

"A man was murdered in his bathroom. Understandable. About what I was going to say in there."

She shook her head. "No need. In a moment like that, emotions surface. Our kiss was nice. No need to analyze it. We cared for each other at one time and those feelings...do they ever go away? I—I mean..."

"Nikki," he interrupted. "Nik."

"What?"

"I was just going to say I was the one that put the rubber chicken on your desk."

It took a second for a laugh to register, then a sudden cough.

She leaned into Keith, putting her head on his damp chest. He held her tight, wrapped in his blanket as well. Two weeks ago, she could never have imagined being in this position.

55

Horrid images of being trapped in the fire dominated Nikki's thoughts. She was thankful to have the other detectives at Headquarters for support. The dry gym clothes were fortuitous, although they had been in her trunk for a month. The other cops wanted to talk about their near-death experience, but Nikki did her best to keep it light.

At one point, Nikki warned, "If a barbequed chicken turns up on my desk, I'm going punch everyone in the dick, including the women."

Nikki and Keith ended up with no ill side effects, except fatigue and soreness. Refusing medical treatment wasn't always the smartest thing. They remained at Headquarters until sure there wouldn't be complications. Despite washing her face in the restroom, she still stunk of smoke.

When they deemed it safe to leave, Keith walked Nikki to her car. They stayed silent the entire way until a few yards from her vehicle. He used those last few moments to hook his pinky with hers. It brought a smile and a little bit of guilt.

"How about we go out for a real dinner soon—a real date. Not tonight, sometime."

"A real date," Nikki repeated. "Step two in your devious plan?"

"*Dating For Dummies* has some good info. I, uh, I have some things to tell you."

"Things? Now, I'm curious. Spill it, Teague."

"Not here, Crispy."

She slapped his arm. "Don't you dare call me that in front of anyone."

"Never. We'll talk. Over dinner. Soon."

Did this have to do with Percy? She nodded with a tilted smile. "Work related?"

"I think we can speak beyond our job." He let go of her pinky, then leaned in to kiss her cheek. "You know something? You're *smoking hot.*"

"That's the last one. I hope it's out of your system." She pushed him away.

"We'll have Bananas Foster. That's the last one."

"Boooo!" She gave him a thumbs down.

"You love it." He backed away with a charming glare.

Nikki smiled like a schoolgirl all the way home. The drive passed in seconds with Keith on her mind. The garage elevator opened, as if waiting for her. As the metal box glided up, her body grew heavy, knowing she was about to lie down. Maybe a hot bath would be a nice treat.

The elevator opened on the fifth floor, and she caught Major down the hall about to knock on her door.

He turned, letting his shoulders slump with a smile. "Thank the Lord."

"What's going on, Major?" She dragged her feet toward him.

"You have to give me your number or something."

"What's wrong?"

"The news showed you at that fire. They're speculating all kinds of shit like a hit is on you."

"I'm okay, as you can see."

Major shook his head. "I wish you could talk to me."

"It's all click bait, Major. Keith and I are fine. It could've been worse."

"I'll say. The video is crazy."

"It's not that I can't talk about the fire—I will—not right now." Nikki almost walked through him.

"Whoa, smoke is all over you."

"It's in my hair. I need a long bath."

"I can give you a bottle of wine to take with you."

That offer lightened her mood. "I'm good. *Major*. What's your real name?"

"My name's Ray. Raymond. Uh, Ray."

She looked at him while sticking her key in the door. "Ray Raymond Uh, Ray, huh? Sounds like WITSEC." She gave a lazy smile.

"That's witness protection, right? May as well be." His face lost some of its humor.

"Talk later?"

"You go take care of yourself, and don't hesitate to bang on that wall if you want something."

"We're not Russian spies. How about we exchange numbers like you said?"

"Next time I see you. Go take care of yourself." He pretended to tip an imaginary cap and entered his condo.

56

FORGET BUTTERFLIES, KEITH had piranhas eating away at his stomach. He had made a tentative date with Nikki to tell her *everything*, no matter the consequences. He entered his apartment and went straight for the refrigerator. A cold beer soothed his throat as he put away his badge and gun.

"I warned you." The voice came from the living room.

Keith's heart nearly stopped, but he wasn't surprised. He knew the intruder. An outline formed on his couch in the dark. "How did you get in?"

"Your key. You told me where you keep it."

"No, I didn't. I wouldn't." His legs froze.

"You told me in the hospital after the accident when you killed Nikki's sister. You were a little out of it at the time."

"That's bullshit." He stepped forward. "That car hit us."

"I couldn't tell if you were still drunk or if it was the morphine."

"I don't remember drinking. And even so, I don't believe I was drunk."

"Doesn't matter how impaired you were, darling. The blood-work proves you were over the legal limit. You are so lucky I was there to intercept that report."

"Lucky me. You must have friends in high places," Keith droned.

"Right people in the right spots. The video needed to disappear. You were the best option."

"That's bullshit. You chose this complicated plan to blackmail me over a simple cash payout to a corrupt cop?"

"A corrupt cop would flip too easily. We needed someone motivated to protect himself. We'd blame you for the cover-up if it came to light. You would be done. Done with Nikki. Done with the force. You would be canceled."

"Maybe I'll go talk to the people who treated me. The doctor and nurses."

"If I find you've been snooping, I'll leak it to the press."

"People would question why my blood alcohol level wasn't reported in an accident involving a death. You'll go down with me."

"Mistakes happen all the time. You're discussing this like we'll stop and change our mind."

"Just tell me why you're here."

"To save your life. They want you gone. I believe you still have value."

"The fire?"

She frowned. "They are not happy. It was a sloppy attempt, but these people generally don't put out hits on the police."

"Who put out the hit?"

"Don't ask stupid questions. Here's where you redeem yourself. Tran requested the FBI's help. They'll be assigning an agent. You need to make sure this fed doesn't dig in the wrong places."

"The FBI will take their cues from us, from Nikki."

"To start. You need to give them harmless tasks that lead nowhere."

"Now I'm controlling the FBI? C'mon. You're close to pushing me over the edge."

"Think of the backlash on Nikki. Her alcoholic ex-boyfriend steals the cell phone from Central Evidence? She'll be hounded by press. The NOPD will never see her the same way again."

"I will steer Nikki. Call it off." He closed his eyes, hanging his head. "I'll handle it."

She stood and walked toward the door. "And I'll hold you to it."

Keith followed her out, taking the key from her hand. He shut the door and fell against it, sliding down to the floor. The back of his head banged against it a few times.

After several moments of collecting his wits, he forced himself up. A shower washed the smoke from his skin. He entered his living room in basketball shorts and a tee, gravitating to the window to watch raindrops hitting the glass. Memories of his father's suicide blinded him like a freight train in a tunnel. It knocked him backwards. This wasn't pity or guilt this time. A guttural yell scratched at his raw vocal cords.

Not today, Dad, he thought.

Morgan's death replaced that memory, coming at him from the opposite direction. He remembered nothing about the crash or subsequent events leading to the ambulance ride and hospital. What he lamented was what *didn't* happen that day. He had gone from the highest high to the lowest low in one fatal moment.

The blinds came down. Keith walked to the kitchen where he opened the safe and pulled out his special gun. The magazine dropped into his hand. He took a long look at the only bullet at the top of the mechanism. A special hollow point reflected light. "Don't be a child," he whispered. "Be a man."

He took the gun to his bedroom closet, setting it on the floor while he searched through packed away items. Inside beat-up cardboard was a beautiful cherry wood chest surrounded by blocks of spongy foam. He pulled out the cremation urn.

"Hi, Dad."

Keith placed the gun, the magazine, and the bullet inside the urn. He closed the lid, running his fingers over the wood. His father had been troubled when he took his own life with that gun. His dad had been selfish and stupid. The man hadn't thought of anyone but himself and never asked for help.

"I wanted to be like you in so many ways. Not anymore."

WEDNESDAY

57

Nikki had slept like a stone. The morning started slow, but her mind was focused.

The coroner was first on her agenda. She left her condo's garage, careful for pedestrians, as always. Before pulling onto the street, she spotted Dread leaning against a light pole near a bus stop. He had his arms folded, offering a slight wave.

She eased onto the curb, looking up and down the street. "Step in my office."

Dread fell into the passenger side. "Nice ride."

Her lungs locked up in mid-breath. "Oh, God. How do you walk around like that." She lowered the window, tilting her head toward the opening. "Wow."

"Sorry. Didn't get to shower this week."

"How did you find where I live?"

"Emma told me you live in this building." He pressed the window button as well. "You'll live."

"I'm not so sure, Dread. *Fuck*." She smiled, and he laughed it off. "There's nothing yet on the beads."

"Okay, but that's not why I pulled up at your place. I'm glad you got out of the fire—you and your partner."

"Do you have information on the fire?"

"Rot got a call about Tchoupitoulas. My Spidey-sense tingled."

"You think Rot set the fire?"

"You don't?"

"It's like the beads, Dread. You overheard a partial conversation mentioning a busy street?"

"I lost Emma's cell, so I couldn't warn you. I did my best to follow him. When I got to the snoball stand, the fire was already put out."

"So, you didn't witness it and it's hearsay." She welcomed the fresh air.

"*He did it.* Somebody called and gave him the green light while I was in the room."

"Still hearsay. Still no contact with Emma?"

"Damn if I can find her."

"What about my witness you're protecting?"

"She doesn't want to talk to you."

"Cut the bullshit! She'd talk to me if you wanted her to. You're seeking me out for a reason. What's your motivation?"

His eyes widened. "Awright. Just don't call me a bitch."

"All my favorite people are bitches. It's obvious to me there's more going on than just Emma. Dread, either you trust me or you don't."

He stared out the window, giving serious thought to something. He turned to Nikki twice before settling in. "All right, yeah. I shouldn't say this shit, but okay. Percy Fields… He's my father."

Nikki blinked at him. "What the F?"

He never broke eye contact. "It's the truth. My mom was a stripper. An addict. He fucked her and left her. She told me in Oklahoma he was my pops, right before she overdosed."

"I'm sorry, Dread."

"Percy don't give a shit, either."

"Have you tried to mend things?"

"No."

"Do you think he's in danger? You wouldn't be waiting for Emma to…"

"… to kill him? No. But anything he gets, he deserves."

"Anything you do to him now would be considered a vendetta. I would have to come after you." She leaned toward the window for air.

"I can take a hint. I gotta make tracks." He opened the door and got out. "There's no vendetta, Chick. He's nothing to me."

She called out through the window. "Can I drop you off somewhere? You can ride on the hood. Air out."

"Nah." He backed away.

"Where you off to?"

"I got a place to shower over by the war museum."

"Keep in touch."

He knocked on the window as it rose. "Hey! Don't let Percy know you know, dig? Use that info while you can."

58

Nikki's muscles tired from standing rigid in the middle of the autopsy room at the Coroner's Office. She thought about Dread, Percy Field's bastard son. If given the choice between the dead bodies lain out before her and Dread's aroma, she'd pick the dead bodies— chicken shit, third. Her life had become about rating smells.

The medical examiner had excused himself for another matter, so she was alone with company that couldn't talk back. There were cameras covering the entire room, so that anyone attempting to contaminate evidence would be caught. The door behind her opened. She looked over her shoulder at Keith with relief.

She refused to face him, yet her body grew warmer. Seconds later, he collected her hair from behind, moving it to the side of her neck. Her head tilted enough so he'd have room to press his lips below her ear. She went from warm to hot.

"We're at the coroner's, *sicko*," she said seductively. "There's monitors."

"So?" He stood beside her. "It's about time you learn my dark secrets."

"Ah, a *necro*."

"I got tired of complaints."

"So sick." She bumped shoulders with him. "You didn't have to meet me here."

"I don't do anything I don't want to."

"Big talk."

"If I don't bathe in smoke or chemicals in an autopsy room, then I haven't accomplished anything."

"Coming here keeps me connected."

"Talk to me in a few months when you have a full caseload. This is all e-mailed in a report."

"I look forward to it." She stared at Saul Green's body lying on the gurney.

"This reminds me we're still alive and kicking." Keith was showered, wearing extra-nice pants and a blue button-down.

"You're dressed for court today, aren't you?"

"Yeah, that love-triangle shooting six months ago. I'll head over in an hour."

Dr. Meachum returned to the room. "We can meet in my office or one of the family rooms. It's rare to get cops here to talk about corpses."

"My mom always used to tell me why stare at a screen when you can go in person?"

"Smart woman. Technology is killing social interaction."

"Is murder social interaction?"

Meachum belted out a laugh, pointing at her.

Nikki turned her attention to Saul Green. "The murders are connected, right?"

"Not so much. Herman Napleton was a frenzied attack. With Frank Brehm, the killer was more thoughtful. Drugged and tortured with the snoball syrup. Saul Green was similar with incapacitating him and murdering him with a blunt object. Different methods, but still signs of the same killer."

"No more panic," Keith mumbled.

"You almost sound proud of her," a new voice to their right said.

Troy Ozwald entered the autopsy room. "I thought I'd save you a trip upstairs."

Keith said, "Must be so convenient to have the labs, EMS services, and coroner all in one building."

"The city did us right after Katrina."

"You mean you didn't like storing dead bodies in refrigerated trucks?"

"I came on after that. The stuff of nightmares." Oz pulled his lab coat back with his hands on his hips and seemed to notice Nikki for the first time. "Hi, Nikki. Haven't seen you here since your sister passed."

"I've come in, just not upstairs. I know I thanked you at the services, but I've been meaning to say thank you again, Dr. Meachum, for handling my sister with respect."

"Of course."

"I'm so stupid." Keith rubbed the back of his neck. "That's why you're coming here."

Nikki closed her eyes, then looked at him. "I had to get over this hurdle, too."

Oz looked inside the thick folder. "Well, the towel matches the lipstick."

"Is that some kind of euphemism?" Nikki smiled, waiting for Keith to join in, but he didn't.

"Not sure how that'd apply." Oz paused to think about it.

"Stupid joke." Nikki waved it off.

He continued, "No prints were on the stationery from your pocket or on Frank Brehm's syrup bottles. Smears, yes. Good prints, no. Same with the toilet lid."

Keith still looked upset about not putting two-and-two together about her last seeing Morgan on the autopsy table. "Go to court. I'll confront Mary Napleton about the towel. She might give us a few more answers."

"You want to question her alone?"

"I'm a big girl. She likes me."

He took her hand. "I'll call you when I'm done. Be careful. Remember that someone tried to kill us."

"Someone tried to kill *you*. People love *me*."

59

It only took two calls for Nikki to track down Mary Napleton at Harrah's Casino. Nikki parked illegally near the front entrance, where a stretch of palm trees looked to be as out of place as a skyscraper would.

The bells and whistles of slot machines assaulted her upon entering, despite the sparse crowd early in the day. Servers dressed in identical, tasteful outfits toured the floor. Nikki took the long, expansive carpeted pathway leading to the table games.

Mary Napleton sat alone at a table opposite a spiffy, seasoned dealer. Nikki eased up to Mary's left side. The sign on the green felt table indicated Caribbean Stud Poker with a hundred-dollar minimum. A digital board listed progressive cash payouts for different hands.

Nikki sat. "This your game?"

"Any table game relaxes me." She placed a bet for a new hand, looking at the dealer, knowing the unasked question. She answered his silent inquiry. "It's fine. She can sit."

"That's a steep bet."

"I request this minimum, so I'm not bothered. Where is your adorable partner? Keith, is it?"

"He's testifying in court. I'll let him know you asked about him."

"Are you two…?"

"It's complicated. If you want easy, you don't want him."

The dealer flipped over a pair of threes. Mary only had an ace-king high. He took Mary's bet.

"I thought I understood these old men who went after young women, but it's more than sex. It's not about the youth; it's the lack of baggage. Why would healthy, vivacious women at my age want the problems and issues with someone else's life?"

"Yeah, but how do you relate to each other? Different experiences—the immaturity."

She spoke to the dealer. "Can you give a moment?"

The man gave a single nod and backed away.

"You must lose a boatload for that kind of respect."

"I also win a boatload. I'm considered a *whale*. Okay, let's lay our cards on the table. You're not here to analyze my love life."

"Well, sort of. You two had sex the night Herman died."

"Sounds horrible, doesn't it?"

"Why?"

"I've been conditioned to give in. Years of manipulation."

"I think I understand."

"Herman had a thing for young girls he could control. But then, he also liked powerful women who controlled him. Fucking Gemini."

"I see."

"I never caught him in the act, just clues. Pictures on his social media. Where his eyes roamed in public. Who he gravitated to at the hotel and in the Quarter."

"No complaints were filed before Emma, right?"

"None. He said his sex life was none of my business. Can you imagine a husband telling this to his wife?"

"Tell me about the black lipstick."

"Mine. He asked me to wear it." She gazed to Nikki's lips. "He wanted me to pretend I was a gutter punk."

"You agreed?"

"You've heard of detachment, right? Herman was into *kink*. It was better for the divorce if I just went along."

"Something tells me your relationship wasn't based on love and mutual respect."

Mary's face aged before Nikki's eyes. "Once I resigned to the fact that cheating isn't personal…"

"How can it not be personal?"

"You said it yourself—our marriage wasn't based on love. Don't get me wrong, I found my happiness elsewhere as well. I had no idea he killed those girls, Nikki."

"Was he rough with you?"

"Sometimes." She thought on it. "He had his fantasies."

"So, that night, he had sex with this last gutter punk he murdered, and then you, too?"

"I pray that's not the case. Why come back to me for sex if he was just with that girl? It's a horrid thought."

"That makes sense. No semen was found."

She sampled her cocktail. "I didn't find out about her until I saw it on the news. He told me I got in his head, from the argument we had here."

Nikki peeked at the side of her neck for a mark, but it was covered. "Does he choke you? Is that part of his kink?"

She caressed where the fingernail indention would be. "The more I…cooperated, the better my settlement. Turns out, I get it all."

"For a moment, I thought you were harboring Emma."

She considered it. "Sharon and I are good friends. Emma is like a daughter without the mother-daughter bullshit. If she had come to me, I'd have helped her."

"Has Emma contacted you?"

"No." She summoned the dealer back, indicating she was done with conversation. "If you want to talk about Emma, I'll need my lawyer. Not because of guilt. I won't say anything that will affect my inheritance. I hope you understand."

"Of course. You say you're friends with Sharon. What about Warren?"

"Warren's a different kind of prick. You want the lowdown, talk to his assistant. Kasie something. You met her as a new hire during the rape investigation. She's involved in the day-to-day now. She's not the type to hold back."

"Like you."

Mary welcomed it as a compliment and placed a new bet.

60

Nikki weaved through happy drinkers in the Grande Esplanade lobby to find Warren laughing with a few guests. A moment later, manager and guests parted, and Warren approached the reception desk. She imagined destination hotels must be like that *White Lotus* show.

He stopped mid-stride in front of Nikki. *"Chick."*

"I don't know why, but it seems your calling me Chick is beneath you."

"Honestly, it didn't feel right coming out of my mouth. Any leads on the arsonist?"

"I'm fine. Thanks."

"I can see that. Did Emma set the fire?"

"It wasn't Emma. She's not trying to kill me and Keith."

"She's really got you wrapped around her finger."

"I'm not here to talk to you. Where can I find your assistant?"

"Kasie?" He lost patience like a switch had been flipped. "So, you don't have news?"

"Only that I spoke with Mary Napleton. She illuminated me on Herman's outside interests."

His face relaxed, relieving many of his wrinkles. "What do you want me to say? That's between them." He started to walk again, but slower. "I have a hotel to run."

"Can we talk a second in your office before I speak to Kasie?"

"If you insist."

Nikki followed him into a small reception area where Kasie Waters typed at a keyboard. She remembered when his assistant first started; most days she ran errands for Warren like a servant. "How are you, Kasie?"

"I'm good. I'm so glad you're okay." The attractive, athletic blonde straightened in the chair. Last time they talked, Kasie touched on her time as an ex-Army Ranger.

They smiled at each other as she and Warren entered his office.

He sat in a large leather chair behind his desk. "You'd be wasting your time with her."

"Did *you?*" She hiked an eyebrow. "Waste your time?"

His lips squeezed into a grin. "You and me have a special type of relationship, don't we?"

"Oh?"

"I don't suppose you treat other victims' families like this."

"Now Emma's a victim?"

"Of sorts."

"You aren't curious about the details of Frank's and Saul's murders?"

"Of course I am. The press is calling constantly. Sharon and I give them the anxious parent sound bites and that's it. I can't believe no one has bit on the reward yet."

"You aren't too broken up over your friends' deaths."

"We're releasing a statement later in the day. The Krewe of Midas parade is canceled, and the ball that would follow."

"Wow, that's huge. I think that's only right. In their memory. And you can't have a party while your daughter is missing."

"And there's that."

She looked around at the Krewe of Midas memorabilia. "You're losing a boatload of cash by canceling, right?"

"It happens. I'm a friend first, businessman second."

"Family man third?"

Warren appeared to shut down, unblinking. A man like him would only say something by mistake due to arrogance, not fear. "Is that all?"

"When I searched Emma's room, I found a box of pictures where my face had been crossed out. Emma would never do that."

"I noticed you didn't take them."

"They're manufactured."

"You're so blind, Detective. Look at the change she went through. The lies. The unpredictability." He got up and poured a small whiskey from a crystal bottle.

"Emma didn't do that to those pictures. But it would be easy to say Emma killed me at trial with those in evidence."

He spoke into the glass while swirling it. "You're crazy."

"I'm not going to be a distraction in this investigation."

"Just a hindrance?"

Nikki tried another tactic. "Have you and Mary been getting along?"

"How does that concern you?"

"You wanted Mary to reign as queen in your parade. She'll be disappointed."

"She understands. There's next year."

"Did you know Emma wrote something on the victims' faces?"

He stared at her. "I did. No reason to lie to you."

"It's nice the gag order is holding up. *Five, four, three*—written with black lipstick. That sounds like a countdown to me."

He took a moment. "Emma always had a flair for the dramatic. I've been considering who's one or two. That's part of the reason we canceled. The members are worried."

"You should all stay vigilant. Whoever was in the video, I mean. It's Mardi Gras. Easy to disappear in the chaos."

His cell rang. "I need to take this. Don't tie up Kasie for too long, please."

61

KEITH LEFT THE courtroom, satisfied with his testimony.

When he checked his cell, he saw three missed calls from an unknown number. Enough was enough. He had to do something.

He drove to hospital where he had recovered from the accident that killed Morgan. Before going in, he checked himself in the mirror. His hair was perfect. He had the right amount of stubble and a touch of cologne. His badge hung from his neck, his shoulder holster hid under his jacket.

He entered Riverbend Medical, following the signs that pointed him toward the laboratory. It was on the third floor, lost in a maze of halls. The reception area had a few people waiting, but he stepped right up to the man behind the window.

Keith showed his badge. "Hi, I'm Detective Keith Teague. I was hoping to speak with your data entry specialist or administrator?"

The man scooted back a little in chair to think. "Ah, you'd want Leslie. Let me check in back."

"Can you take me to her?" He looked at his tag. "John?"

"I suppose." He stood and pointed to a security door.

Keith waited for it open. John nodded. "This way."

They walked down a long hallway, passing offices and rooms with lab equipment. At the far end, they came to a door John opened by swiping a key card. Keith entered a rather large room with several cubicles.

Keith followed John to a woman sitting at a computer in a lab coat. She had curly hair and bright-blue glasses. "This is Leslie."

"Hi, Leslie, I'm Detective Teague, but you can call me Keith. Do you have a moment?"

Her green eyes lit up. "What did I do, Detective?"

"Nothing." He smiled, looking at the receptionist. "I'm good. Thank you."

"I'll escort him out, John."

The man backed away.

"Can we sit?" Keith pointed at her computer.

"Of course." Leslie found an empty chair in the next cubicle and brought it over. "I'm curious what this is about."

After they settled and Leslie clasped her hands in her lap with a pleasant grin, he began. "I have my own personal lab results that were entered into your system about three years ago. I was wondering if we could look those up?"

Her head twitched. "You could get those results by going online to your account or requesting them with a form."

"I have my reasons for coming here. You have access to your server? Administrative rights to do a deep dive?"

"I have certain rights to the laboratory information system, but not administrative."

"Can you look me up? Humor me?"

She swiveled to her keyboard. "It's encrypted and there will be an audit trail. It's better to request your electronic medical record through our site."

He gave her his driver's license. "Please."

She sighed. "I suppose this isn't illegal. Just need your name and birthday. Forgive me if I don't trust you to tell me just anyone's name and date of birth. This is irregular."

"I understand."

She keyed a login and password, then entered his information. A window populated her screen. "Yes, here it is. Oh. Oh, my. Your BAC..."

"Is there a way to find out if this was altered or tampered with?"

"I'm afraid not. These results are populated from automated processes."

"No way to manipulate them? Someone with admin rights and knowledge of the software?"

"I suppose anything is possible. I wouldn't know where to look. Shouldn't you have a warrant?"

Keith sighed. "We can avoid the warrant because this is about my own personal medical history."

She appeared reluctant. "No, there's nothing I can do."

"Can we go back to when this was first entered three years ago? Like a snapshot or something?"

"I can't. We would have to bring in IT and HR and my bosses. There are HIPPA regulations."

Another female voice spoke up behind them. "You stole my chair, Leslie."

"Oh, I thought you left for the day."

The woman eyed Keith curiously. "Hi, I'm Mia."

"Keith."

"Leslie doesn't know the system as well as I do. I'm the admin."

"You heard what I'm looking for?" Keith gave the puppy-dog eyes Nikki has commented on.

"I did. It sounds like you're suspicious of a hack."

"I want verification. That's it."

She glanced back at Leslie's monitor. "Can I drive?"

"Sure." Leslie got up from her monitor.

The lady deftly maneuvered around the keyboard like a wizard, filling in credential windows several times. She opened windows and folders until he saw one file sitting alone. She double clicked on it and another identical version of his lab report was on the screen.

Keith zeroed in on the blood work. "It's clean."

"I don't understand. How did that...." Mia scratched at her head. "Let me check the logs." She sped through some windows and progression bars. "None. Deleted. Hmm. I need to talk to IT."

"Can you print out a copy of that and make a pdf or something to e-mail me?" Keith recognized real concern on her suddenly pale face. "It's my own medical info, right? No HIPAA laws against it."

"But, it's not right. Someone hacked us." Mia stared at the screen. "At the very least, an employee committed a crime here."

"You weren't hacked. I was the target. Mia, Leslie, this is a police investigation. Can we hold off on notifying your IT?"

"I'm afraid not, Detective. This is...criminal. We have our patients to think about and their private information. If it turns out someone got in our system... It would be devastating."

"I agree." Keith handed them each a police card. "At least consider this: If your find no other foul play except the manipulation of this specific report, contact me first before calling any other law-enforcement agency."

Mia took the card. "By that time, I'm afraid the decision will be out of my hands."

62

Kasie Waters had the demeanor of a retired assassin in WITSEC. Her confidence was something to admire. Leadership oozed from her pores. However, Nikki didn't think she had many female friends.

Nikki and Kasie sat with two Cokes at a corner diner in the Faubourg Marigny, a gentrified neighborhood across Esplanade Avenue, two blocks from the hotel. The neighborhood was filled with colorfully bright shotgun homes. The inside looked like a wharf on a pier with low-hanging fishing nets.

"Thanks for not asking me about the fire."

"Thanks for not asking about my deployment. I didn't engage in any combat. I got a nice participation trophy."

"You sound bitter."

"I trained to sit on the sidelines, but… Let's move on."

Nikki's mouth searched for the straw in her Coke. She spoke after a sip. "Warren, right?"

"I realize cops don't water board, but have interrogation techniques gotten that soft?"

"I'll work up to asking who ordered the Code Red."

"Jack Nicholson?" Kasie lightened a little.

"This isn't an interrogation. I just want your opinion on things."

Her skin betrayed her by turning pink. "You want dirt on Warren."

"Think of it as *intel*. You like Sharon, his wife?"

"I do. Sharon has fire. Warren sucks the oxygen out of the room."

"Which puts out a fire. She's a lot more...*herself* without him around."

"Makes you wonder about people's choices. Sometimes I question mine, as in why I work for him."

"What do you think of Emma? Be truthful."

"The kid never had a chance."

"Amen."

"The first time I talked to Emma, she was abrasive."

"But you weren't offended."

"Not at all. That was me at that age."

"Nooooo....."

She broke into a smile. "I was a little bitch. Petty crimes. School suspensions. My dad was like, *you serve in the military, or you're out on the street.*"

"You chose the military."

"I chose the street. Then, I offered the military option to a progressive judge before he was about to sentence me for assault. He liked it."

"Not sure I like a military full of criminals."

"Gives us thugs a purpose." She had some Coke. "Yeah, so Emma was like looking in a mirror. Her attitude was genuine, even if misguided."

"I'm guessing the military prepared you for abrasive."

"No one will ever offend me. Emma's sense of humor was dark and sarcastic. She just didn't care. She has that freedom."

"Has Warren ever hit on you, between us girls?"

"He tested his boundaries when he first hired me."

"Even in this climate? *He said, she said.* Sometimes, that's enough."

"I'm not the litigious type. I take care of my own problems."

"Old school."

"He's old school. *Pat the secretary on the ass* type. I had his arm twisted behind his back, telling him he'd lose it if he ever tried it again. Thought I'd be escorted out on the spot."

"You kept your job."

"He liked it."

"What?"

"Not in a fetish way. He showed me respect after that."

"Makes sense. Predators select their victims. You didn't present as one he could groom, so he left you alone."

"Is Warren a predator?"

"Jury's out. He takes advantage of people. Exploits weaknesses. He bullies."

"Yeah, he bullies people every day. Warren's soft. He compensates."

"What do you think of the Krewe of Midas cancellation?"

"Less work for me."

"Have you come across any insider info on the secret party?"

She leaned forward. "I've only started hearing of this. Is it some *Eyes Wide Shut* bullshit?"

"Could be. Do me a favor. Keep your ears perked."

She gave an incredulous look. "I'm the last one he'll talk to about that. Any other questions?"

Nikki folded her arms, looking at the alligator head on the wall. "Any thoughts on his clique? The Rat Pack. Either dead or alive."

Kasie squinted her eyes. "The creep factor was incredible when Saul or Frank would come by. Herman never looked twice at me. Percy Fields is...he's a fish out of water. He's uncomfortable...yeah. I'd bet his dancers would spill the *deets*."

"Our team interviewed most of his dancers. They don't know anything."

"I wonder if they asked the right questions."

"I'll bet you're right. One last thing. Has there ever been any kind of paper trail that came across your desk that's fishy?"

"He may be ruthless, but the business is on the up-and-up. He'd never include me in underhanded stuff after I *alpha-dogged* him."

"Alpha-dogged. That's the second time I've heard that. Why do you stay there?"

"My salary trumps my disgust. Is this investigation still about finding Emma?"

"There are many branches to this rotten tree. Will you help me out?"

"Affirmative. I'm on the side of the law."

"Then you should be in law enforcement."

Kasie paused in thought. "I should get back." She stood and collected her jacket.

Nikki put on her own coat. "Thanks for this."

"No problem. Don't worry about a ride. I'm going to walk back."

"In the cold?"

"I like it."

Kasie walked down the block. Nikki thought she would be a great female friend—if the soldier chose to reach out. She crossed the street to her car, then called Keith after getting the heat going. "How'd court go?"

"I was very handsome."

"You sound light, chipper."

"How'd Mary go?"

"Oh, I learned some things."

"So did I, Nik."

"Great. Hit the ATM for some singles. We're going to the strip club."

63

THE QUARTER WAS packed with tourists, and there were still six more days until Mardi Gras. Nikki and Keith didn't have to navigate reporters outside the Crush strip club. The media had a difficult time dealing with inebriated people showcasing their stupidity for the cameras, so they avoided it.

Some Drake song pumped from the speakers as Nikki entered first. The bouncer let them through like normal customers.

The place was at capacity, but Keith pointed at a table where three men were leaving. "I still can't believe Green was murdered here yesterday; it's like nothing happened."

They sat at the small table, farthest away from the stage. Sturdy cushioned chairs supported two people if a lap dance dictated. They had beads around their necks in an effort to blend in.

It didn't take long for a cute waitress with a button nose and thin lips to clear the old drinks and give the table a single swipe of a rag. She was wearing a narrow, yellow tube top and took their drink order at the same time. She had a 70s style Farrah Fawcett hairstyle.

"Tell me about this murder." Nikki leaned closer to the waitress.

Her eyes lit up and her tone was that of Betty Boop. "Yeah, in the bathroom. Don't worry, a cleaning crew dis-fected everything."

"They *disinfected* it," Keith repeated.

"Yeah, they dis-fected it." She giggled and rolled her eyes like a doll. "Go take a selfie if you want."

"Any juicy details?" Keith asked.

"Are y'all from here?"

"Florida," Nikki blurted.

"A sixteen-year girl did it and she's in hiding. They think she killed two hotel owners and a chef. But not all of them here. Just the one guy. Crazy."

"What's your name?" Nikki asked.

"Brandy."

That wasn't her name. "My friend needs a dance."

"No." Keith waved his hands.

"I can be your type."

Nikki answered for him. "Can you be gentle with beginners?"

"You're shy?" Brandy twirled fingers in his hair.

"This isn't my thing," Keith added. "I like a nice girl-next-door type. You are far too advanced for me."

Brandy stayed playful. "Aw...not into aggressive women."

"That's my guy." Nikki shook his shoulders with both hands.

"I have just the girl for you. Lemme get your drinks, and I'll send her over."

After the waitress rushed off, Keith tilted his head. "This should be fun."

"So, you said we'd have dinner so you could tell me something. This is sorta like dinner."

"Here?"

"Why not?"

"It's personal. It's sensitive." Keith shifted on his butt.

"This is the next best thing to a dinner date."

He ran his palm across his entire face. "I have some good news, and I have some bad news. It's just that I can't tell you yet."

"Yeah, you can." Nikki slid forward so they were inches apart. "How bad can it be?"

64

Nikki hesitated, speaking over the AC/DC song pounding out the speakers. "You can't tease me with that and then pull the plug. Spit it out."

"I shouldn't have opened my mouth when I didn't have all the info. Turns out, I would've been wrong. Some things have to be sorted first."

"Whatever." Nikki flipped her hand at him.

He leaned forward and kissed her cheek. "I am happy, though. Happy you're here."

"What an odd thing to say at a strip club."

"This place oozes romance."

She looked up. "Here's our guy."

Percy Fields stepped to the table. "Detectives. Are you under-cover?"

Nikki said, "We're here to unwind."

"Unwind, my ass. You want to make sure the place was cleaned."

Keith shook his head. "No, we trust you on that."

"You're here to question my staff again."

"We could've done that outside the club."

Brandy appeared at the table, placing down two Abita Ambers on napkins, deciding not to interrupt her boss's conversation.

"We ordered beer. We're off the clock."

"You're never off the clock."

"We're trying to find a murderer, Mr. Fields. You might show some appreciation for the people who let you open tonight."

"I do. But, not so you can…" His arms waved around the place. "… be all in my shit."

"Your feelings aren't our concern."

"My customers don't need drama." Percy took the third chair and sat. "You can question my employees—again, I might add—with an official visit while they're off the clock. Doing this during business hours is bullshit."

"How many gutter punks are working tonight?" Nikki asked.

"None. Here's the deal, Detective Mayeaux—any woman off the street can come in here and score a ten-minute slot onstage or give a lap dance out here on the floor. Sorority girls. Housewives. Some dancers from other clubs freelance. Any tips they make they split with the house."

"So, you don't check ages?" Nikki drank from her glass.

"If my doorman lets them inside, I have to assume they have identification."

"You think we're stupid." Keith drank.

"Gutter punks are rare. It's easy to tell if one is underage."

"That's pretty loosey-goosey," Nikki said. "Did you have any gutter punks dancing in the past week?"

He frowned. "No. It's Mardi Gras. I'm staffed with regular dancers. Stay. Enjoy yourself, but if I find out you're hassling my girls, I'll ask you to leave."

"One more question," Nikki said as Percy stood. "Is the Krewe of Midas still having its party?"

"Warren told you the parade and ball is canceled."

"No, the *party*."

"Have a good time, detectives." He walked away, straightening his suit.

After several minutes, Brandy approached again, eyeing Nikki. "Mr. Fields told me who you really are. He said not to talk to you while I'm working."

Nikki smiled. "Sorry, we lied."

"Ask me for a dance." Brandy stared at Nikki.

"What?"

"Show me some money. Point to the back room. Make it obvious." Brandy glanced at Keith with a wink, then saddled up to Nikki. "I'm not his type, but maybe I'm yours?"

Nikki followed instructions with a hundred-dollar bill in her hand. "Okay."

Keith smiled. "Go get 'em, Chick."

Brandy led Nikki up a couple of stairs to a black velvet curtain as Percy glared from the bar. They entered a dark chamber draped in dark curtains and a muted red glow. One large bouncer stood at the far end, overlooking the six loveseats used for the dances. Two were occupied. The music was loud enough for their conversation not to be overheard.

Nikki eased onto a sofa, hoping it was clean. "Percy won't punish you for this?"

Brandy straddled her, speaking with a normal voice. "Percy's bark is bigger than his bite. He doesn't want you guys to scare off customers. Besides, *I'm just a stupid girl.*"

"You act dumb on purpose."

"Men need to be smarter than us, so my IQ drops when I walk through the door."

"I'm impressed. I'm assuming you have something to tell me?"

Brandy put Nikki's hands on her hips. "That depends on your questions and how long we dance. It's thirty a song, plus tip."

"How long have you worked here?"

"About a year."

"Have you ever seen Emma Courtland in here?"

She whispered in Nikki's ear while grinding against her. "I've seen her outside the club, but never inside."

"Outside? Like, watching?"

"Yeah, around Bourbon. You see the same faces."

"Do gutter punks dance here often?"

Brandy gyrated with her arms bracing over Nikki's shoulders. "Sometimes. Never for long. They come and go. Percy likes them to try out on Tuesdays and Thursdays."

"Do they make good money?" Nikki tried to focus as the woman pulled down her tube top.

Brandy bucked like a rodeo star in slow motion. "That's the thing. They make great money for a few days, then just stop showing. Gutter punk lifestyle, I suppose."

"Herman Napleton?"

"He came in sometimes. He would take girls into the private rooms for VIPs. These are the cheap seats."

"Do you go in the private room?"

"Nobody turns that down. Mega-money. Herman never picked me. I don't look young enough."

"Do you know a gutter punk named Rot?"

"I know of him. I avoid the punks." Brandy's movements slowed when the bouncer wasn't paying attention.

"How do you identify if dancers off the street are gutter punks or not?"

"Inexperience. Trying too hard. That's how you can tell."

"They come in cleaned up?"

"There's a house in the Marigny where they take showers and get the right outfit to come dance."

"Where?"

Brandy slithered up and down Nikki's body, like a sexy snake. "I don't have an address memorized, but I think it's on Frenchman."

"Frenchman? I need that address."

She kissed Nikki on the corner of her lips. "I'll have the address for you before you leave here tonight. Promise."

"As tempting as you are, I'm straight. But, I'll be honest, you present a good argument."

"We're all fluid, but I respect your choices."

"Thank you. If this address helps me, I may consider coming back to find you."

"Flirt."

65

KEITH HAD DELAYED telling Nikki he had been drunk the day of the accident. Thankfully, he waited, as that wasn't the case at all. However, he still broke the law by stealing evidence. If he mentioned his blackmailer's name, Nikki would become a dog with a bone.

He pulled into the driveway of his darkened home.

Still paranoid about having an intruder in his house, he checked up and down the street for the odd car. He shut off the engine, releasing the seat belt. Strip club aroma wafted off on his clothes. Like a contact high, his skin had absorbed stripper lotion. This would be a prime example of circumstantial evidence.

He and Nikki enjoyed the best place they've ever been since the accident. She agreed this wasn't a good night to consummate their reconnection, to check that box. They shared a nice kiss before parting ways. As he climbed the steps to the front door, his cell rang.

"You visited the club?" the voice questioned.

"Yep." He took another step.

"You went snooping at the hospital."

"How the hell do you know that?"

"I thought we understood each other."

"I didn't find anything. They told me I needed a warrant."

"You made a very big mistake, Detective. There's no coming back from this."

He leaned on his porch railing to look out onto the dark street. "The FBI agent is reporting to us tomorrow. What's my next move?"

"You don't have any." The call ended.

Keith exhaled, shaking his head. By tomorrow morning, with the proof he uncovered, this blackmail nonsense will be over and he'll take the punishment. The fire came to mind, along with the decision to pack a bag and find a hotel for the night. He opened the door, closing and locking it behind him.

Stale sweat caught his nose.

Movement to the left caused him to launch a blind haymaker.

His punch landed.

A different set of hands grabbed Keith's jacket, throwing him backward. There were two of them. He struggled on all fours, reaching for his gun. Before he could pull it from the holster, a massive weight landed on his back, and he collapsed to the floor.

He was pinned. "Who are you?"

The man collected both arms to his side while pressing down. Zip ties secured his wrists. This guy was large and strong like a wrestler. Keith's sidearm slipped from its holster.

"Stop struggling," the man said in his ear.

The oxygen had been squeezed from his diaphragm. "What do you want?"

The man got up and pulled Keith to his feet at the same time. He faced a third man sitting on the sofa in the dark. "You're a catfish swimming with sharks, Detective Teague."

66

Dread lay on his back crossways at the foot of Rot's bed. Flower kept him company, sitting upright and holding his hand. She was scared, that much was evident. A few traveler kids were in the warehouse, but they wouldn't dare go upstairs.

"I'm a good dancer. Let me show you."

"No."

She let go of his hand. "Is Rot taking me across the river?"

"No, I am. We'll meet him at the Frenchman house. I just wanted us to clear up a few things before we go." Dread sat upright.

Flower sprung up on her knees, throwing her arms around his neck. She attempted to kiss him. "Why don't you like me?"

Dread pulled away. "I'm not fucking you because I *do* like you."

She fell back on her butt. "That don't make sense."

He grabbed her hands again. "Sex is not why people will like you or love you."

"That's all guys ever want."

"And you give it. That's what they take from you. It's not what you want."

"I don't care."

"You do. I want you to try something."

"What?"

"Don't have sex with anyone for six months. No matter who you like or who likes you. Six months."

She couldn't compute. "Six months?"

"You've been doing it your way. You're alone."

"I have Rot."

"You're *alone*. Try it my way. What's the worst thing that'll happen?"

"I'd still be alone. I was twelve when…"

"Don't. It sucks that someone in your past life took advantage of you."

She looked like a scolded child.

"Rot wants to trade you for sex, you understand? He's no good for you."

"Men treat my mom the same way."

"That's rough."

"Most punks say you're a good guy."

Dread checked outside the room even though they were alone. "The people you're going to dance for are the people that raped Emma and protected Herman Napleton after he killed other traveler kids."

"I won't get arrested when you call the police?"

"You're a minor. None of it is your fault in the eyes of the law. You'll be fine. Once this is over, I'll pay for your way home. Hell, the cops will want to pay your way home."

"So, you'll stay at the Frenchman house with me?"

"The whole time." Dread patted her knees. "Let's do this."

Tears collected in her eyes. "I'm going to throw up."

"Throw up, if it'll help."

"I can't do this, Dread. I don't want to be here anymore." She looked around as if she had a plane ticket somewhere.

Dread stared at her. "Where is home?"

"Texas."

"Will your family welcome you back?"

"My aunt will."

"Let's call your aunt, then."

"You're not mad?"

"What kind of friend would I be if I didn't support you? I wouldn't be any better than Rot." He touched her chin. "I'll tell him you came to your senses."

"What about the club? Percy?"

"I'll find another way."

THURSDAY

67

"*WHERE ARE YOU, Keith?*" Nikki kept a lilt in her voice while speaking into her cell. "I missed lunch for this. You're not answering my texts. You're forcing me to leave a voice mail." She moaned in exasperation. Her sight focused on a blue house on Frenchman but a block away from the bars and shops. "I'm at the address. I knocked. No one answered. Just watching from my car for now. Call me."

Nikki adjusted the heat, wishing she had eaten breakfast. She considered how close the Grande Esplanade was to this house, right on Frenchman Street where Herman Napleton prowled. The area had changed over the years. Residents strolled the one-way streets of the gentrified neighborhood, walking distance to anything they might need.

Minutes before giving up the stakeout, Rot turned the corner on foot. He wore sunglasses but checked up and down the street before climbing the stairs to the same house she swatched. *Thank you, Brandy.* Rot opened the door, but stopped.

Nikki scooted low in the car.

He took two steps to the railing on the small landing, then stared at her. He waved.

Nikki berated herself for being *made* by a gutter punk. She straightened and exited the car, approaching while he shook his head. "So obvious."

"This can't be your house," Nikki said.

He turned to the door. "Why not, Detective Mustard?"

"Funny, coming from a man named Rot."

"They call you *Chick* now. Great street name."

"What's going on here?"

"You're following the wrong guy, Chick."

"You're not going to get under my skin with that shit. I like the nickname." She walked up the steps.

"I want the reward for finding Emma. Shit, I'd turn her in for free, but I'd take the money. You're wasting your time with me."

"I think you tried to kill me and my partner."

"Kill you? Are you fucking delusional?"

"I have my sources."

"Dread?" He laughed. "Let me tell you a little something about your *source*."

"It wasn't Dread. There were loads of witnesses driving by, moron."

"Whatever. Dread's got his own agenda. I haven't figured it out yet."

"What's your agenda?"

"To survive the day—and then, the next." He leaned against the doorjamb.

"What concerns me is who would give you a key to their house?"

"Is house-sitting a crime?"

"Oh, you water the plants, do you? Feed the chickens?"

"Wait…you're not following me. You were watching the house. Fuckin' Dread."

"It's not Dread. He won't give up shit on you. We tracked Herman Napleton to this address from his GPS."

"Emma's face is all over the news, and yet you have no idea where she is. That don't make you look too good."

"Is she in *there?*" Nikki pointed.

"House is empty."

"Can I come in with you?"

"No."

"You don't have a choice."

"You don't have a warrant."

"I see a transient entering a house that isn't his. I have every right."

"No." He paused. "No." He shook his head. "No. You can't."

"Hands." Nikki showed him cuffs, securing him to the railing.

"This ain't right."

She hooked the other cuff to the rail and left him there. "Don't move. I have my gun."

"Nothing's there!" he shouted through the open door.

Nikki yelled back from the front room, still with a visual on Rot. "You might as well tell me who owns it. I'm going to find out."

"I house-sit. That's all I'm saying."

Nikki looked around the front room with a similar layout to Frank's place, both being shotgun homes. It was furnished with a few items. Hardwood floors. A beautiful mantel to a fake fireplace. One room opened to the next, leading to the rear where the kitchen resided in this style of home. Nikki stopped at the second room, where the bed was exposed to anyone walking through.

She approached a dresser with a large mirror. Several items were spread out on the surface, including jewelry. She whispered, "You lied, Rot. Emma hid out here."

Nikki heard a mechanical humming from the kitchen and reached for her Glock. She had unsnapped her retention strap and gripped the gun. The refrigerator caused the sound. That awful gutter-punk stink wafted passed her nose.

Rot.

As the sidearm came out of the holster, a sting on her neck

caused her to spin, facing Rot as he held a syringe in his hand. She'd been drugged. His other arm blocked her weapon.

"How did you get out?"

"After our first meeting, Frank got me a cuff key." He held up the needle. "And you know I have experience with this."

"What an...asshole." She faltered backward until finding the bed. The room swayed.

A sick grin on Rot's face was the last thing she saw before falling backward on the mattress.

She could just make out his voice. "It's perfect that you showed up here. Saves me the trouble of finding you. Oh, your partner's not coming, by the way." Rot spun her so that her face pressed into the covers, pulling her arms back. "I'm going to kill you, Chick. You won't escape twice."

68

Nikki opened her eyes to something covering her head. A light source filtered through the material. Her arms and legs were spread out—*tied up*. She was on a mattress, somewhat upright on pillows against a headboard. The air she inhaled was hot.

It was disorienting and claustrophobic, like in the crawl space of the snoball stand. Soft material brushed against her face. Best she could tell, it was a pillowcase. The cloth wasn't opaque. Last thing she remembered was showing up at the house—and Rot.

"Help!"

Her body rocked to wiggle something loose. Neither arm had enough slack to cause damage. It rubbed like a rope. Her feet couldn't kick out, either. Despite being in a brain fog, she was a prisoner. A shadow moved across the room.

"Help!" Her volume came out weak.

A blow to her gut released her breath. She gasped for air. Noises in the room confused her more. Body odor, mixed with food. "Rot?"

His voice filled the room. "Every time you scream, you get hit."

"I won't scream."

"Good."

"You were going to kill me."

"The only reason you're alive is because of your cell's GPS. Wouldn't be the smartest plan to kill you here and leave evidence."

"Take the hood off my head, at least."

"No—you get no advantages."

"Because you can't look me in the eyes. Rot, listen to me. The police already have you connected with this case. If I turn up dead, you will be arrested. You will go to prison for the rest of your life. Think this through."

"With no proof, no trial."

"Detective Teague is coming here."

"He's not a concern anymore. Why do you think he's not with you?"

"Who told you that?"

"The fire didn't work, so…here we are."

"Rot, let me go while the charges are just kidnapping. With cooperation, you'll walk. Don't make this worse."

The weight of his body dipped the mattress as he pressed on her thigh. His forehead bumped hers. "I'm not mad you talk to me like I'm stupid. You're trying to save your life. You'll say anything."

"With our ridiculous justice system, am I wrong? It's like they don't want to put criminals in jail."

"So, you're calling me a criminal." He backed away. "In another life, you and me would've worked good together."

"Did you kill Frank? There was a needle mark in his neck."

"Really? Interesting."

"What's your plan? You can at least tell me that."

"We wait until dark. I put you in your trunk. I drive you out to the East. You send a text to Keith that you found something out there. Then, I put a bullet in your head and set your car on fire. It will be assumed you were followed and killed."

"No murder is perfect. You're going to miss something."

"If you don't see a hole in that plan, then it's pretty good." A door closed. "My friends in high places will protect me. My friends in low places are coming in as we speak."

Multiple voices overlapped. As they grew closer, she recognized the female voice. Nikki squirmed again to keep her arms and legs from going numb.

Dread said, "What the hell have you done? Are you crazy?"

"Chill," Rot responded.

"What's she doing here?"

"Emma?" Nikki struggled even more. The restraints pulled at her skin. Another punch to her stomach released all her air.

Rot sounded riled up. "So this is Emma! About time we meet. Dude, where's Flower?"

Emma called out, "Nik?"

"Run, Emma!"

A smack resonated, and something hit the wall hard.

Dread yelled out, "Fuck, dude, why'd you hit her like that?"

"What'd he do? Emma?"

"She's going to ruin everything. We have to kill them both. It pisses me off I can't collect the reward."

"Fuck, you are."

"Dread, is Emma okay?"

"She's out cold, Nikki."

Rot's voice turned excited. "Holy shit. I'm a genius. We don't need to kill Mayeaux in the East."

"We're not killing anyone."

"Emma is going to kill Detective Mayeaux, then herself. That's what the police are going to find."

"No one will believe that." Nikki imagined Dread was standing between her and Rot by their voice proximity.

"This is where we separate the men from the boys. I'll kill you, too, Dread. Don't go against me."

Nikki heard movement off to the left where Emma had been

discarded. Was she stirring? She prayed that Rot and Dread weren't paying attention.

"No, I agree about Mayeaux. She's a cop. We have to. But, we don't have to kill Emma."

"You're in fantasyland, Dread. Emma don't need this life. We don't kill her, she's gonna spill what we did here."

"You're right. Them or us. They both need to die."

"Damn, you're making me proud, *my brother*."

Nikki couldn't believe her ears. "You can't side with Rot."

Dread slapped her head. "Shut up, Nikki. You've been playing me all along."

"We pull this off, Dread, we're going to impress a lot of rich people."

69

"You say you're smart, Rot. But, this isn't smart." Nikki expected another punch to the stomach with her protests, but none came.

"It's all about survival, sweetheart. Things changed." More sounds of rustling to her left.

"Where's Keith? At least tell me that."

"Dead," Rot said. "Shut up about it."

"Take the pillowcase off my head." A presence moved in front of her like an eclipse.

"Where's her gun?" Dread asked. "You got it?"

"Shit. Where the fuck is it?"

Her Glock fired three times in rapid succession, causing Nikki to clinch. But the bullets weren't meant for her. "What happened? Dread!"

"Jesus Christ, Emma!" Dread shouted.

There was complete silence. Hints of sulfur penetrated the pillowcase. Nikki made out soft breathing that rose to hyperventilating. *Was Emma shot?* A heavy set of hands grabbed her forearm. "What happened? Who was shot? Emma!"

"She's good," Dread said. "You gotta run, Emma—Go!"

"Stay strong, Nik," Emma whispered. The shadow moved away from her vision.

"She's gone." Dread said calmly. "Don't move."

"Take this hood off. Dread, you're supposed to be helping me!"

"I am. I'll untie you. Hold on." He didn't say anything for a moment.

"Is Keith dead?"

"I don't know."

Dread tugged while cutting through the rope, and her hand became loose. Her ankles came next. She fumbled spastically to pull off the pillowcase, finding a vacated room. Her eyes settled on Rot, with saturated clothes. His eyes were still open, staring up at the ceiling. With the struggle of trying to rise too soon, she fell to the floor next to Rot's feet, as her muscles weren't ready to obey her commands.

Some people could get suspicious of *her* if she kept ending up next to dead bodies. Her Glock and cell were nowhere to be found. Real panic set in.

Hearing the squeal of tires outside forced Nikki to her feet, stumbling forward and falling again onto her arms. When she rushed outside, her Accord was turning the corner toward the Quarter. She patted her pocket, knowing they must've found her key fob. Whether that was Emma or Dread in her car, she had to chase after them.

Someone had her gun.

70

NIKKI'S FEET FOUND purchase, hitting flat but still not in line with her shoulders. She tumbled forward onto her knees. "Crap!"

She held the railing on the stairs of the front porch. Running down the street would be a futile pursuit. After maintaining balance for half a block, she encountered a cyclist on a mountain bike. The front tire swiveled trying to guess which way the woman would dodge.

Nikki stopped her cold.

"I'm a cop. I need your bike. Please." She presented a police card from her back pocket.

The young teen climbed off the bike with wide eyes. "Yeah, yeah. Okay. Don't hurt me."

"I'm not stealing it." Nikki wasted no time climbing on the bike, handing her the card. "Call this number. I'll get it back to you, I swear."

The adage about riding a bike came to Nikki as she gained speed, heading down the quickest path to the Quarter. Her balance stabilized as the bike's momentum kept her upright. Before getting to the French Market, she spotted her car abandoned halfway up on the curb with traffic at a standstill. Without her cell, she couldn't call in for backup. However, Emma was on foot while she had the bike—an advantage in the Quarter.

Her speed slowed for pedestrians on the access road just to the right of the French Market, which was a long canopy of vendors and merchandise stretching a couple blocks. She assessed the jumble of patrons within, shopping for bargain clothing and souvenirs. The foot traffic on the path turned chaotically dense as shoppers trekked back and forth from the parallel shops.

Nikki ditched the bike and ran into the heart of the market, where twenty yards ahead she spotted a lone female weaving through the shoppers like Indiana Jones at an Egyptian bizarre. *That had to be her*. She picked up footspeed and kept pace as the more sprite girl maneuvered a little quicker.

Emma performed the oldest trick in the book by pulling down displays of merchandise, causing chaos and blocking the path. Nikki thought she might lose her, however the teen did something stupid and left the cover of the market to shoot across the pathway into a parallel building.

Nikki felt the same fatigue as the night of Napleton's murder. She panted while forcing her legs to continue. Emma ducked into an antique store with entrances on each parallel street. Nikki avoided knocking over the oddest objects, from medieval torture devices to ancient kitchen utensils. There were posters, dolls, and wigs as well.

The shop owner yelled something about police.

Once on the opposite street, she could see Emma with an entire block to make up. Nikki willed her legs to cooperate and closed the gap with renewed vigor. The tourists multiplied the closer they got to Café du Monde. Anyone in a car at this end of the Quarter was stuck.

The visual of Emma got lost in the swimming heads, but she stayed on a straight line. Nikki passed the outside seating at several establishments, one being the Gazebo Café playing live music, but no one paid attention to the two crazed women barreling through.

The band sounded like a movie's chase soundtrack. Where was a cop when you needed them?

The distant blaring of trumpets grew louder. She couldn't believe with Emma's face posted all over the news, no one recognized her. However, those images were before the goth makeover and radical hairstyle. Doubt crept in that Emma had stayed on this path. Her steps slowed, wondering if she lost her in another shop. This was a disaster.

Powdered sugar and lattes from Café du Monde filled her lungs. Nikki had to run alongside traffic on the street if she'd have any hope. That proved to be a good decision as she bypassed the meandering masses in clips.

Sirens blared nearby. Once in front of Café du Monde, just the sight of wall-to-wall people in Jackson Square gave her pause. Her legs were noodles. Emma had eluded her.

A squad stopped in the middle of Decatur with their flashers and the window down. The other cars were trying to make room.

The driver said, "Detective Mayeaux. We got a call about a pursuit."

Nikki recognized him from Headquarters. She got into the back seat. "Head to Canal. Emma Courtland is out here somewhere."

They put the call in to dispatch that Emma Courtland was spotted in the area and to concentrate their patrol. Even with their siren, the traffic had nowhere to go, and tourists continued to cross the street. "There, they'll let you pass on the left. Go up on the curb, if you can."

"Left or right at the fork?" the cop asked upon coming to where the Decatur split into two directions.

"We're already going left."

Emma disappeared again, she convinced herself. Once at Canal Street, a streetcar on her right glided through a turn to head toward Uptown. "There! Get in front them."

The squad turned onto Canal, the widest *street* in the world, where the traffic could change lanes to allow the squad to pass. It didn't take long to cross over the tracks and stop the streetcar.

With her badge out, Nikki boarded the refurbished relic from the past, taking inventory of the riders. Without a place to hide, she knew Emma hadn't gotten on. A very tiny part of her was glad.

She turned to the cops that had followed. "She's gone. I need a ride back to the Marigny—Frenchman Street."

71

NIKKI DIRECTED THE two officers to search for the bike Nikki borrowed. That person would get reimbursed one way or another. She arrived back at the Marigny murder scene. Neighbors on Frenchman had called in the gunfire, and the block had been secured. Perez and Jonesy coordinated efforts.

The threesome met up on the sidewalk in front of the house. Nikki asked, "Has anyone heard from Keith?"

"We can't reach him. Lan is sending a car to his house." Perez looked her up and down. "Are you okay? What happened?"

She drank water Jonesy handed to her. "The victim's alias is Rot. Other than that, no identification. I came here on a tip and thought Keith would meet me. Jonesy, can I try Keith on your phone?"

"Sure." She handed over the cell.

Nikki dialed, however no one answered. "Shit."

"He invited you in?"

Nikki lied. "I told him to wait on the porch."

"The handcuffs attached to the rail are yours?" Jonesy pointed.

"Yeah… I still told him to wait."

"Lan's not going to like that. I'm guessing he picked the lock?"

She nodded. "He surprised me from behind and drugged me,

but Emma intervened. She and Dread. My gun is missing. It might be in the house. I don't know. I gotta get in there."

"We looked around in there. There was no gun. Who shot him?" Jonesy asked.

"I was tied to the bed with a pillowcase covering my head."

A black woman with a confident stride approached in a FBI jacket over a sweater and dark pants. "Detective Mayeaux?"

"That's me."

"I'm Special Agent Rolanda Woods with CID. Lieutenant Lan Tran requested our assistance."

"Lan told me you were coming." Nikki tried not to sound sour.

"Your Lieutenant caught me up. I tracked down the deed on the address before I came. It's owned by Mary Napleton, as part of her husband's estate."

Nikki wiped her face. "Won't Mary be surprised."

"Your sidearm is missing." Rolanda pointed at the empty holster.

"It might be in the house, but I think Emma Courtland has it."

"That's opening a can of worms. Lieutenant Tran said you're starting three days leave after we finish here. With a missing sidearm? Indefinite suspension if I'm not mistaken. You need to report to Headquarters when I'm done with you."

"Yeah, I figured."

"For now, let's make a plan to hand off the baton."

"My partner is missing Agent Woods, so you'll understand my attitude." Nikki's stomach pinched when she said that, fearing what Rot had told her. "Look around the house. Search the backyard with some uniforms, question the neighbors about daily activity and Emma sightings."

"Sounds good. Everyone can call me *Ro*. Pick up Mary Napleton?" she asked.

"We don't have to." Nikki pointed at the woman as she made her way past the blockade alongside Warren. "Let them through!"

"What is going on here?" Warren stopped short. "Did you find Emma?"

"Who called you?" Nikki asked.

Warren stuck his chin out. "A friend in the NOPD."

"Emma was here. I lost track of her in the Quarter."

"It's Mardi Gras. Good luck." Mary patted at her hairdo.

"Perez, Jonesy—Can you two swing by Keith's place? There's a key under the frog in the garden. If it's not there, break in. See what you can find."

They nodded and left.

Nikki continued, "Mary, did you know Herman owned this house?"

She frowned. "No, but it doesn't surprise me."

"Warren, what about you?"

"I had no idea he owned this property."

Nikki stared at him. "Emma knew about it."

"If Herman and Emma were carrying on, it makes sense."

Mary raised her voice. "When are you going to wake up, Warren? Herman was a monster."

"I've known him for decades," Warren stressed.

"And you've known Emma since birth."

Mary reached out and touched Warren's arm. "You and Sharon are the only ones that share the opinion that Herman was innocent."

Nikki rubbed at her pink wrists from the rope. "This appears to be a cleanup house for the gutter punks. Emma probably didn't realize Herman owned it, otherwise, she wouldn't have hidden here."

The forensics tech came out of the front door holding something in her gloved hand. "Found a cell, Detective Mayeaux. Yours?"

"Bring it down here." Ro turned to Nikki. "Check your messages before we put it in evidence."

Nikki broke away from Mary and Warren to examine the phone with Ro watching.

"I have a new message, not from Keith." The text from the

unknown number stated to meet at the corner of Bourbon and St. Peters in an hour.

"An asset?" Rolanda asked. She slipped it into an evidence bag. "We'll pick him or her up."

"A source. No offense, Ro, but I have to meet him alone or he'll scare, and we'll get nothing."

"I can't let you leave the scene to work the case. Plus, you have to take me through what happened before reporting back to Headquarters."

"Is this an FBI case now?"

"No, but until a new detective is assigned, I'm in charge." Rolanda sealed the bag. "Walk me through the scene, and then in about an hour, I'll trust you to find your way back." She offered a sly grin.

72

"I GAVE THE entire account to Agent Woods and left her at the Marigny scene," Nikki explained to Lan on a prepaid phone she had picked up at a Canal Street discount store. She'd have to get along without her cell until Oz cleared it. "I'm meeting Dread in few minutes."

"AIB is already breathing down my neck about your missing gun. I don't want you anywhere near this case."

"Tell them I'm on my way in." She figured the Administrative Investigation Bureau was inevitable. "I pinky swear I won't go near it. I'm meeting a friend, not named Dread."

"Nikki."

"I'm getting a bite to eat before I come in. How's that?" She waited a beat. "Any word on Keith?"

"No word. Perez just called me from his house."

"Oh, they got in. What'd they find?"

"No sign of a struggle. His car and car keys, wallet and phone were there. The door was closed, but unlocked. They took the cell in case a call comes in."

"That's not good, Lan. Rot all but told me he's dead."

"Don't think the worst until there's a reason to."

"Right. I'm trying hard to keep my shit together."

He paused. "So, you're heading in?"

"I'm heading in soon." She ended the call.

Nikki took her time in the approach of the designated corner where Dread wanted to meet. The shifting crowd revealed the Lucky Dog vendor ahead. To her right was Dread sitting on the sidewalk, leaning against the wall. Next to his hip was a Big Ass Beer.

He glanced up. "I want to be buried in one of those Lucky Dog carts."

"That'd be something."

"You gonna arrest me, arrest me. Fuck it."

"Calm down." She stood before him as a sea of tourists parted around them. He tried not to look her in the eyes. No other gutter punks were around. With a look to the left and right, she sat next to him. "You wouldn't happen to have my gun on you?"

His head rolled against the brick until facing her. "I don't need that heat. Emma took it with her."

"Mind if I...?" She reached out.

Dread spread his arms as Nikki proceeded to check for her Glock.

"Your smell is better. Downgraded to awful."

He grinned. "I cleaned up."

"Thanks for letting me pat you down. I had to be sure. Was Rot telling the truth about Keith?"

"Rot was frontin'."

"Now, Rot is rotting."

"Dark." He finished his beer. "Rot lied. Killing a cop is too big. He would've been...different about bragging."

"This is a stupid question. Where did Emma go?"

"We split off. I expected you to come with a squad of cops."

"That's still going to happen. It'll be better for you if you come into the station. I'm off the case, pending an investigation."

"'Cause of the gun?"

"They take that very seriously. And they will be looking for you.

Once it gets out that Emma has my gun, these cops out here won't think twice about shooting first."

"I'll think about it."

"What happened in that house?"

"Rot was killed." He grabbed his beer.

Nikki shook her head. "Don't do this bullshit, Dread. I'm Emma's friend. You have to trust me."

"I thought... I thought I could stop him... I tried to stop him."

"Emma saved my life, didn't she?"

"If I'm not under arrest...let's walk."

Nikki stood and took to his side. "Talk to me."

"I'll admit, I was looking to stick it to my deadbeat dad who likes to fuck women with no other options."

"Okay." *Where was this going?*

"I blame him, and I hate him. But, I don't think he has a bad heart."

"Spoken like a son. If it makes you feel any better, there was no black skin in that video. All small white dicks."

Dread pulled his head back to take her in. "Something is seriously wrong with you."

"Gotta be to be a cop."

"Guess I can't run from my DNA, right?"

"Give me something, Dread. You called this meeting knowing I could slap cuffs on you."

They entered Jackson Square, heading toward the river. "Let's go to the Moon Walk. I like the view."

"I just chased Emma down Decatur earlier. Why'd she come this way?"

"Got to imagine she was running toward safety."

"That makes sense. She headed toward Canal, staying close to the river."

They walked past general parking near the Mississippi and onto the Moon Walk, which was a bricked path along the river with benches and an unobstructed view of the powerful current and the Crescent City Connection. The same view she had from her condo, just a different angle.

"I have no idea if Emma will even contact me again after that."

"She will. That's why you need to keep yourself available."

Dread sat on a bench, putting his hands in his jacket's pockets. "I think my father is helping move women. Rot and Frank—they had something with Warren. They talked about Emma's dad nonstop."

"Do you think Percy was complicit in Emma's rape?"

"I think he knew."

"We have our eyes on Percy. If he makes a bad move, we'll jump."

"Good, 'cause my plan to bust him with a minor fell through. The girl went home, by the way."

"That's good, I suppose." She turned on the bench to face him. "You told me you'd contact me if you saw Emma. You didn't."

Dread hunched with his elbows on his thighs. "I didn't know she was going to be on Frenchman. I dropped that girl off at the bus station and planned on telling Rot his girl was gone. Emma stepped up to the house at the same time, honest. She probably wanted a shower. I would have called you, but then, you were already there."

"All the planets aligned. Thanks to this little ordeal, I'm suspended indefinitely. Off the case."

Dread huffed. "I don't want to run anymore."

"Don't be surprised if the police take you in. I gave my statement and you're not a suspect, so I doubt they'll arrest you. Your statement about Emma saving my life will go a long way. Don't make me regret letting you go."

FRIDAY

73

Nikki stared up at her ceiling as dawn announced itself through the edges of her curtains. She convinced herself that without a body, Keith was being held captive. An occasional tear rolled down to the pillow. Anger and sadness wasn't a good mix.

Rot's voice didn't have that—well, *dread*—when he spoke of Keith at the Frenchman house. She believed Dread when he said Rot lied. As much as she'd love to stay under the covers all day, Keith deserved her full concentration.

She forced down a small bowl of cereal with a coffee. The news played as white noise. Keith's face occupied the screen with a concerned anchor giving personal commentary. Emma's face joined his, side by side. Thousands of tips were pouring in, all wanting the reward. A press conference with Lan leading the charge followed. DA Collins jockeyed to be in frame.

Why hadn't Nikki fought for their relationship earlier? She abandoned Keith after the accident. His hurt was real, and she ignored it. She had tossed aside one of the best things in her life. Now, there may not be a second chance.

Yesterday's recounting to Lan, her union rep, and Agent Rolanda Woods had been tough. Lan brought in a federal investigator for extra resources, however only Keith understood the Emma factor.

Nikki had fought between the truth and editing the truth. In the end, Keith's life depended on full transparency.

Lan didn't think she'd be found negligent, but having the service weapon stolen warranted the suspension. She put the bowl in the dishwasher, noticing a cup and a plate that she hadn't used. An alarm pinged. The plate had a brown smear.

She checked the peanut butter. It had been moved. The loaf of Bunny Bread wasn't tied the same. After a moment of reflection, she went to the bathroom and realized the guest towel hanging on the bar was damp.

Emma.

Nikki checked her entire condo. Emma had used the spare key from the hallway to get in. Plus, she got past Major. No one else besides Keith had knowledge of the key.

Emma hadn't left the gun, so what did she need it for? Warren?

Nikki would've hoped for a three-page letter explaining things, at least. Why risk even coming here for food and a shower? Had she planned to surrender? Did she change her mind? Murderers often showed erratic behavior on their spree.

She opened her front door still in her nightshirt, walking to the far end of the painting on the hallway wall, checking between the frame and thin cardboard backing. The key was still there, however not placed in the correct spot. The video surveillance in the lobby was still busted.

"What's going on, Nikki?" Major closed his own door, dressed for the day.

She looked around the floor. "I can't find one of my earrings. This diamond pattern doesn't help. Just thinking it might've rolled over here."

"I find whenever you drop something that small, it always ends up farthest away from where you're looking. I call it the *blueberry effect.*"

"Ain't that the truth? Yeah, it was cheap. I think it's a goner. Where you off to?"

"Errands. Haircut. I never have much going on. Wine and king cake tonight? Help me find the baby? It's always under the purple icing."

Nikki smiled. "Let's see how my day goes. Say, Major, did those sensitive ears of yours pick up on anyone in the hall yesterday?"

He thought about it. "No, although I wasn't home part of the day. Why?"

"Ah, my partner is missing."

"That's not good."

"It was on the news this morning. I thought maybe he stopped by here, but I guess not."

"If your partner is missing, then…" He stepped forward. "Nikki, be careful. You're investigating people with lots of money. *I mean it.*"

Nikki stepped in her threshold. "Always am. Thanks, Major."

74

KEITH WAS LISTED as a missing person, which only threw the press into a frenzy. The general public was desensitized to the frequent crime, but watching these reporters gather outside Headquarters made her thankful for keeping the story in the public eye. These days, a missing cop got a thirty-second segment on the news, and then it was on to the weather.

Nikki had snuck into Headquarters again to answer more questions with Internal Affairs. Oz delivered her cell minutes before, having cloned it. Every cop available did what they could to help find Keith. Agent Woods checked other places of interest such as the abandoned Six Flags in New Orleans East and the Lakefront Marina.

Lan stepped up to her as other cops answered the hotline. "You can't loiter. Go home. I'll keep you updated."

"I can answer calls."

"No, you can't. Go on home."

Nikki meandered out of the building without a plan. She was in the parking lot as her cell rang with a number she didn't recognize. "This is Detective Mayeaux."

"Hi, Nikki, it's Kasie, Warren's assistant."

"Kasie, hi. How are you?"

"I'm good. You said to call if anything came across my desk."

"You have something."

"I'm right outside the Marquis Hotel. Warren had me hand deliver a package to Mr. Fields."

"Do you know what it was?"

"No idea, but Warren was deliberate in handing it to me with instructions. His body language was different. I think it's something."

"Well, that's interesting. His instructions?"

"He told me only give it to Mr. Fields. Mrs. Napleton and Warren's wife Sharon are having drinks together at the hotel restaurant *with* him as we speak."

"Thanks, Kasie. I'm going to head right over. I won't let on you're my source."

"That's the only reason I called. I trust you."

⇜

Nikki's little interruption of Percy's gathering at the Marquis Hotel wouldn't be appreciated by either Percy or Lan. A chat wasn't police business, and his hotel restaurant was a public place. Knowing Warren's connections, the Midas krewe got word she was suspended. Stirring the pot was better than doing nothing.

She entered the hotel lobby, turning toward the dining room styled with modern furnishings, intimate tables, and sleek, straight lines. Purple, green, and gold reflective tassels steamed overhead. There was a long wall with one-way windows to the outside world.

The threesome sat in the corner at a round table with a white tablecloth, where each had their backs against the wall. The majority of plates had been cleared, but they still enjoyed cocktails. Percy wore another fitted suit. Sharon and Mary were more casual.

"Well, isn't this an unexpected meeting." Nikki took note of the little box sitting in front of Percy.

They each looked up. Percy initiated the greetings. "Evening, Detective Nikki Mayeaux. Any news on Emma or your partner? It's on every news channel."

"Your partner is adorable. I do hope he's okay."

"Thank you. Since I have free time on my hands, I stopped by to check in."

"Yes, your suspension," Percy said.

"What's in that pretty box?"

Percy placed his hand on it. "A personal gift."

"Odd-size package. Too thin to be a Rolex."

Sharon answered, "He wouldn't tell us, either."

"Sounds like we all want to know, Percy." Nikki sat. "Mind if I join you?"

"Please."

"C'mon, open the box."

"I dare you," Sharon chirped. She said it in an ineffectual way.

Mary rolled her eyes. "I really don't care. Harrah's is waiting for me. Coming, Sharon?"

"I'll walk you out."

"Ladies, don't leave on my account."

"Not at all." Mary touched Nikki's shoulder. "Lunch was over an hour ago."

Percy received a kiss on the cheek from each of them. "We'll talk later."

"Bye, ladies." Nikki waved.

He raised his hand for the server. "Can I offer you something? Tea?"

"Nothing for me, thanks. I heard some interesting news."

"What's that?" His arms rested on the table with the box between them.

"Dread has been forthcoming about your close relationship."

His eyes found the table. His nose twitched. "I see. Only you?"

"Just me. That's between y'all. Thing is, he got close with Emma and told me a few other things."

"Spit it out, Detective."

Nikki mirrored Percy's position. "It's about the rape video that disappeared. I can't go into specifics."

He exhaled. "I was Switzerland with that entire ordeal. That's my only regret."

"I guess that makes you clean in all this."

"You're being facetious, but it's the truth."

"The truth is that Emma was raped. But the truth don't pay the bills." Nikki continued before he commented. "You're still going to accept what's in that box from Warren?"

"It's nothing."

"You don't have to be Switzerland anymore. Your krewe is falling apart."

"Our krewe has many prominent members and will remain strong. If Herman raped Emma, then there's justice in his murder."

She pretended to write in a notebook. "Oh, that's good. I'm going to use that. It's funny, Emma mentioned justice, too."

"Justice is hard-pressed to be served when those who dispense it don't care."

"Half of you is full of wisdom, the other half is full of crap." She took a sip of water with melted ice. "I have one other question."

"Which is?"

"My partner disappeared right after the night we showed at your club."

"I expected an accusation. Come back when you have your badge."

"Expect a few visits from the NOPD. They get upset when something happens to one of their own. She looked at the box again. "Can I see the invite?"

"Why not?" Percy hesitated, then opened the box, taking out the long, narrow card. He handed it over. Nikki cradled it in her palm like ancient parchment. It was written in a pretty script font with gold foil and embossing.

"There's no location or time." Nikki studied it. "It doesn't give any information but the name of your krewe and the year. Is this like *The Da Vinci Code?*"

Percy reached out to take the card back. "Time and place are revealed the morning of the party. However, it's canceled."

"Yet, Warren still sent this to you."

"As a memento. The printing is done in Europe way ahead of time."

"Are you guys a sex cult? Is that the whole deal? Like Masons or Illuminati or something along those lines?"

Percy hiked an eyebrow. "Amazing where the imagination takes you."

"It's a fact that these organizations exist. Your denial is very telling. What is that saying? *Me thinks thou doth protest too much?*"

He frowned. *"The lady doth protest too much, methinks."*

"So intelligent. Pieces are coming together." She stood to leave. "Can I just say one more thing?"

He huffed, folding his arms in wait.

"Your son is a smart man as well. If I were you, I'd do what I could to include him in your life. Once you break through this initial wall, he'll be more forgiving than you think."

75

Rot's murder drew varied reactions from the punks at the West Bank warehouse. Dread ignored the comments and questions while packing his rucksack. No matter the trouble, they looked out for each other while together. Otherwise, out of sight, out of mind.

He had just enough money for a bus ride to Tampa, Florida, where a few friends would take him in for a bit.

His relationship with Emma was real, but ill-fated. Perhaps he'd visit her in prison. These traveler kids weren't his *people*. This wasn't walking out on Emma or breaking a promise to Nikki. Each of them had her own agenda, and Emma had her own demons to sort. If he stuck his nose back into the investigation, he'd end up in prison, too.

Traveler kids were already scavenging through Rot's belongings. He glanced up the catwalk every so often as they took things. There was nothing Rot had of value. His back was turned to the common room when the door by the bay shut, which he paid no mind. However, everyone went silent at once.

Goose bumps formed for no reason. He looked over his shoulder to see a man and woman. Warren and Sharon Courtland. He was in a suit, shaking his head at the living conditions. Sharon was dressed for church.

"Emma isn't here."

"We were looking for you," Warren said.

"How did you find me here?"

Warren looked at his wife and chuckled. "I like him."

Dread twisted, falling back on the mattress. "I'm packing to leave. Don't worry. I'm never coming back."

Emma's stepfather said nothing as several punks circled the wagons. They acted as a pack of wolves, waiting for Dread to initiate action.

"We need to talk. Can you tell your…*friends* to back off, please?"

"They won't do nothin' if you don't do nothin'."

Sharon clasped her hands by her mouth. "This is about Emma."

"Partially…" Warren added.

Dread stood, motioning the punks to stand down. "There's nothing else I can do for her."

"Love what you've done with the place."

"You've been here before?"

"I own the building." He glanced at Sharon. "We—own the building."

"You?"

Warren stepped closer. "You think it's luck that the police never come here? I allow you to squat here. I allow all of you to live here."

"Rot was in your pocket."

"A useful piece of shit, that guy was."

"So, you're here to kick everyone out?"

He laughed. "That's why I like you, Dread. You're not a scammer like Rot. You don't look for the profit in a situation. Sharon thinks since Emma trusts you, we can trust you."

"Trust me for what? You tried to accuse me of Napleton's murder and raping Emma. But, it was your own friend."

"A grown man and a sixteen-year-old girl show up on our doorstep? What am I supposed to think?"

"Dread, may I speak with you? Alone?"

"I got this, Sharon."

"He's not going to respond to a hard ass. Let me reason with him."

Warren's eyes narrowed. His jaw set. "Of course. Have at him, dear." His hand presented the moment.

"Walk with me, Dread." Sharon started for the other end of the warehouse.

Dread's eyes were wide as he walked beside her. "Nice power play."

"You don't know the half of it."

76

"CALLING TO CHECK up on me?" Nikki drove into Keith's neighborhood while speaking on Bluetooth.

"I called to inquire how you're doing," Lan explained. "And to tell you something I shouldn't."

"I love you, Lan."

A television went mute. She pictured Lan's wife setting down a green tea while he sat in his study. "An employee from Riverbend Hospital called into the hotline. She said Keith was at the hospital yesterday, early afternoon."

"Was he hurt? How is he?"

"No, he isn't a patient. He visited their labs."

"For what? Who called in?"

"A data entry specialist. He checked on the blood work after the accident…with Morgan. I had her come in for a statement."

Her car pulled to Keith's curb. "Why look into that? He wasn't drunk."

"The report said otherwise."

"Bullshit. The hospital would have disclosed it."

"The administrator, Mia Duong, said they uncovered the original report, which was doctored, no pun intended. After her IT team found no other hack or compromise in data, she reported it."

"Someone faked his blood work? Why?"

"That's the question. The timing with your video evidence tampering is suspicious."

"I need to talk to this woman."

"No, you don't. She's off-limits. As you are with this case. Don't make me regret telling you."

"You told me because you know I won't sit still."

"I'm getting a warrant for Riverbend Hospital. You'll only contaminate that effort if you show up there. We'll find out whose fingerprints are on this data breach. Speaking of prints, the report came in on Saul Green. No Emma prints in the Crush bathroom. I'm guessing Emma brings gloves with her now."

"It's easier to dispose of gloves than find a place to scrub her hands clean."

"That's a good assumption." A plate clacked. Perhaps, a tea cup? "Collins wants to put a detail on Warren, but no one can find him."

"Two missing men." The engine stopped. "If Warren thought he might die, he'd be shitting himself. He wasn't worried at all."

"We'll talk more in the morning."

"Enjoy your tea."

A pause. "How did you know that?"

"Elementary, dear Tran. Gotta go. I'm at Keith's place."

"Wait, what? You're breaking up. You said you were going to get some food?"

Nikki ended the call.

⁓

Nikki had lived at Keith's Mid-City home for nearly three months. Like herself, he kept a second spare key outside that only she knew about in the garden, but since she still possessed her old key, it didn't matter. She planned to redecorate the entire house. He would've fought it, but she'd leave him a man-cave to die for. *Die for. You can't be dead, Keith.*

The living room hadn't been disturbed. Nikki flipped on the light. A quick tour proved Keith hadn't fought off an attacker. Nikki had lectured Perez and Jonesy on the art of the search, and they listened when they had come here. The house was still tidy.

She repeated a mantra that no one found a body. His bedroom came first. The mounted television opposite the bed reflected her image on the black screen. Memories returned of watching an episode of *Breaking Bad* every Saturday night after sex. It was their *cigarette*, Keith joked.

She hadn't played an episode since, and she wanted to see how Walter White ended up. But, not without Keith.

Perez had bagged his cell, keys, and wallet. Oz needed to go through the phone. She looked under the bed and in the closet—nothing unusual stood out. On the dresser in a frame was a picture taken of them at Pat O'Brien's piano bar. He leaned back on her while her arms wrapped around his neck.

Why would someone alter his blood work, making him appear drunk?

Nikki opened the dresser drawers, finding the same socks and shirts. One drawer revealed an old cell. She remembered the protective case, having a Saints fleur-de-lis on it. Her finger held the power button, waiting until it started up with only twenty percent battery. The security code was the date they met.

The wallpaper presented a zoomed in picture of herself, smiling wide. She selected the photo gallery, seeing a long string of selfies of him and Nikki. It all came rushing back like floodwater. Many pics contained Morgan as well. Some she hadn't even seen, where he and Morgan acted out for the camera.

The last pic taken was Morgan and Keith cheek-to-cheek, holding up an open ring box two days before her sister died. It was an engagement ring.

WTF?

Confused, she switched to the text threads. The top messages with Morgan caught her attention. She understood that they probably sent a few notes to each other, but she needed context to that picture.

They had texted several times that day, just hours before the accident. Her little sister asked if he was ready. *Ready for…?*

The engagement ring.

Oh, God. Keith was going to propose the day Morgan died.

The back-and-forth texting was all about the secret proposal at Audubon Park and Morgan's excitement to be included.

Nikki tossed everything from the drawers. The last one had a jeweler's box shoved in the back. She stared at it through a blur of tears.

Her knees gave, and she fell onto the floor against the bed after a moment of letting herself cry with the ring in her lap. She almost put the diamond on, but the ache of taking it back off might send her over the edge.

SATURDAY

77

It took a bottle of wine Major had gifted to help Nikki sleep. She stayed in bed most of the morning. She couldn't wrap her head around the fact Morgan was killed while on their way to Audubon Park where Keith had decided to *pop the question*. Would she have said *yes?* They had only been living together for three months, dating seven months before that.

A shower and coffee helped clear her head. How did Keith not say anything after all this time? Anger surfaced for withholding such a bombshell. Keith and Morgan shared a secret. After sitting with that knowledge, she realized it wasn't anger, but emptiness for the possibility of what might've been.

If Keith was dead, she'd never get to slap him, and then forgive him because he was the man she wanted to marry—the man she *will* marry. Sitting around the condo wasn't constructive. She may have been taken off the case, but why couldn't she go out for fresh air and visit a potential friend?

Nikki brought takeout jambalaya and Barq's Root Beer to the Esplanade Hotel to have lunch with Kasie in her office. Digging for more info from Warren's assistant was a *gray area* as far as police involvement.

After fielding Kasie's questions and concerns for Keith, Nikki guided her toward Warren.

"Some people don't understand what it takes to put on a parade," Kasie continued, conducting an invisible orchestra with her fork. "For the whole city to do it."

"Did Warren let you get involved with the krewe before it was canceled?" Nikki pretended to enjoy a bite.

"To a point."

"You have a list of the members?"

She shook her head. "Warren made it clear that's off-limits and I signed an NDA. But most of these guys brag about riding."

"An NDA? Figures. Where are the floats?"

She sipped her drink. "Warehouse on the West Bank."

"Why are you even here on a Saturday? Endymion's tonight. Biggest parade of the season."

Her eyes rolled. "Today's the most hectic for me. The Saturday before Fat Tuesday. A friend is riding in Endymion, and Warren said I'd leave early."

"Great."

"Not great. Warren hasn't shown, and he's not answering his cell."

"Is that typical?"

"Never, unless he's in a meeting that I didn't schedule."

Nikki pulled out her cell. "Where does he stand for Endymion? Does the hotel have a spot?"

"The hotel rents out the Tabby Cat bar for hotel employees. We get wristbands to go inside. Near the corner of Carrollton and Canal. I talked to several people already there. He hasn't shown."

Nikki stared at her cell as it rang. "He's not answering for me, either. I'm sorry, Kasie. I have to go. If Warren contacts you, call me."

"Do you think...?"

"Just being cautious. I'm sure he's fine." She didn't sound convincing.

✖

Nikki drove down St. Charles Avenue to the Courtland house. It wasn't a parade route today. She told Lan about Warren not answering her calls. The traffic lightened the closer she got.

The gate opened after a buzz, and Sharon invited Nikki inside the house without much of a greeting. Nikki followed her to the sofa, where she was watching a true crime show with a glass of white, which Nikki declined when she offered.

"I tried calling first," Nikki started.

"Oh?" Sharon curled her legs under her butt. "I might've been in the bathroom."

"You don't return calls?"

"I didn't want to deal with any distractions. Whether you found Emma or not. Either one is not a good outcome."

"Do you know where Warren is?"

"At the hotel or Endymion. Maybe he's with your friend Dread."

"Why would he be with Dread?"

"Warren has some bright idea that Dread can help him find her. Last I saw them, they were heading into the Quarter."

"Dread and your husband. This isn't a joke?"

"I wish."

Nikki checked her cell for messages from Dread. "No one can reach Warren."

"He's been like that for years."

"Did he say where they were going to look?"

"That woman there on this murder mystery show, she killed her husband. For seven years, they've been trying to build a case. Looking over her shoulder. You think she freed herself? It's just a different prison."

"You can't disappear, Sharon. Emma is going to need you."

Sharon took a drink. "No one needs me."

"Sharon, my partner is missing."

"So's mine, according to you. Maybe Dread will kill Warren and then Mary and I can live together in a New York apartment. The odd couple. Have a seat, Nikki. Let's see how this woman explains her DNA being at the scene."

"I live that show. Let's talk instead."

"I'm leaving Warren. My bags are packed and in the car. I was waiting for Warren to tell him face-to-face. Then, I got into the show."

"That's huge. I'm proud of you."

"Thank you, Nikki." Sharon looked away from the television.

"I'll let myself out."

Before Nikki could reach the front door, she heard Sharon catch up from behind. "Wait."

They turned and faced each other. "What is it?"

Sharon leaned in to give Nikki a nice, if not awkward embrace. "Thank you for being Emma's friend."

78

Parking spots along a parade route were like unicorns when arriving late. Residents allowed friends and family to park on their property, but most were forced to walk a long way with ice chests and supplies. Nikki left her credentials on the dash alongside a fire hydrant. Endymion wouldn't arrive for a while.

The crowd enjoyed walking the street to different music sources. Nikki dodged kids and families to find every vantage point. She stepped onto a bench in front of the Tabby Cat for higher elevation. Warren wouldn't be in a suit, and who would he be with? Percy? What other friends in the circle did he have?

Attending a parade was an affair where no one was a stranger. Someone offered Nikki a beer, which she took to be polite. Another put beads on her with a kiss on the cheek. Nikki let it happen, as it was all innocent. A kid offered a slice of King Cake. People danced.

Nikki was allowed into the Tabby Cat by a hotel employee vouching for her. She made a round inside the small establishment, not seeing Warren. Everyone in the line for the bathroom denied his presence. Several sober people even confirmed he hadn't arrived yet. She left for one more look outside.

It was obvious as she weaved through the masses that she'd never find Warren, especially if he had teamed with Dread. Sirens whipped down the route, clearing the street. The flambeaux marchers marked the start of the parade. The tradition started with Mardi Gras itself when parades were at night. The group of black men carried propane torches like picket signs. Coins gathered in the street at their feet—tips for dancing.

She started back to her car as the first float appeared. Warren might already have the number two on his face. Then, a second thought hit her. What if number two ended up being Keith, and she was number one? No, that was ridiculous.

Her heart sank when she returned to her car, leaning with two flat tires on the driver's side. No other vehicles on the street were damaged. Closer inspection indicated punctures. Could've been stupid kids walking by or some drunk local who didn't like where she parked. Either way, she had to call headquarters to send mechanics to change the tires in the morning.

Nikki had the rideshare driver drop her off in front of the condo. She entered the lobby adrift. A text came in while taking the elevator to her floor. Agent Woods apologized for not being available, but said they would talk Monday morning. Nikki responded with an okay that turned into a thumbs-up emoji. She was too tired to care.

Without paying much attention, she left the elevator, turning toward her condo while checking her e-mails. She looked up in time to see Major standing by his door, talking on his phone. He hung up, presenting a big smile.

"Shouldn't you be at Endymion?" Nikki asked.

"I was leaving, and now my knee is bothering me. I might have to skip this one."

"You okay?"

"Just need a pill and some rest. Want to partake in a little red instead?" He opened his door.

"Why are you in the hall?"

"I just knocked on your door. A few more seconds, and you would've gotten a call."

"Bad knee, and you're out here instead of a text?"

"Texting…that's for kids."

"What's going on, Major?"

"Fine. You got me. Let's go in my place, and I'll tell you what's on my mind."

"I have a lot going on, Major. I really don't have time for this." Nikki stepped past him to her door.

Major took a few steps with her. "Can you at least go in my place and get my cane? I've fallen over before." He reached down, grabbing his leg.

A thump from behind Nikki's door caught her ear. "That came from inside."

He shook his head. "Sometimes these old buildings. The plumbing makes the place sound haunted."

She held her hand out to him. "Stay here. Get ready to call 911."

"Nikki—wait."

She spun to him. "What?"

"There's an FBI agent in your condo."

"What? How do you know that?"

"Because I'm FBI." Major reached into his back pocket and held out his credentials. "Wait here."

Nikki couldn't process Major shifting his attitude on a dime. Without her sidearm, she had to let this play out. She stared at Major as he opened the door. Nothing was disturbed at first glance. She followed him inside.

"York, come on out."

She held out her hand. "Stop right there. Show me your creds."

The meek-looking man held up his hands. He was balding, with soft eyes, and didn't appear excited. "I'm Agent Evan York."

"Major, what the hell is going on?"

79

NIKKI WAITED WITH folded arms as Major spoke to his ASAC on his cell, the Assistant Special Agent in Charge. He stared at her with compassion. "Yes, sir." Pause. "Yes, sir." Pause. "Yes, sir, I will." He ended the call.

"Well?" Nikki let her arms drop.

"Let's all have a seat." Major walked to the table with two working knees.

The second man followed with less confidence. He was a cubicle agent, not used to being in the field. They both sat, waiting for Nikki.

She kept standing. "Talk."

"We have an ongoing operation involving Warren and his associates that bled over into your Herman Napleton rape and subsequent murder case."

"You've been in your condo for months just to record me?"

He gave a single nod. "I was placed here when you received the rape video. It's not an assignment I wanted. Maybe you should sit."

"What? With a little merlot? You planted listening devices?"

"The time frame on the *tap* expired. We were pulling them."

"Great."

"Our spotter downstairs missed you. You should be none the wiser."

"Sorry my car trouble interrupted my routine."

"This wasn't personal."

Nikki's eyes widened. "Major, I thought you were my friend. No, not personal at all."

"We are friends. That's genuine."

"Don't go there. Is Agent Woods a part of this?"

"She's been read in. That's why she was delayed in reporting."

"What's the bottom line?"

"Bottom line, you're clean."

"What evidence allowed a warrant to tap my place?"

"The night you let Emma stay here days after the video was placed into evidence. That opened the door to evidence tampering, obstruction, and conspiracy."

"What's your part in this, York?"

"I'm tech. A surveillance agent."

Nikki squeezed her eyes shut to think. "What's your real name, Major?"

"I'm Special Agent Greg Bailey. My friends call me Major."

"Greg Bailey." Nikki tugged out a chair and sat, but not close to the table. "What am I supposed to do with this?"

"You can start by continuing to call me Major."

"We're not friends."

"We're on the same side. I was doing my job. I still am." His voice went softer. "Our interactions were genuine. I think of you as a friend."

Nikki smirked at him. "How could I possibly trust you?"

"Let's start with your partner, Detective Teague. He's alive. He's under our protection."

Nikki sprung up, but found her knees too weak for support. "You have him?" Her eyes watered. She put her hands to her cheeks. "Thank God."

"Detective Teague has been under surveillance for a while. We picked up a credible threat on his life the same day he visited the hospital lab."

"Damn. Does this have to do with the blood report?"

Major never broke eye contact. "Yes. He briefed us on everything that's happened."

"Was it blackmail?"

Major, or Greg Bailey, went to the refrigerator for three waters. He passed them out. "Yes."

"Do you have Emma, too?" Nikki took a long drink of needed water.

Major clasped his hands. "No. We can't go into details about our investigation..."

"Bet you been dying to say that to me."

"The Krewe of Midas is a criminal syndicate. It started out as a good ol' boy's network but grew into bribery, fraud, extortion—you name it."

"What did the blackmail entail? And why? What could he do for them?"

"Detective Teague is the one who stole the cell phone from Central Evidence."

"*He* did? That's crazy. He wouldn't."

"He confessed."

"I – I have no words...no fucking words."

"It's up to your department on charging him after this all plays out."

"He'll be cleared."

"We're building the best case we can at this point, for the ones still alive."

"You're not going to tell me who blackmailed Keith because I know this person."

"You're not in danger. You weren't conspiring with Emma Courtland."

"I'm suspended, as you know. What happens now?"

"We continue like normal."

"Normal." She ran her hand across her face. "We can't get ahold of Warren. You might be losing another target."

The two agents looked at each other. "We can't locate him, either. What happened at the Marigny house on Frenchman?" Major asked.

"I got drugged. Blindsided. Emma killed Rot with my sidearm, and she still has it."

"She's building quite the résumé," Greg commented.

"I want to talk to Keith."

"You will. He's in a safehouse," Major offered.

Nikki exhaled, calming herself. "Why is it you don't have Warren's place tapped?"

Greg and York glanced at each other again.

"Oh. You guys are unbelievable. So, you heard my interactions with Sharon."

They both nodded. "You skirted the law, but said nothing warranting action."

Nikki's cell rang. She answered with less urgency since Keith was safe. "Hey, Lan."

"A uniform spotted Emma at the foot of Canal and attempted to apprehend her, but she got away."

"You're kidding. How does that happen?"

"Rookie. Didn't call for assistance. She was last seen outside Harrah's. Patrol established a perimeter, but they're holding back so she'll expose herself again. For the record, I forbid you to get involved."

"Wouldn't dare. My car is still in the shop, anyway."

"Have you considered gambling on your time off? Take a ride-share."

"I love to gamble."

80

"MAJOR, YOU'RE DRIVING. Let's go find Emma, guys." Nikki clapped her hands.

An immense weight lifted off her shoulders knowing Keith was safe in the FBI's custody. It eclipsed Major's betrayal. After securing her personal firearm in a shoulder holster under her jacket, she led the charge out of her condo to track Emma at Harrah's Casino near the foot of Canal. York followed in his own vehicle to be another set of eyes.

Nikki had formulated the plan on the drive. It was simple. Major would walk around like a tourist near the front since Emma never met him. York would hang out pretending to be waiting for his ride, and Nikki would circle Harrah's in Major's car. In heavy traffic, she pulled over and let everyone out.

Nikki circled the casino. Orange barriers diverted traffic into and around the valet line. On occasion, Major acted lost. Emma wouldn't go inside the casino because she'd be escorted out just as fast, not to mention the cameras. It brought about the question: Why would Emma be at Harrah's in the first place?

Was she looking for Mary?

On one of her trips around the block, Nikki's cell pinged. She pulled over to read a message from an unknown number.

I see you Nik maybe next time

Nikki needlessly checked the surroundings. She texted back *dont run lets talk* but it was undelivered. After a groan of frustration, she found Major and York, tapping the horn to collect them. They gravitated to the street, looking in the window with trepidation. She waved them to get in.

Major asked, "What happened?"

"Emma texted me. She spotted us or me, I don't know."

"Damn. Anywhere else you want to check while we're out here?"

"No, but if we ever find her, she'd be a great case study in living off the grid."

York patted Major's shoulder from the back seat. "I'm out past my bedtime. I'm going home. It was nice to meet you, Detective Mayeaux."

"You too, Agent York."

"Major—Greg. *Major Greg.*" She rolled her eyes. "I need you to come into Headquarters tomorrow and brief my lieutenant and the DA about Keith and your involvement. At the least, we have to stop using resources and manpower to look for him. We need this to be a joint investigation."

"We'll help out, but it won't be *joint*. We can't share everything."

"Whatever you say. Since you were embedded, who's the actual lead agent on your investigation?"

"Can't say," Nikki and Major said in unison.

"I'll give you a ride there." Major flashed a grin.

"Great."

"Heading home?"

"Your home?" Nikki hiked an eyebrow. "Are you going to keep living there now that you're burned?"

"Business as usual."

"You go. I want to run an errand while I'm out here." She opened the door.

"An errand this late? You want company?"

"No, it's not case related. I'll catch an Uber." She got out of the car.

"You're going to see if Mary Napleton is at a table."

"Maybe." Nikki waited with a tight-lipped grin.

"Keep me updated."

She backed away from the window. "This isn't a joint investigation, Major. We'll talk tomorrow."

Major's car disappeared into the mass of taillights on Canal. Nikki looked to the rear of Harrah's where gamblers turned in to valet. The evening neared 9 p.m. Street parking was so difficult; either you walked to Harrah's, parked in a garage, or you gave it to the valet. She walked along the hedges and past the palm trees.

What had Major said in passing the other day about Harrah's?

She mumbled under her breath, "No, it can't be that easy."

81

NIKKI STROLLED UP to the busy valet line at Harrah's, where a kid with mutton chops handed a ticket to a Tesla driver. Several employees jetted back and forth as gamblers came and went. The faster they ran, the better the tip. A tall kid with a buzz cut and thick glasses squeezed behind the wheel.

She flashed the gun in her holster as the window slid down. "I'm Detective Mayeaux. What's your name?"

"Josh." Both hands were on the wheel as he hunched forward. "Where's your badge?"

"I forgot it at the station. Josh, you recognize her?" She held up a picture of Emma on her cell.

"Yeah, from the news."

"I'm asking if you saw her *here*."

"Oh." He turned pink. "No, I don't think so."

"Another question for you, Josh…y'all park cars in the tunnel under Harrah's, right?"

"Yeah…" He wasn't sure what to follow with.

Nikki held up a twenty-dollar bill. "Can you take me down there?"

"Why are you giving me money if you're the police?"

"Because you can say no, Josh." A second twenty appeared. "I'm basically paying you to take me around the block."

He checked the surroundings. "Get in."

Josh turned the radio down for the ride. He pulled up to a huge nondescript beige wall along St. Peters. Carved out of the expansive side of the building were an entrance and exit to the parking basement. He pulled up to the iron gate and a swing arm. The Tesla descended into the cavern, leveling off to a wide parking area. Other valets were handling cars as well. He parked in a spot with a large number 2 painted on the wall in yellow.

"I gotta run." He opened the door.

Nikki got out and looked around. "Thanks, Josh. You ever go down to the far end?"

"Nah, creepy down there. I think they had offices somewhere down here, too. Dunno." He nodded and ran toward a booth where they secured key fobs.

She journeyed to the opposite end where parking became sparse. Despite the vast width, it grew oppressive and confining. Why build anything so massive underground in New Orleans, in the saturated earth? Numerous columns supported steel beams extending overhead. Gigantic sump pumps still worked to care for water seepage.

The 700-foot-long tunnel had sparse lighting the farther she traveled. There were discarded pallets, barrels, and crates. Rats looked at her funny before continuing with their business. The bitten victim under the overpass came to mind. Nikki's cell showed one bar. The cold damp gave it a creepy, apocalyptic horror-movie vibe. Her heels echoed as she moved forward.

Just that fast, her sense of direction jumbled. The distant sound of engines roared closer to Poydras than Canal. When she reached a wall with no exit, a set of stairs leading down presented itself. A simple sign reading OFFICES showed the way. *Another floor down?* While descending further into the subterranean nightmare, she lost the last bar on her phone. This could be another stupid situation where she didn't call for backup. She regretted sending Major away.

The door opened to a damp and musty hallway with no light source. Her cell's flashlight scanned for movement, or if she had to be honest, more rats. This *basement of the basement* was meant for a handful of offices. Street names were on the walls, indicating more than two hallways. The floor was dated tile, and the drywall had gaping holes and water stains.

Within two steps a light came on, triggered by a motion sensor. *That helps*, she thought. Nikki put the cell away and held her personal gun with both hands next to her thigh while entering the first empty office.

A distant *clack* caused Nikki to freeze. Her hairs stood on end. She looked down the bleak hall where the sound originated. The light source behind her went off as another light above came on. She took cautious steps on dirt-stained tile toward the next open door. Her gun aimed as her body swung into the doorway. The hallway gave just enough light. The large office had a mattress, magazines, and books.

Found you, Emma, she thought.

The light switch on the wall still worked. There were several rat traps set up, with one unfortunate creature with a crushed skull. No evidence of Emma or a captive Warren jumped out. Nikki holstered her weapon and checked that she still didn't have reception. The light in hallway faded to half power, then went dark.

The room by flashlight had nothing specific pointing to Emma. This could have been anyone's trash. Was it a coincidence that this became Mary Napleton's favorite spot to hang out?

The revelation of Mary giving Emma the Mercedes key fob *before* she and Herman argued in Harrah's almost bowled her over. While Herman's car was valet parked down here, Emma was able to get in the trunk undetected. That would mean Emma was in the car when Herman picked up the gutter punk on Frenchman and killed her. That probably fueled her rage.

The light in the hallway came on again. *A rat?* The door to the stairs closed with a metallic finality. *A rat didn't do that.* Nikki ran from the room to the exit, triggering more lights. The footsteps grew distant. She couldn't take the stairs fast enough.

Once back in the subterranean garage, she scanned left and right, not seeing anything. Noises echoing off the ceiling messed with her radar. Car doors shut and voices bounced off the walls. Nikki rushed toward the Valet area, fearing she was too late.

"Hey!" Nikki stopped one of the boys getting out of a car. "Did a female run out of here?"

"Nope." His brow furrowed. "Who are you?"

"Commissioner of Valet Services. You're doing a great job."

She ran up the incline of the exit lane and onto the street to find it empty of foot traffic. Emma just lost a great spot, and she was running out of places to hide. Mary Napleton had some explaining to do.

SUNDAY

82

"THIS GOES AGAINST every regulation," Internal Affairs Officer Jane Zeigler said. "Detective Mayeaux is on suspension."

Agent Greg "Major" Bailey nodded from his seat in the war room. "Detective Mayeaux is instrumental in our investigation and being a federal case, she was at Harrah's on my instruction. You don't have a say."

Nikki stuck her tongue out at Zeigler, immature but worth it.

The IA officer ignored her. "Does this have anything to do with the Napleton murder or Emma Courtland?"

"It does. Did I mention this is a federal investigation, Officer?"

"You did." She pulled out a chair. "I'll stay, if you don't mind."

DA Simone Collins walked in. "Well, the gang's all here."

"I explained the details to Simone before you got here." Lan sipped his coffee, steam rising in his face. "Nikki, how late did you stay with CSU under Harrah's?"

"About midnight. From the looks of it, the most they'll get is her fingerprints and rat droppings. It was a place to sleep—not that I could, in that horror."

Lan tapped on the table. "How'd no one report a gutter punk in the valet parking basement?"

"These valet kids… they're hyper-focused on the in and out. I can see how she'd slip in without them noticing or even caring."

Jane Zeigler sighed. "So, no gun recovered?"

"I think I would've led with that. But, we need to talk about Keith. That's why I brought my neighbor, friend, and spy to Headquarters."

Simone shook her head. "Invite one fed, and they multiply."

Lan smirked. "Emma is still our case. Can't say I'm not pissed about the resources we wasted to search for Detective Teague, but I can understand if you're investigating one of our own."

"I didn't say we're looking at one of your own."

"You didn't *not* say it," Nikki chimed in.

Officer Zeigler perked up. "Wait, you're investigating someone in our office?"

"I didn't say that. Everyone is making assumptions."

Lan asked, "Why don't you state the rules from here on out?"

Major nodded. "I'll tell you what I can, of course."

"Of course."

"I had a meeting with my bosses last night. Our case has been diluted."

Nikki said, "Because your targets are being killed."

"I'm dealing with Swiss Cheese here. Herman Napleton was our main target. Tim Donovan—or Rot—is dead. Saul Green had a small part. Heroin supplier Frank Brehm, we wanted to flip him."

"You're casting a wide net," Lan said.

"Widespread corruption, LT. There is a task force of White-Collar Crime agents going through a mess of financials on these people. Oh, and this is confidential, Officer Zeigler."

"Understood."

"You still have Warren Courtland and Percy Fields," Nikki said.

A cloud hung over Major's head. "They've kept themselves pretty clean. That's why your murder investigation is on the front burner now."

A tapping on the door indicated Perez needed to enter. He poked his head in the doorway. "Nikki, Percy Fields is here with his lawyer. I stuck him in A. He said just you or he walks."

"Speak of the devil." Nikki looked at Lan as she started for the door. "He brought a lawyer?"

"He's ready to talk." Lan followed her. "Are you good with this, Officer Zeigler?"

"Federal case, right?"

⸗

Nikki delayed long enough for Lan to start recording video. She entered with a curious and friendly expression. Three bottles of water were placed at the center of the table. "How are you, Percy?"

"Nikki. This is Jack Beal."

"Esquire." The older lawyer in new threads had a strong grip.

"Good to meet you."

Nikki aligned herself opposite Percy as he leaned back in the chair, with one foot thrown up over his knee. "Bet you're surprised to see me here."

"With a lawyer, yes. I can only imagine you have information?"

"Jack is a criminal lawyer I found outside the Midas circle. They wouldn't be pleased about this."

"No more NATO?"

"None of the members know I'm doing this." Percy continued, "He's here so I don't meander into a jail sentence."

"Okay. You're here with good intentions, I imagine."

"My life is a shit-show. I want out of NATO, as you put it. I want to put my kids' needs first."

"Dread? If you help this case, we'll help each other." She oozed sympathy. "My intuition tells me you're a good guy who maybe did some bad things."

"Hold your judgment." His eyes closed. "For about twenty

329

years, Herman and the Krewe of Midas threw their private Mardi Gras party with anonymous women, strippers, and yes, cleaned-up gutter punks."

"Underage?" Nikki glanced at the lawyer.

His expression fell flat. "No one asked. Some were dressed young. Pigtails. Catholic school outfits. Fetishes were entertained."

"These women didn't come from your club?"

"Some did. They were legal."

"They're witnesses."

"Not good ones. We wore masks."

"Okay. Sorry, go on."

"The women agreed to all activities. There was drugs and alcohol. Each year, the king gets the first pick of who he wants to have sex with." He paused. "And I do believe that minors have been chosen. No one asked their age, like I said."

"How young would you say?"

"Fourteen? Fifteen, maybe."

Nikki tried not to show her disdain. "You were okay with this?"

"I rationalized they were the age of consent—seventeen and eighteen—just dressed up to look young. I wasn't in a place to rock the boat."

"You could have declined to attend."

"I was inner circle. If I refused, then I'd be an outcast. Almost the same as ratting them out."

"Any pictures or video exists?"

He shook his head. "No electronics are allowed."

"Where did the video of Herman come from?"

"If it was real, then someone broke the rules. The fact that Frank couldn't get into the phone tells me it wasn't his."

"I agree. Someone probably freaked out when that cell went missing."

"I can't speak to that. Every year Herman picked younger and younger, and the other members knew who he'd pick."

"Were you aware that some of these girls were murdered by Herman?"

"I didn't know that. Once the party was over, I never saw the gutter punks again."

"No one did." Nikki scooted forward and leaned in. "So, why are you here? So far, nothing you said is hard evidence."

This time, he turned to his lawyer before speaking. "Dread is my son...and Emma is my daughter."

83

NIKKI RUBBED AT both her temples. "Emma is your daughter?"

"They are both my children." He nodded.

Nikki let out an exasperated laugh. "I've been speechless a couple times during all this, but Percy—you take the king cake."

"Can we move past your shock? Warren brought Emma to these sex parties. Starting at twelve."

Nikki waited through silence. "Why?"

"Herman *wanted* her."

"Napleton just snaps his fingers and members bring their underage daughters to him?"

"Herman offered him a piece of the hotel."

The lawyer said nothing.

Percy fidgeted. His eyes darted. "The first year was a test. To acclimate Emma to the situation."

"In case she freaked out?"

"We never lost sight of her. She had some drinks, passed out on a sofa in plain view. The second year Emma attended, they disappeared to a private room."

"You participated?"

"*Never.* She was masked, like everyone else, taking drugs. And then at some point, everyone takes a girl to a room."

"Did anyone *care* for her afterwards? It doesn't matter if she was unconscious during the act, she would *hurt* when she woke or sobered up. She was a child, your child."

"Yeah," escaped in a breath. "I remember the second year when I suspected it happened, I called Warren. I asked how Emma was doing. He said *fine*. Like it was code. I'm sure Warren either told her to stay quiet or Sharon assumed she had sex with a young boy or something. Maybe Emma never complained at all."

"When's the last time you spoke with Warren?" Nikki pushed a bottle of water in front of Percy.

He succumbed and took a healthy swallow. "Friday." A weight looked to have been lifted from his shoulders. "No one can get ahold of him."

"Does Dread realize he's been protecting his half-sister?"

"They are both aware."

"So, did Emma find out she had a brother after she became a gutter punk? Or did she become a gutter punk because she found out Dread was out there?"

"Emma learned about the gutter punk life from one of the party girls. When Warren told me she started to run away for days at a time to live on the street in the Quarter, I contacted Jamal—Dread. I asked him to look out for her. I had to tell him the truth."

"How'd he take that?"

"He hated me even more. That responsibility should've been mine. I'm a piece of shit. But, that was fine compared to the alternative."

"Alternative?"

"Winding up dead of a heroin overdose on the street."

"Emma's birth must've been a shock to Warren. Can't imagine him seeing that in the hospital."

"Sharon wouldn't embarrass him at the birth like that. There was no hiding she had the indiscretion, but we were all supportive. In public, they worked it out."

"It's plain to see that Warren always held it against Sharon... against Emma. He never suspected it was you?"

"He knew it was me. It was a *don't ask, don't tell* situation. We all pretended."

"Emma hasn't confronted you about being her father?"

"She never did. We ran across each other in the Quarter. Never said a word. She hated me—all of us."

"And you think you're not on her list?" Nikki looked at him with a tilt of her head.

"I know what you're thinking. *I'm her father, and I allowed those men to rape her.*"

"That's guilt you're going to have to deal with."

He tried not to cry. "I was trapped. The money. The secrecy. I was surrounded by power but had none—*never had any*. I sold my soul for... *for Mardi Gras beads!*" He broke down, shedding real tears.

Nikki slid a pad and a pen to him. "Write down what you told me. Include names, dates, and places. You've done the right thing, Percy. You're helping Emma now, that's what's important."

Percy took the pen while his lawyer consoled him.

"I'll leave you two alone," Nikki told Jack.

84

NIKKI STOOD OUTSIDE the interrogation room with Simone, Major, Zeigler, and Lan as Percy concentrated on writing down his statement. She scrutinized Percy through the long, narrow panel of glass in the door. He wiped at tears and conferred with Jack, who acted more like a friend than a lawyer.

Simone said, "Mr. Fields' statement is great, but everything he said about the party is hearsay."

"You can't use any of that? He's a witness," Nikki stressed.

"He's a great witness for laying the foundation, even placing members at the party. The jury will eat it up."

"But."

"They served minors alcohol and drugs, but he didn't witness the act. These victims are nameless. The people who make up the Krewe of Midas are judges, politicians, CEOs. They wear masks. I need proof or we have nothing."

"Back to square one?"

Simone waited a beat. "Are you still even pursuing Emma?"

"Why do you think I was at Harrah's? We're squeezing her out."

Major looked at everyone. "Percy's confession is great, and Simone is right that his testimony could sway a jury. It's not enough."

"Do you have any cards to play, Agent Bailey?" Collins folded her arms. "Can you prove girls were trafficked to these judges and politicians? Can we handcuff Warren with financial fraud? Bribes?"

"We have questionable transactions—contributions, but no smoking gun. Not yet. Mary Napleton won't flip, and Sharon doesn't have to testify against her husband." Major turned somber, looking at Nikki. "Without Warren, the case goes away."

"The other Midas members are nervous. Percy will be Warren's proxy at any meetings or interactions. We wire Percy up to talk about the party." Nikki looked for confirmation from everyone.

Lan said, "Do we risk releasing him? He's Emma's target, whether he thinks so or not."

"It's important he keeps operating." Nikki ran her fingers through her hair. "What about Keith? Using him as bait?"

"Bait?" Simone asked. "Someone was hired to kill him."

"And failed." Nikki answered, "Mary Napleton is the key. We thought Emma got in Herman's trunk at the Esplanade, but I believe she got in the trunk in the parking lot under Harrah's while Herman and Mary were arguing."

"Do Keith and Mary Napleton have a relationship?" Simone asked.

"Mary is sweet on him. She was flirting."

"You want Keith to seduce her?" Simone put her hand over her mouth and laughed, looking at the floor. "You just—throw anything at the wall to see if it'll stick? Seducing a witness? Lan, what are you teaching these detectives?"

Agent Bailey interrupted, "It's been proven the old cliché of yelling and punching the desk during an interrogation isn't as effective as empathy and sympathy. Not everyone has the stomach to tell a pedophile they understand their desire. Flirting is another form of manipulation. It's a way to display power."

"It sounds ridiculous."

"We can't put Keith back into circulation without the press

making a fuss. What's our story on finding him?" Lan looked to Major.

"Don't stray far from the truth. You say he was put in protective custody and is being kept out of state. The ongoing investigation prevents us from commenting. Let the press speculate all they want." Major pulled out his cell. "That's all contingent on Keith agreeing to be exposed."

"He'll agree. Make the call," Nikki said.

Major nodded. "We'll bring him by your condo while we prepare his house. We'll place him with round-the-clock surveillance for anyone looking to complete the hit."

Simone said, "I'll make a statement to the press about Detective Teague being released from federal protection and that he's staying with friends or family."

Lan signaled the end of the meeting. "And I'll write up a warrant for Warren's office first thing tomorrow morning," Lan added. "If he's a missing person, we have that avenue to explore."

Nikki raised her hand. "Oh, Lan. What about my car?"

"It's fixed—ready for you in the yard. Get a squad to drop you off."

※

Nikki settled into the driver's seat of her Accord, none the worse for wear. She rushed home to be ready for Keith's arrival. This time, instead of seeing Major outside her condo door, it was another man with sunglasses, a cap, and thick stubble. Keith was sitting against the wall, under the painting that held her spare key.

He stood. "It's me...Keith....Keith Teague."

Her smile almost hurt her face. Her hand clutched her chest. "Yes, you are."

Nikki's pace turned into a run, closing the gap. He caught her in his arms, spinning her several times. Their lips waited while staring in each other's eyes. Then, like magnets, they kissed.

"I thought you were dead," she said.

"I couldn't reach out."

She let her hands fall to hold his. "Why didn't you tell me about the ring?"

"The ring? You searched my house—shit."

"I know you wanted to propose."

"I'm sorry…"

'No, don't." She touched his cheek. "Let's go inside."

MONDAY

85

EMMA ENJOYED A Coke and a small bag of Zapp's chips at the end of the pier, staring over Lake Pontchartrain. The crunch filled her ears. The camp had been in her mother's family for generations, and after Hurricane George wiped out all the ones along Hayne Boulevard in New Orleans East, her mom rebuilt.

It was the only one of a hundred camps to come back, adding to the social media *ain't dere no more* movement that started to remember the places New Orleans lost after Hurricane Katrina.

Rebuilding was difficult to keep on the down-low, but Sharon and Warren didn't advertise, and they had the juice to make it happen without fanfare. It was their own private escape. The place was their retreat, a sanctuary. When Warren went on business trips, Emma and her mother would make their escape, playing *bourré* and fishing. The fact that the cops still hadn't showed at the camp proved her mom still loved her.

The simple structure appeared rickety and unstable on purpose. It stood on pylons, leaning in places. Mosquito netting made up the walls of the main house, and warped boards added character.

To find this secret, one would have to cross over Hayne Boulevard, climb the levee, and traverse railroad tracks. By all accounts, it looked condemned and never had trespassers. Afterall, there was nothing to steal. She preferred this to the Harrah's tunnel, but it was so far away from everything.

A fish jumped in the calm water.

Emma folded the empty bag of chips into a square and put it in her pocket. The distinct squeal of hinges alerted her, about a hundred yards out. The boards bent under pressure behind her. She palmed Nik's gun in her lap. The last creak ended behind her back.

"It's just me."

"Not sure if I'd be more relieved if you were the cops." Emma looked at Dread.

"You want to hold on to Nikki's gun? She's in trouble for that."

"Don't you think I know that? I almost left it at her condo, but I might need it in an emergency."

"Is this coming to an end?"

She squinted out to the horizon at a sailboat. The sun had settled on her left, but a shimmer remained on the calm water. "Turn myself in before I go put a bullet between Warren's eyes?"

"I found him." Dread sat on the deck, hanging his legs over the water. "He's waiting. It's up to you. As your brother, we're in this together."

"Where is he?"

"He came by the warehouse with your mom. I think it's best if I show you."

Emma put the gun in her backpack and stood. "Great; let's go."

86

Nikki stirred before her alarm clock. Keith's warm body rolled over when he sensed her movements. He proceeded to spoon her with a snug fit. Her hand rested on his forearm draped over her waist. She soaked in the moment.

A gentle peck found her neck. "This is so much better than cuddling with that fed in the hotel."

"What was her name?"

"Stanley."

She spit a little with a laugh. "Yeah, Stanley sucks. I'd ask what you had planned for the day, but since I'm sidelined, you get to go have fun while I'm stuck here."

"They'll fire me for stealing that cell."

"Who blackmailed you? Do you know?"

"I don't."

"You're lying, but I do it enough not to hold it against you. I know you weren't drunk."

"We'll figure that out later. I'm due in at Headquarters." He propped his head up on his hand. "Major kept me updated. They set up cameras and surveillance on my house."

"A statement's being released this morning that you're okay." She smiled. "They should report you're not in town."

A text arrived that Major would knock in five minutes—*time to go...*

Keith sighed. "I'd better start moving." He kissed her, then got up. "You don't mind if I head out?"

She examined every inch of him from under the covers. "No. Tell the gang I said hi. Damn, I want to go in with you."

Keith dressed, leaning over for one more lingering kiss as a light rapping came from her door. He put on his makeshift disguise and left the bedroom. After hearing Major's muffled voice, the front door closed. Nikki inhaled his pillow one more time. She showered, brewed a half pot of Community Coffee and Chicory, and turned on the morning news.

After checking for messages on her cell, she opened her laptop and performed another search for Krewe of Midas. The same pictures of the floats, masked riders, and parade routes populated. She'd even found an image of Sharon and Mary as a float passed behind them.

Nikki scrolled several pages before coming across a picture of a warehouse containing rows of floats in storage. "Huh." She sat back.

The link on the picture led to a tourist's guide to Mardi Gras, offering no new information. A search for the krewe's warehouse also came up empty. She called Kasie.

"It's Nik. Did I wake you?"

"I already ran two miles and dressed for work, although I'm not sure why I came in. Warren's still MIA."

"We have a fed helping us search."

"Right. Agent Woods already questioned me."

"Warren's being listed as a missing person today. But, that's not why I'm calling."

"How can I help?"

"Can you tell me the West Bank address where the Krewe of Midas floats are being kept? I can't find anything online."

"Only a handful of non-members would be privy."

"Is it a secret?"

"No clearance needed, but most of the public is clueless to where any of the krewes keep their floats. Vandalism and trespassing. Hold on, I have the address."

Nikki tapped the cell against her lips after hanging up with Kasie. A search warrant would be the best way to go, but DA Collins' comments about judges being members of the krewe came to mind. Not to mention, she's on suspension.

She collected her things and shut off her coffee pot to leave for Headquarters. Perhaps imminent danger would come into play and they won't need a warrant. When she opened her door to leave the condo, her nose bumped into the barrel of a gun.

She almost didn't recognize her sidearm from the other end.

Beyond the gun was the last person she expected to see.

"Emma."

87

EMMA PUSHED NIKKI back into the condo as if surrounded by a force field. She closed the door. "It's good to see you."

"Thank you for saving my life, but I need my gun."

"Not yet. Give me your other gun." Emma's alert face showed no emotion. Her jet-black hair fell into her focused eyes.

"Worth a shot." Nikki reached for the butt of her Sig Sauer and handed it over. "I'm not on your list, am I?"

"Don't ask dumb questions."

"Right. I'd be dead right now, several times over. So, you didn't cross out my face in those pictures?"

"I have no idea what you're talking about."

"Just your stepfather covering all the bases."

Her exterior broke a little. "We need to end this."

"A little hard to do while you're pointing my own gun at me."

"Let's go. You're driving."

"You're lucky I just got my car back or we'd be ridesharing."

"Thanks for not freaking out."

Nikki walked into the hallway, not expecting Major to pop his head out the door. "The West Bank?"

"Yes, the West Bank."

Nikki let Emma keep the gun aimed at her. The danger was

minimal, discounting an accidental discharge. Emma thought she had control. They got in her car in the garage and left without incident.

Emma instructed her to turn onto the Crescent City Connection heading over the Mississippi River to the West Bank. She gave the directions without extra remarks. After Nikki's first five questions weren't answered, Nikki also kept quiet.

The morning rush prolonged the trip. When it became clear that Emma didn't need to talk, Nikki tried a new tactic. "No comment about the night Herman died?"

"What about it?"

"I was there to kill him, too. If you had waited one more day."

She sat twisted in the seat, facing her. "Did you plan to kill asshole Saul and dickhead Frank?"

"If their faces had been on the video…" Nikki looked at her for a moment. "Maybe."

"I don't blame you for the cell phone or the video. Warren has friends in high places."

"The FBI is investigating those guys, you know. Put that thing away before I hit one of our famous potholes and it goes off."

"It won't. Why are you smiling?"

"Because we're going to that warehouse whether you have that gun or not. Is that where you have Warren?"

"It's not what you think."

Nikki felt relief in Emma saying anything. "Tell me, then." Despite the gun, Nikki reached out to caress her hair.

Emma avoided her touch. "I'm not Morgan."

"I never said you were."

"You never had to. When you let me stay at your place, I could tell there was something behind it. The way you talked about her and shared the pizza like we were besties. You weren't a cop with me."

"Is that so bad? You remind me of someone I loved. The bond

we share is real. Who cares if you remind me of Morgan or if I fill a void your mother created?"

"Don't go there."

"What's going to happen at the warehouse? Why don't you Scooby-Doo this plan for me..."

"Scooby-Doo the plan?"

"Explain. Before your time. It's a joke."

"I know Scooby-Doo is a dog. Whatever. No more talking." Emma relaxed the gun.

Minutes later, Nikki pulled up to the address and parked in an empty lot. They stepped out of the car and into the chill near a large, bland warehouse. Emma waved the gun at a service door.

Upon entering the unsecure entrance, the aroma of spray paint and cleaning products wafted by. Rows of huge floats were positioned end to end, about twenty in all. Gigantic heads made of papier-mâché stared off in the distance. The door closed behind her.

"Go that way and take a left after the crawfish float."

Nikki let Emma direct her to an open area in the middle of the warehouse. Not seeing anything on the ground, she heard muffled noises from above. Nikki spun while looking up, until she saw Warren taped to the king's throne on top of the colorful float. A large number 2 marked his face.

"Emma..." Nikki turned, but she had vanished and still with her sidearm.

She looked back up at Warren, fighting against his restraints. He'd spotted her and struggled even more. Nikki climbed on board the multi-colored float with a huge King Midas head at the mast. A bird's-eye view revealed nothing. Was Emma going to let Warren go? Did she take off? What was her endgame?

Warren attempted to yell something through the tape. Nikki held up a hand to quiet him while stepping near. The tip of a large knife was stuck upright in the floor, likely placed there to strike fear in the man.

Nikki pulled the tape off his mouth. "I'm getting you out of here."

"Emma isn't the one to worry about."

"Don't worry about Dread."

"No, you fool. It's that *bitch!*"

"He's talking about me, Nikki." Sharon's voice carried through the warehouse rafters. "My daughter brought you here because she doesn't appreciate what I've done for her."

Nikki spotted Sharon standing at the rear of the float, pouring gasoline down its sides. "It was you? In Napleton's garage?"

"A mother would do anything for their children." She continued to splash the gas.

"Don't do this, Sharon. This is crazy. Warren's going to prison."

"I didn't plan on having Emma as a decoy, but she was the obvious choice for you, right?"

"You know I was on her side."

"Her resourcefulness worked out well."

"If Emma doesn't want this, then you're not doing it for her."

Sharon disappeared off the back of the float, but kept speaking. "I'd get down, Nikki. Let the bastard burn. I doubt you can free him before this float goes up in flames."

The distinct sound of a Zippo lighter flipped open.

88

"I'M COUNTING TO five, Nikki. Because I like you."

"Just like your victim countdown?"

"I suppose."

"Sharon, you're throwing your life away." Nikki couldn't see where Sharon hid.

"5 - *Herman Napleton*."

Nikki pulled the knife from the floorboard. She used it to cut the duct tape from Warren's feet.

"Hurry," Warren pleaded.

"4 - *Frank Brehm*. You're trying to save the man who ordered your hit. He ordered the snoball stand fire. 3 - *Saul Green*."

"She's lying," Warren hissed.

"You want the gag again. Shut up. He should go to prison, Sharon." Nikki sliced the tape, not caring if Warren suffered cuts in the process.

"The party is a sex auction. He sells young girls to the highest bidder! 2 - *Warren Courtland*."

She almost got his legs freed. "The FBI is on to him, Sharon. They have a case. A federal case. He's not bulletproof."

"He arranged the rape of my daughter for ownership in the hotel!"

Warren answered back, "It was never violent—it was *ceremonial*."

"You cock sucker!"

There was no name for *number one*.

Nikki cringed at the distinct whooshing sound of fire behind the float, followed by a bloom of smoke. Sharon strolled within sight of Nikki again, flipping the lighter's lid. "Jump off the float, Nikki. It's spreading fast!"

The panic from the snoball fire consumed her thoughts. Nikki cut his arms free as the heat pressed against her skin. The flames licked up the sides of the float, along with Warren screaming in her ears. These behemoths were made of nothing but flammable material. It would only take seconds before engulfing.

Warren used his free legs to rock and push the throne from its cheap base. He tumbled through the wall of flames and off the float. A thud hit the concrete with the sound of breaking bones, but it could've been the chair breaking apart. It wasn't the best idea, but at least he was on the ground.

A sudden combination of frosty fog and smoke overtook the fire. The flames died out while hearing the swoosh of a fire extinguisher. Nikki ran to the back of the float, where Emma and Dread were spraying the fire. Because of the flammability, most floats were equipped with their own fire extinguishers.

The smoke had collected at the ceiling, triggering the sprinklers. Stale, dark stink water rained down on them. It was better than an inferno.

"Dread?"

"I'm sorry, Nikki. Sharon tricked me. I had no idea about this."

"We have bigger issues. Where's Sharon?" Nikki shouted over the spray of water. She descended off the float to the floor.

Emma dropped the extinguisher after the sprinklers consumed the flames. "I don't know. But she's not going to stop until he's dead."

They both peered at Warren, trying to crawl with broken parts of the chair still taped to him. He cornered the float like a snail.

Emma handed Nikki's gun to her. "Sorry about this, too."

"Thanks. We should get him before your mom does."

"Should we?" Dread asked.

"No one else is dying, if I can help it."

"I dream about the day he goes to prison," Emma stated.

They caught up to Warren in the manufactured rain. Nikki asked, "Why did you bring me here instead of calling the police?"

"You're the only cop I trust to do right by my brother. And he agrees." They faced each other, standing near Warren's broken leg. "Help this bastard get out of here, or my mom will kill him."

89

THE RELIEVING SOUND of sirens grew far off in the distance. The fire department was on their way, alerted by the sprinklers still raining down. The distinct pattern of police sirens were evident as well.

Nikki was soaked and cold; her fingers were numb. She'd come full circle from the night of Napleton's murder, only this time, the killer didn't run.

Mary Napleton's voice called out over the sprinklers behind one of the tractors. Nikki wasn't sure what to make of her appearance. Mary materialized between two floats under a large umbrella. "Oh, my!"

"Wait here, Emma." Nikki trotted over to her.

"Is that Warren? He looks injured."

"What are you doing here, Mary?" Nikki wiped water off her face. She took a step with the gun in hand.

"Sharon called me. She wanted to show me something with the king float. I got tied up in traffic." Mary strolled, as if shopping. She took Nikki's free arm to walk with her under the umbrella's protection closer to the gathering surrounding Warren. She dressed more casual than usual, in tight jeans and a ruffled blouse and jacket.

The sirens were closer. "You and Sharon worked together to murder Emma's rapists?"

"Dear Lord, no. I just didn't ask questions." She stared down at Warren who flipped over onto his back, breathing heavily and spitting out water. Mary was deadpan.

"You didn't give the key fob to Emma. You gave it to Sharon. That was Sharon in the Harrah's garage."

"I didn't ask for what."

"That makes you complicit."

"The membersvoted me Queen of next year's parade. I came by to check on the floats to find this chaos." She side-eyed Nikki. "Perhaps Warren should be attended to?"

"It's a broken ankle. He'll be fine."

"*That's not what I meant.*" Her eyes were sharklike under the shade of the umbrella.

"The police will be here in seconds. It's all over."

The sprinklers stopped. Only the sound of water dripping surrounded them. Mary collapsed the umbrella.

A familiar metallic sound clicked behind Nikki.

Sharon's voice projected. "Drop your gun."

"I thought you ran." Nikki held the gun up first, before lowering it to the wet ground. "Don't kill him, Sharon."

"*Oh, no—don't kill him,*" Mary's sarcastic voice mocked while shaking the umbrella of drops.

Sharon had crazed eyes. "Love you, Mary. Stand aside. I want Emma to do this one. Emma!"

Emma appeared like an unbalanced wet cat. Her soaked hair was matted to her face with running mascara like something out of a horror movie. The collar of her tee shirt hung low enough to see cleavage. Her ripped jeans held all the water they absorbed. She trembled.

"It's over, Mom."

Dread stepped behind Emma. "Your mother won't shoot you."

Emma moved closer. "No one witnessed the other murders, Mom. You do this one, you're not getting away with it."

Mary put an arm around Emma. "Don't make your baby girl kill that horrible man. That isn't healing for her. She'll be arrested. That isn't your mission." Mary then slid close to Sharon and rubbed her shoulders from behind, speaking in her ear. "She's suffered enough."

Nikki couldn't believe their conversational tone. They stood in a circle around Warren, who was moaning with his arms over his face. He would probably go into shock soon.

"Do it!" He curled into a heap.

Nikki tried to figure her next move, but there was no way to rush Sharon before she could pull the trigger. And Sharon wouldn't hesitate to make one more dead body. The sirens were right there.

"Mary's right. Look at your daughter, Sharon," Nikki protested. "This will break her."

Emma stood over her stepfather. "He's done, Mom. I want him to suffer...in prison."

Warren attempted to speak. His hand raised to Emma. "I'll be dead before I ever make it to trial. Do it."

Sharon's entire body shifted as she aimed her gun at Warren. "For the love of God—are those your last words? No better than Frank."

"You want last words, you bitch? I let Herman rape your daughter. *Do it.*"

Emma extended her hand for the gun. "Give it to me. I'll kill him."

Sharon tilted her head like a disappointed parent. "You're lying, dear."

Firefighters entered, but stopped when they saw the odd gathering. Sharon held up the gun as a show to keep them from encroaching. Warren clumsily reached up for her leg, snagging the material. "Pull the trigger."

"Calm down, Warren. It's going to happen. I'm just sorry that I won't get to do the number-one person on my list."

While Nikki didn't want to bull rush Sharon, Emma never had

that trepidation. Just as Sharon pointed the gun at his face, Emma leapt, knocking her mother over.

The gun fired.

90

THE BULLET STRUCK the edge of Warren's shoulder, likely tearing flesh away. Other than that, everyone was fine. The police were able to enter and take control of the warehouse. The firefighters were allowed to assess the damage, but had to wait, as it was a crime scene.

Dread had helped subdue Sharon after Emma tackled her mother. Side by side, with their arms around each other, the brother and sister had distinct similarities. This was a hell of a thing to bond over. Major separated them to hear Dread's account.

Nikki and Emma huddled with blankets, watching as the medics wheeled Warren toward the ambulance. Broken bones ensured a hospital stay while Major would work with Simone to build a solid case.

Lan and Simone questioned Mary off to the side while Sharon waited in a squad car in cuffs. Unless Percy or Sharon conjured hard evidence against her, Mary would probably walk away unscathed. Nikki would be okay with that. In Mary's twisted mind, she was being a good friend.

Charges against Dread depended on the DA. He helped Sharon kidnap Warren to put him on display. Instead of just killing her husband while he slept at home, she wanted him to watch his friends die in a spectacle. Whatever Dread's intentions to help Emma, kidnapping was still a crime.

The medics loaded Warren into the ambulance with his wrist cuffed to the gurney. Emma said, "He's going to go free."

Nikki put her arm around her. "Not this time."

The ambulance doors slammed shut.

Nikki looked over at Sharon, who just stared forward in the squad car. "I didn't ask your mom; who was going to be number one?"

91

SIMONE COLLINS HAD prayed to find Warren dead when she arrived on the West Bank scene. First, Emma hadn't killed anyone. Second, it had been Sharon under their noses the entire time. This could have been nipped in the bud from the very beginning if Warren could control his wife.

While questioning Sharon with Lan, it was clear that she would keep her mouth shut. But, the way Sharon peered at her. The woman had something planned. An ace up her sleeve. It would be Simone's job to offer Sharon a deal for her testimony. Surely, the feds would be in on it.

Simone couldn't operate by her own rulebook with this one. The Midas boys were worried about exposing their network. They had to be mounting evidence for a scapegoat. *Would it be me?* she thought. There was no way in hell to squash testimony in a trial. Bribes would come to light. Sweat beaded on her forehead.

Nikki and Emma stayed huddled together in a curious manner. What were they planning? Simone couldn't shake the paranoia. Emma pulled something out of her pocket, like a cell phone. It was a recording device. Simone acted casual, stepping closer to listen. Their voices traveled in the large, open space.

"What is this?" Nikki asked.

Emma handed the device over. "It's a recorder. Just press PLAY." Nikki found the button.

Emma: *You have the video. What happens now?*

Collins: *We examine the video. It may not be legitimate.*

Emma: *Legitimate? What does that mean?*

Sharon: *Yes, Simone. What does that mean? I want them arrested. I will testify.*

Everyone in the immediate area of the warehouse had stopped whatever they were doing. They listened to voices coming from the speaker. Simone's feet froze in place. Everyone stared at her.

Collins: *Deepfakes are all the rage. The video is dark. You can't make it out.*

Emma: *That's me. It's easy to see that bastard when he took off his mask.*

Collins: *The defense will tear the video apart in a trial. They'll call you a liar, a slut. Are you prepared for this?*

Emma: *Why are you trying to talk me out of this?*

Collins: *Sharon, we don't want this to go to trial.*

Sharon: *We? Besides me, Percy Fields is a witness. We have Emma. Hearsay can be allowed.*

Collins: *Yes, hearsay laws can be allowed in some conspiracy cases. (hesitates) Consider who you're naming, Emma. These are men with deep pockets who will drag out every unsavory detail of anything your family has ever done in court.*

Emma: *So?*

Sharon: *Yes, I agree. So?*

Collins: *They will bring up your affair with Percy Fields and name him as Emma's father. Fields will be labeled a trafficker and say you're complicit. They will discredit him. Anything Warren has done.*

Sharon: *You're not bringing this to trial.*

Collins: *This will never go to trial.*

Sharon: *They got to you.*

Emma: *Got to her? What do you mean?*

Collins: *They didn't get to me. They've always had me. Don't be stupid, Sharon. This is how the game is played.*

Emma: *We have the video.*

Collins: *I'm sorry, Emma.*

Nikki stared at Simone, projecting her voice. "Agent Bailey. I can understand why you didn't give me Keith's blackmailer." She handed over the recorder. "I believe this is evidence."

"I wanted to wait until we were back at Headquarters, but now is good, too." Major motioned for an agent to arrest her.

"Warren told my mom that Simone has an offshore account."

"You're taking that conversation out of context," Simone tried. "I was only preparing you for the realities of a trial." The agent secured her hands behind her back.

"Liar!"

Major announced, "We have many conversations on record between Warren and Collins. She's been on our radar for a while. Anything you want to add, Keith?"

Everyone turned in the direction Agent Bailey already faced. Detective Teague walked onto the scene, making a path to Emma and Nikki. He too never took his eyes off Simone. "I already gave a statement to Agent Bailey about your blackmailing me. I also recorded each conversation."

"I want a lawyer," Simone managed with weak volume.

"I hope you get one as good as yourself," Nikki returned.

"It ends with you." Emma wiped a tear.

Emma pulled a cylinder-shaped object from her pocket and walked up to Simone. Nikki followed a few steps behind, but not yet attempting to stop her. Simone backed up, but had nowhere else to go with the agent behind her. Emma twisted the base of the lipstick.

"What are you doing with that?" Simone asked, leaning in with all the confidence she could muster.

Emma reached up with her empty hand, cupping her at the back of the neck. The lipstick rose to her forehead, and in one quick stroke fell straight down the slope of her nose and to her chin, ending the countdown.

She placed the lipstick into Simone's jacket pocket.

ONE YEAR LATER

92

FAT TUESDAY FELL on a sunny day, with temperatures in the lower sixties. The streetcar on St. Charles sat idle for the festivities. Nikki and Keith's picnic setup near the tracks avoided trampling by parade goers closer to the street.

The Zulu parade approached with a lazy attitude. Their thick blanket was spread between two large groups of college kids from Tulane. Nikki wore a Brees jersey and leggings, while Keith had sported a long-sleeve purple, green, and gold striped shirt and sweatpants.

Keith selected a beer from the cooler. "Emma is a different girl... woman, if truth be told."

Emma threw a Frisbee with a Tulane boy who had started flirting with her in the most innocent way. Emma was in a layered plain tee, looking more grunge than anything, with her hair in a ponytail. She wore no makeup, resembling nothing of the girl named Punisher. She ran and laughed like a kid. It was heartwarming.

Nikki said, "Therapy is good for her. She's excited that Jamal pled down to a two-year sentence for his testimony against Sharon."

"Given partial visitation to Percy helped, I'd imagine. So glad she found a cousin for a foster family."

"Percy did some evil things, but he's trying to step up. It's hard to imagine everyone in your life letting you down."

"You didn't let her down." Keith reached to secure her hand.

"Mr. Teague, I do declare…" She scooted a couple inches closer.

Keith's face opened. He almost laughed. "This wouldn't be a bad proposal site, right?"

"Asking to gauge a proposal reaction is not how that works." Nikki leaned forward and kissed Keith as he rested back on his elbows. "I read the texts between you and Morgan. You two had your secrets, didn't you? I love that you had that kind of relationship."

He turned red. "Ah, yeah. If that day had turned out different. We'd be married right now."

"If I'd said yes."

"I'm a catch."

"Your dead mom told you?"

"*Yes.*" He pushed her. "I was going to propose at the Tree of Life."

"Tree of Life? How cliché. How beautifully, wonderfully cliché."

"It's an amazing spot."

"But, not original. It's not us."

"How about next to a Dumpster fire behind a Burger King?" He smiled.

"Make it Popeye's, and I'm in." She gave him another soft kiss.

"If you caught me a year ago, you'd think my house *was* a Dumpster."

"You need a woman in your life."

"I could call Cristal from El Salvador."

"*Asshole.*" The word was a laugh.

"I guess I have to plan a proposal worthy of us, then."

She pulled out a ring box. "No, you don't. I got it covered." She opened the box to reveal a black diamond engagement ring designed for a man.

"Holy shit." Keith sat up to inspect the ring.

"Well?"

He embraced Nikki, falling back into a prone position with her. "This isn't how I imagined getting engaged but, yes. You know it's a yes."

They kissed again, until noticing Emma standing at the edge of the blanket recording it with a cell phone. "This is so amazing!"

"Get down here, *best woman*." Nikki waved her into the hug.

ABOUT THE AUTHORS

J.D. Barker

J.D. Barker is the New York Times and international best-selling author of numerous novels, including DRACUL and THE FOURTH MONKEY. His latest, BEHIND A CLOSED DOOR, released May 13. He is currently collaborating with James Patterson. His books have been translated into two dozen languages, sold in more than 150 countries, and optioned for both film and television. Barker resides in coastal New Hampshire with his wife, Dayna, and their daughter, Ember.

E.J. Findorff

Award winning author E.J. Findorff hails from the vibrant city of New Orleans, where he was born and raised. Deeply influenced by his surroundings, Findorff uses New Orleans as the evocative backdrop for many of his gripping novels. He has a talent for weaving intricate tales infused with the city's unique culture, history, and mystique.